PERFECT TWIST

First Edition

First printed in the United Kingdom

Published by Green Fairy

Paperback ISBN: 978-1-9196222-0-0
eBook ISBN: 978-1-9196222-1-7

PERFECT TWIST

T J GRISTWOOD

BOOK ONE OF THE PERFECT SERIES

Dedication

Perfect Twist is dedicated to those who see beyond the illusion and choose to live and love freely, without boundaries or restrictions.

Playlist for Perfect Twist

Some authors love to listen to music while they write. I'm one of those authors. This is the playlist that gave me inspiration for each scene in the book. They are all on Spotify. Enjoy!

Soma – Return of the Jaded
My Boy – Edit R Plus, Dido
Organic Cold Brewed Hipster Funk – Martin Roth
Evening Fog – Modd
Lanarka – Sebastien Leger
Wanna Die for You – Netsky, Diane Charlemagne
Aitne – Monkey Safari Remix T.M.A, Monkey Safari
Evaporate ft Paul Wetz – Edit – Durante, PaulWetz
District Seven – Broken Mix Joris Voorn
Menabelle – Sebastien Leger
Come Together – Mixed, Nox Vahn, Marsh
Tethered, Wrapped Around – Dekker
Heavy – Haux
Spinning Around – Kylie Minogue
Whole Lotta Love – 1990 Remix – Led Zeppelin
Dawning – Monrroe, Emily Jones
Nothing – Original Mix, Humanature, Colussus
Believe – Maduk, HEBE
Safe – Monkey Safari
1992 – Marsh
Leave Yourself – Cassa
Need to Feel Loved (with Zoe Durrant) – UnClubbed, Zoe Durrant
Fire – Xinobi, Vaarwell
You Might Say – Sidsel Endressen, Bugge Wesseltoft

Chapter One

The young man standing behind the shop counter is trying to get my attention.

Despite his best efforts to communicate with me, my brain is currently not functioning properly. All I can hear is a ringing in my ears and see that his mouth is moving.

"Sorry, what did you say?" I mumble.

He gives me an irritated scowl. "I asked if you wanted me to check this lottery ticket?"

I continue to stand at the counter with a confused and, most likely, pathetic look on my face. In my defence, I'm ridiculously hungover right now. Suffering from an almighty self-induced come down from my previous night's exploits. He could be a high-class hooker offering me a night of free pleasure and I would have responded with the same vacant expression and response. I must have handed him a forgotten lottery ticket with the twenty-pound note that was stuffed in my jacket pocket as I paid for my cigarettes.

"Yeah, sure why not," I say looking out the window of my local corner shop while the impatient queue behind me shuffles and snorts at the delay I am now creating.

I take the packet of cigarettes and my change and shove them in my pocket. I'll need the cigarettes to make the joint I intend to roll as soon as I get back to my flat. A nice, fat spliff will help me recover from the night before and then I'll fall back into a coma for the rest of the day.

The machine sucks up my ticket and then produces a

surprising beeping noise that causes the guy serving me to let out a sound like someone being throttled.

Turning to face him, I take a deep breath waiting for the inevitable 'sorry that's not a winner mate'. But that's not the response I get. He looks at me, back at the screen, then at me again with a look of sheer disbelief.

He, somewhat reluctantly, hands back the ticket with a shaky hand. "You should keep a good hold of that mate," he says. He then pulls out a pad and scribbles something onto it before sliding it across the counter at me.

I pick up the note and read what it says. The queue behind me is getting hostile and I step to one side so he can get on with his job and I don't end up saying something I shouldn't to the good people huffing and puffing behind me. I'm cranky at the best of times, my temper a ticking time bomb even without a hangover.

Jackpot. Call hotline, is scratched across the paper in a rushed spider-like scrawl.

I stuff the note and the ticket back into my pocket and stumble out into the street. The sun is so bright today, I am blinded by both the thought I may have just won a serious amount of money and the sunlight reflecting off the bus stop before me. He must be playing a joke on me; I don't believe for a moment I could be so lucky. Any minute, some guy with a camera will pop out, waiting for me to start jumping up and down with joy while they record it all. Right before they tell me it's a complete hoax and I'm the main star of some prank comedy show.

As I head back to my block of flats, I'm slightly paranoid someone will do just that. I take the lift instead of the stairs, trying not to faceplant or throw up. The mixture of alcohol, ecstasy pills and vigorous sexual activity – all part of last night – were now swirling dangerously around my frazzled body.

It takes me an hour before I am even remotely able to switch my TV on and check the lottery numbers on Ceefax. I have my joint in my hand, a glass of lemonade and the numbers now on screen before me.

The ringing in my ears begins again as I stare at the evidence before me. It seems my forgotten lottery ticket, purchased before last week's draw, has matched every single number. It looks like he's right; I need to keep a good hold of this piece of paper. My ticket is worth twenty-five million pounds.

Taking a long, delicious drag on my joint, I reach for my mobile and dial the number on the back of the ticket. It takes a while for anyone to answer but, when they do and I give them the details of my ticket, I am pleasantly surprised to find that I am now one lucky bastard and my life has suddenly taken an unexpected turn for the better in an instant.

It wasn't a prank after all. And I'm insanely grateful the guy in the corner shop gave me back the ticket and didn't keep it for himself. I shall have to bung him a big cash thank you at some point.

Several thoughts rush through my mind after my call, the primary one being how the hell am I going to handle this? How am I going to protect this fabulous revelation and keep myself anonymous and safe in a world that is greedy and invasive? The guy I spoke to at the lottery said I can keep my win completely private, stay out of the press and they would help me do this. They have scheduled a face-to-face meeting to verify my ticket and talk through my options on Monday.

I said a big 'yes, thank you very much' to all of that.

Why?

Firstly, due to the fact I am currently working as a consultant psychologist in Harley Street. Which fundamentally means I'm paid serious amounts of money for keeping my mouth shut and my ears open, while my clients pour their hearts out to me.

Secondly, due to the fact I present the world with what it wants to see from me. The portrait of the perfect man who seemingly has it all. Doctor Jackson Doyle, the man with a great job, a trendy flat and a handsome face with a friendly smile.

What a crock of shit. The truth of the matter is as follows.

I am basically one big fuck-up: I'm a liar, a fake, a magician of illusion. Transgression – that's what really gets me going. You see, what I keep very well hidden from most people (apart from my best friend, Ash) is that I lead two entirely different lives.

I've basically managed to wing my way through life. Juggling a lot of balls, as most of us do, and impressing the world with the seemingly easy way that I manage to do it. Hiding my real existence behind a fancy suit and a sexy smile.

I trick the world into seeing what they want to see. Doctor Jackson Doyle is a clean-cut law-abiding citizen. A respectable, professional man with no secrets or hidden agenda. How naïve they all are. I didn't try hard to pass my degree, my master's or land a successful practice in Harley Street.

Somehow, through sheer luck, I've always landed on my feet.

Yes, I am one of those annoying people. And now it seems, a *very* wealthy annoying person.

I am, without a doubt, a man that loves his recreational drugs. My preferred cocktail being weed, coke, ecstasy and, of course, alcohol. Each one providing me with that little taste of something different to stimulate, dampen or just blow my mind.

But most of all, I love women *and* I love men. I am, you see, bisexual and, just to add an extra bit of flavour to the mix, I most definitely enjoy a bit of controlled kinkiness every now and then – who doesn't?

I have no doubt that most of the clients that visit my practice would probably have a coronary if they knew those titillating little snippets of information about me. If they could see it was really 'Jax', the narcotic-consuming libertine that sat in front of them as they revealed every intimate problem instead of Doctor Jackson Doyle they would most likely turn around and walk straight out of my door. And if the outside world were to learn of my win they would, without a doubt, love to chew up and spit out those pieces of my life.

Regardless of the fact it is now the new millennium and we live in a world where we can be whatever we like, people still love to judge.

I have a sick feeling in the pit of my stomach that, if my current lifestyle were exposed because of my sudden increase in wealth, I would be like a celebrity facing the firing squad. People would judge me and my blissful life of naughty drug habits and sexual preferences would give them some very juicy fodder to feast on.

I could be a target for the less-than-desirable humans of this world that still find homosexuality a threat. Ash and I had a close shave last year when we arranged to meet for a pint at The Admiral Duncan in Soho. If Ash hadn't forgotten his phone and insisted, we return to his flat to get it, we could have become victims of the horrific bombing that took place that very day. It threw a dark shadow of fear over the gay community and created a new wave of paranoia in our lives. That paranoia still clings to me now. And no matter how hard you try to keep your private life private; someone will always find a way to expose you if they dig deep enough.

I've always made sure to keep the professional and the personal aspects of my life very much separate for that very reason. Stay away from judgement or scrutiny. I remember my old professor at university gave me a stern lecture on such things.

"Remember the boundaries, Jackson, they will keep you and your clients, safe. Without them, you are quite literally going to be fucked," he would preach to me, in that bellowing schoolteacher voice I can still remember to this day. I loved the old boy. He was a little like me, talking 'street' instead of 'Harley Street' when the occasion was appropriate.

I think about last night when Ash persuaded me to come out to Heaven, a club we visit when we are both in the need to let off some steam and get a little crazy. It's a place to find adventure, a little bit of decadence wrapped up in a shiny package and, if you're lucky, you can find it with both sexes. Just the way we like it. Sometimes we even manage a double-tap. Great fun.

He got busy dancing with some guy that looked like he'd come straight out of the Village People, whereas I homed in on a guy with his girlfriend who looked like they might just be up for some 'triple fun time'. The music was pumping and the bass vibrating. The air practically dripping with sexual pheromones. It didn't take me long to work my magic.

It's always been like that. Maybe it's my looks; maybe it's my charm. Who the hell knows? All I do know is that it took less than an hour before I was back at their place, having more fun than your average person would on a Friday night. I've always had a way of bringing the hidden kinkiness out of people. One of my many hidden talents. Fan-fucking-tastic.

The night was a little hazy after we'd switched around a couple of times and I found the effects of the ecstasy pills starting to slide. I called a cab and made my way home, stumbling into the lift to my flat, thanking the gods it was now Saturday, and I could lie in my comfy bed all day if I wanted to. I left, as I always do, without leaving my number or having to deal with any emotional bollocks I may have created by sweeping in and persuading them to indulge in kinky sexual acts they may be too embarrassed to mention ever again in the cold light of day.

Ash had text me to say he arrived home safely and was happily sucking off his Village People lookalike. Nice one Ash.

But now, the day after our fun-filled night, it seems my life has suddenly become an entirely different kind of interesting. With sleep unachievable and the need to fix a joint my only mission, I'd staggered to the corner shop, totally unaware my day was about to become something other than the original plan of sleeping off my hangover.

As I sit looking at the golden ticket in my hand, I resign to the fact that I will need to be at least semi-sober before Monday and ready for what is about to unfold.

Whatever that may be.

Chapter Two

Ash looked at me as if I had, quite literally, grown another head. "Stop fucking with me Jax, it's not big and it's not funny. Are you coming out with me and Jo tonight or not?"

I'd called him as soon as I'd finished talking to the lottery hotline.

Asking him to come over and join me for a beer late in the afternoon was not uncommon, especially after a big night out. We usually sat and watched some crap on the TV, smoked a few joints or drank a few beers and then decided whether we were up for a repeat out on the town or a wank to some porn that I would download.

He had not expected me to tell him I'd just come into twenty-five million quid.

Hell, I wasn't even someone that religiously brought a ticket each week. It was a spur of the moment purchase; a 'fuck it, why not?' idea. I never thought I'd win the bloody jackpot. I had money. Not huge amounts, obviously, but I was comfortable with my practice income and lived in a very decent flat in Notting Hill. I had a crazily extortionate mortgage but very little debt as I was paid well in the dirty Harley Street world of 'charge a fortune and worry about the morals later'.

"I'm not joking Ash. I've won the lottery, twenty-five million to be exact. Every single number on my ticket matched perfectly. A guy's coming on Monday to verify the ticket and talk me through my options," I said.

Ash looked at me, his beautiful brown eyes glittering eerily like he was about to cry. "You're a fucking idiot, Jax. Now answer the question, are you coming out tonight or not?"

I laughed. A full belly-laugh. He wasn't going to take this as gospel until I'd showed him my bank balance. Well, fuck him. I'd show him soon enough. "Yeah, why not. I'm up for a celebration, my friend," I replied with a cheeky grin.

He took the joint I offered, kicked his legs up on my coffee table and snorted in response. I watched him tap a text to Jo, our good time girlfriend who sometimes likes to join in with the fun and games. She's single, just like Ash and I. Bisexuality often equals a lifetime of being single. It's far too complicated for the 'normal' people of the world to process and we are often left to mourn the possibility of a meaningful and loving relationship the regular mortals of this world seem to find at some point in their life.

I don't mourn. I relish in my singleton status. I fucking love it. I'd be bored shitless if I had a wife and two-and-a-half kids. Hang me by a rope if that ever happens. Who, in their right mind, would want to deal with someone like me anyway? Someone who always wants to experience the pleasures of the flesh and earthly temptations regularly as if they've been deprived of it. Ash is the only person I know who can tolerate my behaviour in much the same way I tolerate his. We are like brothers-in-arms on a single mission in life: to consume in excess.

The night is set. Jo, Ash and I are going out to the local wine bar. A pretentious, pretty place, filled with pretty dim-witted, young things that are ready for the picking. We are the three musketeers: three darkly dangerous and, quite honestly to the sparkly young things that may cross our paths, predators without remorse. Jo is the perfect sidekick to our double act. She accepts us for what we are. Two guys that like to party hard and bat for both sides.

She asks for nothing more than our company and our protection. We take care of her. She's our female secret weapon that helps to draw in the next willing contestant when we are on the prowl. We've never had sex with her but we often help set her up with a girl or guy she may like, we make sure to check them out first. Make sure they are at least sane and have no dark intentions. (I know that sounds hypocritical coming from me.) I can almost smell the more devious of our kind.

If someone has anything other than just casual fun on their mind, we pull her out. So far, we've managed to keep ourselves out of harm's way in this dark world we swim around in. My fascination with walking on the wild side, pushing boundaries and flitting between partners has unfortunately given me the reputation of a dominant playboy. It also hasn't gone unnoticed that Ash and I often work as a team. It helps I have a strong alpha vibe going on. No one messes with me. Unless I want them to of course.

Jo arrives and, after two lines each, we are ready to take on the world. The evening goes by in a blur of cocktails and flirting. Jo picks up a vivacious girl with red hair who is dripping with sexual energy and seems a little more mature in her attitude towards us three 'misfits' than most. Ash is more interested in watching tonight and I never say no to giving a show.

We head back to my pad at one in the morning, slightly charged on tequila cocktails and the thought of what's about to happen. The redhead seems keen to party and I dim the lights, flick on some tunes and chop some more lines. Ash is sitting on my couch; his legs open showing his ample package with a sly smile on his pretty face. He is very pretty.

Redhead and Jo dance a little while I snort my first line

and grab the bottle of tequila I have stashed at the back of the drinks cabinet. The thought of how the hell I'm going to deal with the guy from the lottery on Monday with another monster comedown makes me smile.

I'm already working out what I'll say to Hilary, my receptionist, in the morning as to why I'm not coming into work and that she needs to reschedule my appointments. No scratch that – I won't be coming in, full stop. I'm going to disappear for a while. Take some time out and think about my options.

Ash lets out a "fuck yeah" as he lifts his head after inhaling his line of coke. His eyes are popping out of his head and the vein on his forehead is pulsing like it's about to burst. I hope it doesn't. Jo now has her tongue down Redhead's throat and Ash and I are grinning like two kids in a candy shop.

Happy days indeed.

Chapter Three

Okay. So, the guy from the lottery has just left. It's four o'clock on Monday afternoon and the sun is shining in more ways than one. He confirmed my ticket as genuine and I'm now the happy recipient of twenty-five million quid. Fabulous.

I watched him go through the motions, analysing him – as I always do with everyone I meet– as he talked through what would happen next, how the money would be wired into my account after his financial advisor had been to see me and asked me if I wanted to go public with my win.

I reiterated my 'no thank you very much'. I'm not about to expose to the world that I'm now a rich bastard. Not just a rich bastard but one who, if the press chose to dig a little deeper into my life would discover, is just a little bit dark and dangerous.

I'm more than happy to keep my new wealth a secret.

The only person who will know I'm now very well off is Ash. That's if he'll actually believe me, which trust me, eventually, he will. He's a fucking idiot but I love him; I always have and always will. He's always been the one and only person who has totally accepted me for what I am: fucked-up and a little bit wicked. With a shiny smile.

I'll take some time out, think this through properly so that I don't end up snorting the entire fortune up my nose or blow it on a shitload of useless crap I don't really need. Don't get me wrong, I intend to have fun with this money. A lot of fun. But that's a moot point, isn't it? What the hell do you do with that amount of money? You need to plan, that's what you need to do. After some serious partying, of course.

A week of serious partying with Ash results in the loss of more brain cells for both of us. I get Hilary to reschedule my appointments for in another months' time and have her tell everyone I've had to go abroad for the funeral of a close family member – which is total bullshit as I have nothing to do with my family anymore. Now, I'm ready to disappear.

Which is probably just as well as it's getting harder to avoid bumping into previous conquests. I will need to widen my territory if I want to avoid any uncomfortable situations in the future. Ash has finally come to terms with the fact that I'm now set for life. His first words were, "You lucky bastard, why in the hell would the universe give such an amazing gift to a shithead like you?"

I just smiled at him. My shark's smile. He knows I'll see him right. He is my wingman, my brother, my lover, my friend, my everything and I'll always make sure he is first on the list of things to be taken care of. He also thinks I'm insane when I tell him I'm going to take some time off in the countryside and think about what I'm going to do next.

His suggestion of hiring a yacht and sailing around the Med for the summer, fucking, drinking and debasing whoever was unlucky enough to cross our paths was not really on my agenda. I, for once in my life, want to do the right thing with this weird shift in my life's path. I mean, come on, who gets an opportunity like this?

Very few, that's who.

So, here I am with an oversized duffel bag on my shoulder walking down the towpath of a canal in Wiltshire, heading to the barge I've rented for a month. Crazy, eh? Yep, that's what Ash thought. "You could at least hide in the Caribbean, arsehole. Why the fuck are you going to some shithole when you can take your pick of places across the world?" he spat at me in distaste when I told him my plan.

To be honest, I'm not entirely sure. Yeah, I trawled through travel magazines, the internet and scoured for places the beautiful people would head for in these circumstances but, for some weird and totally unfathomable reason, I ended up booking a canal barge in Wiltshire. I just stumbled across it.

The website described it as *a widebeam canal barge sitting on the glorious banks of the Kennet & Avon canal.* The literature tempted me with total solitude and a slow pace of life and, most importantly it seems, no one to stop me sailing the bloody thing if I'm twatted off my head.

Sounded perfect to me.

They sent me the instructions a few days ago. It was like learning from psychology textbooks, easy when you have an eidetic memory. That's a photographic memory to the layperson. Fuck knows who I inherited that from. But, who cares, it's a wonderful gift to possess.

Plus, I'm not great with flying. I've travelled, don't get me wrong, and been to plenty of places in the sun but, for now, I just want something easy, familiar but off the grid. If I get bored, fed up or lonely, I can just get on a train back to London, pick up Ash and head out to some other destination.

Besides, with Ash hanging around I can never think straight, usually because we are taking far too many narcotics and have our dicks in places they shouldn't be. With a problem like mine – ha ha, *problem*! – I need to escape to a place where no one knows me and I'm not likely to bump into any clients who want to know why I'm not available to sort out their problems.

At this precise moment, I couldn't care less if they are self-harming, traumatised from losing a loved one or just unable to deal with the fact their partner has left them for someone else (of the same sex). Yep, I'm going to be a selfish bastard. And now a very rich, selfish bastard.

So now I'm an expert in the art of starting, steering and living on a canal barge. Easy peasy. I intend to just sit on the deck and watch the world go by with a big bag of weed. I know, it would have been impossible for me to not have at least one form of naughty pleasure with me on this quest of 'doing the right thing with a large sum of money'.

Weed helps me think. It helps me calm down and it makes me laugh. A lot.

I took a taxi to a pub called, funnily enough, The Barge Inn, in a place called Honey Street, in the middle of God knows fucking where. It cost me a small fortune. But hell! Who cares when you have shitloads of money? I wasn't going to sit on the train with a massive bag full of clothes and weed all the way from London to Wiltshire. No way.

Ash told me to keep in touch – and not to masturbate too much. He knows me too well and has placed bets on how long I'll actually last on this stupid quest. I'm determined to make it at least a week before I cave. One good thing is the fact that the weather report is suggesting a heatwave for the next week or so. Bloody marvellous. I can chill out, get a tan and really think things through.

I walk past the pub, which seems nice enough and, most likely, a place I'll frequent for some decent food (I'm not the best cook). I head down the towpath. The instructions said the barge would be moored a short distance down from the pub.

The sun is shining and I'm starting to sweat carrying this big-assed bag on my shoulder. There are a few boats moored by the pub and they all seem okay. The boat I've rented is called *The Water Witch* and is apparently wider than your usual canal barge, fitted with all mod cons, including a bath and a shower. Thank God.

I'm yet to see the water point mentioned in the pamphlet. I'll have to ask someone at some point where that is and how long it will take to navigate my way down the canal to find it. I'm not fazed by this. I'm resilient with most things. In fact, I'm smiling as I think about taking *Ms Witch* out for a spin at some point.

Even if I sink the bloody thing, I can afford the insurance. I'd rather not sink it, however, and I'm glad I requested that she be fully stocked on my arrival with a full tank of water, diesel and food. I paid extra for that, of course.

After twenty minutes of trekking, I round a bend on the towpath. I'd not anticipated that it would be so far away from the pub. I'm frowning by the time I see it but am glad that, at last, I've found my oasis in the desert. *The Water Witch* is sitting flush to the bank, gleaming black and sexy in the shadow of a large willow tree.

She looks fat compared to the other boats I've walked past but decadently wicked, as if she is grinning at me awaiting my presence and like she already knows who is about to step aboard. The front of the boat is painted with a dark-haired temptress, her hair flowing behind her as she rides her broomstick. Naughty.

I like her immediately, with her name painted in bright red and her stockings flashing from under her dress like a very wicked witch indeed. The artwork is incredible and whoever owns this boat clearly takes care of her. She is perfect.

The gangplank creaks slightly as the water pulls the boat gently in a slow slide. I step on, hiking my bag up higher on my shoulder as I place my boot on the metal of the engine compartment. The air is thick with heat and sweetly scented from the fields on either side of the canal that are high with corn. The sound of bird song and the rustling of the reeds fills my ears.

It's sublime. Idyllic.

Throwing my bag on the floor with a thud, I wrestle in my pocket to find the key.

Chapter Four

Hot air blasts me as I step down inside the hull of the boat. Now I'm smiling. This boat is tip-top, perfect for me and decked out with some comfy furnishings. The kitchen I've stepped down into is small but modern, the open-plan design reveals a large living area beyond with a huge wood burner in the corner – I won't need that if this weather keeps up.

A long narrow hallway leads off to a bathroom and then two bedrooms, one with bunk beds and the master, at the front of the boat, with doors that open giving the most amazing view out onto the canal. The bed in the master bedroom is huge and takes up most of the space. I can already see myself, spliff in hand, lying on it naked without a care in the world.

I'm more than happy with my chosen hideaway.

I open all the windows and let the air circulate, immediately sending a cool breeze down the length of the boat, casting out the stifling heat. I strip naked in the bathroom and step under the shower, the water is freezing but exactly what I need after working up a sweat.

I'm happy to find the owner has left a bottle of tequila and beers in a cool box filled with ice, which is still nice and cold, just as I'd requested. Top score on TripAdvisor coming up for them. I've showered and changed into shorts and a vest within fifteen minutes of my arrival. I don't hang about.

Beer in hand. Spliff already rolled. Sorted.

Half an hour later, sitting on the roof of the boat in a deckchair, I'm beginning to wonder if Ash is going to win the bet and I'll be home within two days. Don't get me wrong, it's beautiful here and just what I asked for but I'm already bored shitless.

My spliff is unwinding me nicely and the beer is still cold but I'm feeling a little strange perched up here watching the ducks and swans float by. Just as I'm about to cave and ring Ash, I hear someone approaching along the towpath. My ears perk up and my eyes adjust in the bright sunshine to see a person coming closer on a pushbike.

It's a woman. A young woman. There is a god.

She's cycling at a leisurely pace, her face upturned to the sky with a slight smile on her lips as if she's daydreaming. She doesn't see me at first, sitting on top of this black beast, but I certainly see her. Her hair is dark, a beautiful ebony black, the top section is spiked, almost in a Mohawk with intricate braids woven into the sides of her scalp. Wearing short shorts, biker boots, a tiny vest top and sporting a thousand brightly coloured bracelets she looks like a sexy character from some futuristic comic book. Her arms are decorated with tattoos. Lots of them in swirling feminine patterns.

Very intriguing.

She comes to a screeching halt beside *The Water Witch* as she spots me, her face like an open book as she takes me in. It's priceless. I grin at her and salute her with the beer. She's very pretty, with soft features, full lush lips and dark blue eyes. They scan me with what looks like shock. I often have that effect on people.

"Hi," I say flashing her my best 'I'm not a crazy person' smile. She's holding her bike steady, her feet now on the ground, as she stares up at me. It seems to take her a while before she can respond.

"I didn't know anyone had rented *The Witch* for the summer," she says in a voice that is warm and sultry like molasses. As I'm sitting with my legs open, my crutch on full display, I wonder for a moment if my tackle is hanging out of my shorts. I shift discretely and watch her eyes take in the movement. Oh, she's fish food for sure.

"Yeah, I've come down from London. Taking some time out for the summer," I respond, still smiling.

She nods slowly. "City boy, eh?" She says in a tone that suggests she's not impressed in the slightest.

I laugh with amusement. "I suppose." She's still staring at me, scanning me, and I suddenly feel vulnerable as if she can see through my carefully constructed walls and has full view of the real person inside. "I'm Jax. Nice to meet you."

She smiles in return, but it doesn't quite reach her eyes. She's a little wary of me, that much is obvious. "Jade. I live on the next boat down."

I raise a brow. Interesting, I have a neighbour and a very pretty one at that. She surveys me one more time then pushes up on her pedals and begins to cycle off again.

Just as I begin to think that's the end of it, she turns around and winks at me. "See you around, City Boy."

I can't help the shit-eating grin that spreads across my face as I watch her pert arse disappear down the towpath. Despite this girl being the exact opposite of what I usually find attractive, she's caught my attention and may turn out to be my only source of entertainment while I'm here. My grin morphs into a sly smile as I think about how it might be good for me to shake things up a bit. Dip into a new paint pot and get messy with someone that won't just roll over in submission at my first sexy smile.

This girl with her tattoos and funky style seems like someone that may be a good challenge.

Oh, I do hope I see you around little Jade. I really do.

That evening I manage to cook myself something that resembles a half-decent meal. The small kitchen is easy to navigate and has everything I could possibly need. The owners have kindly stocked the fridge for me. I take my plate of steak and salad back up to the roof, which was becoming my favourite place to chill, with another cold beer.

It's still light at nine o'clock. I haven't seen a soul since Jade. The solitude of this place is both soothing and unnerving. There is nothing here but Mother Nature and she is bursting around me in abundance. The sound of the birds and the trees rustling in the evening breeze is almost hypnotic; the way the barge moves silently back and forth, tugging against the ropes, is surreal.

I call Ash to let him know I've arrived here in one piece. He's amused by my description of the place and tells me I'll last another day before I end up calling him after arranging another taxi back to London. I'm determined now to hang in here and make good use of this time alone.

I haven't been alone for a long time. In fact, as I dig into my steak and sit silently watching the sun go down from my rooftop terrace, I ponder on my incapability of being without distraction or stimulation from others for too long. I don't like my own company all that much. It's like seeing myself staring back in the mirror, the realisation that I'm trying to be something I'm not.

Normal, nice. Boring.

I never used to be like this. As a kid, I was easy going, friendly, fun, in a normal, kid-like way. Then puberty began and I quickly deduced I was far from normal. I would fantasise about things the other kids did not and became very good at hiding my sexual preferences. My parents had no idea.

I learnt the hard way, of course. Got fucked-up a few

times for being a 'faggot' when I experimented in my teens. My father always gave me that odd look when I would come home beaten to a pulp; I think he always knew something was amiss. My mother, funnily enough, seemed totally oblivious to my dangerous wanderings at the weekends, when I would go out searching for something to scratch the itch.

Of course, I brought a few girls back, played the part of the 'normal' heterosexual boy. But the shit really hit the fan when, one night, my father walked in on me and a boy from my maths class when we were supposedly studying. I had his dick in my mouth and was sporting a hard-on even I was proud of. He literally beat the shit out of me for that unexpected show. A good Catholic boy would never, ever indulge in such a wicked sin. Everything he had ever preached to me as a child was broken in that moment. He was disgusted by my behaviour and angry as hell that I could defy him in such a way.

I left my family home at the ripe old age of seventeen. I never went back. I knew I could never fit in and, quite frankly, I didn't want to.

I left college, took myself up to the big city and somehow managed to get a job working in some shitty insurance company. I took night classes, even slept rough for a while and learnt how to take care of myself when things got rough. I became a good fighter as well as a good lover. I learnt to trust my instincts: when to get the hell out of Dodge and when to stick around.

Some of the things I did to survive during those early days still play on my mind. But I did them because I had to and, quite frankly, because I could. I've always had a way of manipulating people, taking what I wanted from them easily. Like a predator would; without a second thought. I had always been good at studying, could retain information easily and quickly and made my way up within the small company I worked for.

I could sell anything, even shitty insurance. I made money quickly. I even taught myself how to trade stocks. That's how I got by in the early days. But I became bored very easily and it was my fascination with people, and the fucked-up things they do daily, that led me down the psychology route and, eventually, to becoming a full-time shrink.

Life, despite the initial disadvantage of leaving my parental home at an early age, was easy for me. I met Ash in a club when I was twenty-five; he was like a moth to the flame and I fancied him something rotten. Who wouldn't? He's a shockingly beautiful man. Slightly effeminate but still rough and edgy, he'd been down a similar route to me. His family were completely dysfunctional and paid him little attention as a child. He'd also left home at an early age.

He'd experienced a rougher start down the bisexual byway but had finally settled when he landed a job in a city recruitment agency and had started to make good money. He'd also lived on the streets for a while and knew exactly what it was like to be me. Well, without the photographic memory and abilities to sort people's shit out. I still laugh my arse off at that one. Who would have thought it, with my background and secrets? But, so far, I've winged it very nicely, thank you very much.

Ash knows all my secrets and I know his. He's never judged me for the fact that I became a petty thief in the early days; I would seduce women and take their money and jewellery after we'd had sex and they were sleeping soundly. I would disappear without a trace, leaving them satisfied – but with an empty purse.

My morals were a little clouded in those days. Gay men were easier to control as I've always been dominant, something they often loved. I would take what I could from them too. Ash says I was merely surviving, doing what I could to put food in my belly and, eventually, a roof over my head.

He's the only person I know that could justify my behaviour when it was, in fact, wrong. We would never, ever destroy the trust we have in each other and, funnily enough, we both have the unnatural ability to never get jealous. In fact, I've never had a jealous thought in my life. I believe we should be able to be with whomever we wish whenever we wish. Why trap ourselves in monogamy when there is a whole world of different sweets to choose from?

I think Ash and I were probably separated at birth. We are like twin souls, who no one truly understands. Of course, everyone wants a piece of us. The irony. Ash is beautiful, witty, a bit of a bitch and fantastic in the sack. People radiate towards him like he's some kind of magnet. I can see why.

We are very careful about how we conduct ourselves in front of people. Like chameleons, we change colour and shape and fit into each scenario perfectly: best friends, work colleagues, sexual playmates. We can work each role like a perfectly choreographed dance without letting the illusion slip. Hence why work believe I'm a 'normal' man in his prime, with good friends, a good job and lots of girlfriends; only a select few get a glimpse occasionally of the complexity of who I really am.

Ash says I remind him of some Australian beach bum, with my chin-length hair that curls naturally and is bleach blonde. I tie it back for work, which I know gives some of my female clients a little thrill – I see it in their eyes when they first meet me in my pinstripe, three-piece suit and my fancy office. I'm nothing like your average shrink.

I've had my fair share of stalkers, but I can see it coming

before it happens and cut the supply off immediately. I can handle anyone and pretty much anything. You see, the wonderful thing about being me is that nothing whatsoever can shock me or upset me. Tell me anything and I'll analyse it, play with it, unravel it, and then solve the problem. Simple.

I remember a guy who came to see me with severe panic attacks. He had no idea he was gay. Not one tiny bit. I had to delve slowly into his psyche, gain his trust, push a few buttons. When he eventually came to terms with the fact his feelings of being out of control, were purely a result of his refusal to accept who he really was, it was like the floodgates had opened. He was ecstatic and horrified all at once. I helped him on his new path and, a year later, he came back to see me, happy in a gay relationship with a man he had met recently.

Another happy customer.

Chapter Five

After finishing my meal, I pull out my packet of cigarettes and light one up, watching a swan float by looking like some regal fun ride. It's still warm and I'm not wearing a top, just shorts and no shoes. It's liberating.

I walk around my flat naked most of the time. Wearing a suit for work all day makes me feel restricted and, by the time I get home, I can't wait to strip off and let it all hang out. I contemplate sitting up here looking out over the fields in my birthday suit but decide there's a good chance some dogwalker will come down the towpath and report me for indecent exposure. Not the first time it's happened. Luckily, it was before I gained my practice in Harley Street.

I'm happily puffing away and taking swigs from my cold beer when I see a shadow on the towpath in the distance. Two, in fact: one person and one that looks like a dog. It's black and shaggy, not too small, not too big. I smile as I see Jade approach. She is walking her dog. Cute.

My dick instantly twitches, eager to jump up and see to her. Down boy. Her dog runs ahead and is suddenly up my gangplank, looking up at me sitting on the roof, wagging its tail and panting with its giant tongue lolling out to one side. I'm grinning back at it like we are both of the same species.

"Bob, leave Jax alone you little shit," Jade shouts at him. I laugh. She reaches my boat and tries to call her dog back; he's sitting down now, just looking up at me.

"It's okay, he can probably smell the steak," I say watching her as she starts to look a little agitated by her dog's lack of discipline.

"He's a bugger, just runs off at the slightest whiff of food, terrible scrounger," she says.

She's changed from the shorts and vest into a dress. It shows off all her lovely curves; her tits and long legs. She looks like dessert to me. I smile at the biker boots she's still wearing. An odd match to her new outfit. But they suit the rebellious aura I'm picking up from her and wonder what they would look like flung around my neck. Bob is still sitting there looking up at me like I hold all the answers to his doggy food problem.

I don't want her to rush off yet. I stand up, stub my fag out in the ashtray and start to step down off the roof just as the dog becomes excited and jumps up at my legs. Jade steps onto the boat and tries her best to restrain him. He's the craziest dog I have ever seen, his fur is like dreadlocks, and he has tiny black eyes and the cutest little nose. I don't usually like animals but this one is intriguing me, like its owner.

"I'm really sorry. He doesn't usually make such a fuss over people."

I look at her and reply with a smile. "I'm not like most people."

There is a pause as if she is holding her breath. I like that I have stunned her a little. She will be fun to play with. "Would you like a beer?" I say, indicating the cool box sitting beside us. She is petting Bob who is staring up at me as if I can still provide him with steak.

"I really need to walk Bob but thanks for the offer."

She's going to take off before I have even had a chance to stick my claws in. "Okay. I could do with a walk, been sitting up here since I arrived. Mind if I join you for a bit?" She's biting her lip looking a little confused and wary. Perfect.

She tilts her head to one side as if assessing me for any unseen threat, her hair falls across her shoulder as she does. She has loosened it from the braids and it is wavy and quite long. I'm instantly imagining pulling it back into a long ponytail, tugging it hard as I fuck her from behind. I catch the shift in her expression as she stares at me oddly as I unashamedly run my mini porn film through my brain. Her eyes flick suddenly to my bare chest. I smile again knowing full well this girl is totally aware of my horny vibe.

"I'll grab a shirt," I say. I haven't even waited for her to say yes. Taking control. It's what I do best. She is, as I knew she would be, waiting for me when I reappear wearing a T-shirt. I know she clocked my nipple piercing: I saw her lick her bottom lip as she took me in. Ash and I were both pierced on a day of boredom one weekend. He had his cock pierced; I had my nipple done. It's the only rebellious declaration I have on my body, both men and women seem to love it and I'm the first to admit it does increase sensitivity.

We take off down the towpath. She remains silent as Bob wanders off in front of us sniffing the grass and doing his doggy thing. I can sense the cogs in her brain whirring. I look at her in my peripheral vision, she is looking straight ahead her eyes downcast. Her chest is a little red, a slight blush of what looks like either embarrassment or arousal blooming across her gorgeous tits. Perhaps she's trying to work me out, understand why a city boy would be interested in hiding out on a canal barge for the summer alone. I'm already keen to find out more about her. Not just because there's no one else here to talk to. She's caught my interest, that's for sure.

"How long have you lived on a boat?" I ask as we walk. She looks up at me and I'm momentarily blinded by the depth in her blue eyes. They literally sparkle.

"Two years. It's a nice way of life, close to nature, away

from people." I nod digesting this. She finds people difficult to be around, prefers the peace and quiet of the countryside, which means she has most likely had some trauma in her life and has run away. Interesting.

"Different," I comment. She is still looking at me, trying to work me out. I like that. I see no sexual interest in her eyes but her body is indicating something different. Her breathing is a little fast and her hands are clenched by her side as if she is trying not to grab something or someone. I'm really enjoying this.

"Yeah, I suppose so." She says nothing more. Her reluctance to elaborate tells me she is going to be a little more difficult to win over than my usual conquests.

"It must be nice in the summer living out here. But a little more difficult when the weather changes, eh?" I ask. Bob comes bounding back to us with a stick in his mouth. Jade takes it from him and throws it down the towpath, he runs off like a massive ball of black dreads and leaves a plume of dust in his wake.

"You get used to it," she replies as if my observation is a minor detail. Her left boot is clinking slightly as she walks, the sound catches my attention and my eyes wander downwards. Something's wedged into the side of her boot and is sticking out over the top catching the buckle as she lifts and drops her foot. It's a pocketknife. She's packing, which makes her even more interesting to me. The fact she doesn't take her safety for granted in this place in the middle of nowhere makes me feel a sense of pride in her resilience. I smile at the irony she may have a darker side to her character just like me.

This girl has a story to tell and I want to hear it. "Don't you get lonely?" I ask her smiling.

She looks back at me as if I'm crazy. "No, never."

We walk for a bit more in silence, just enjoying the sweet

summer air and the last glimpse of the sun as it slips down over the horizon. We reach the pub quickly and she calls Bob to her, fastening a lead to his collar.

"Well, I should head back really," she says, looking at me as if I should stay here and let her walk back on her own. Fuck if I'm going to do that.

"Hey, the night's still young. We should have a quick drink before I walk you back," I say giving her my best smile. I start to think this girl is going to take off again before I have had a chance to dissuade her when she smiles back at me and nods slowly.

"Okay."

I take that as a positive and I'm glad that I have some cash in my pocket. I run a hand through my hair. It's loose and starting to curl annoyingly over my eyes. I see her watch my movements like she is trying not to be affected by me and my rugged good looks. Well, that's what Ash says anyway.

"What would you like?" Bob is sitting on my foot and panting again, his beady black eyes smiling at me like he knows I'm on the prowl.

"I'll have a cider, thanks." I nod and extract my foot from under her dog, heading into the pub. I glance back at her and watch as she takes a seat outside in the far corner of the garden looking over the canal.

I'm glad she's not decided to ditch me as soon as my back was turned.

Chapter Six

The inside of the pub is a real psychedelic headrush; a hippy's heaven. Pictures and paintings of crop circles and all things weird and UFO-like cover the walls. I feel like I've just stepped into a scene from *The X Files*. Everyone knows everyone and I'm clearly the outsider here. I've never seen anything like it in the city.

The guy behind the bar takes my order and eyes me warily. I've already taken note of all the exits, the people sitting around and the guys at the end of the bar who, if they knew I liked dick as well as pussy, would have no problem beating the shit out of me. You have to be constantly on alert when you are, what the average straight citizen of this world, may consider as a threat or a freak. Watch your back, take everything in like a goddamn SAS soldier. I've been caught out in the past entering new territory and flirting with the wrong people. I must have one of those faces that creates problems, especially when someone's girlfriend has taken a fancy to me and it ends in a standoff.

I pay for my pint, Jade's cider and some beef jerky for Bob, the dreadlocked dog. I wonder if he is named after Mr Marley himself. I hold the jerky in my mouth, the two pints in my hands, cursing silently in my head as they slosh a little as I navigate my way down the steps. It's beginning to get dark and the garden's lighting illuminates Jade sitting, patiently, waiting for me. She has her back to me and is looking out over the canal, by her feet the dog is now sprawled out like a rug. She has the most exquisite outline, sleek and slim, her hair is over one shoulder giving me a good view of her slender neck. I imagine holding it, biting it and restraining her a little with my thumb pushed into the curve. My cock twitches again. It's been a long time since a girl has caught my interest so much.

I normally go for blondes: big busty ones with lush lips. I don't usually like brunettes or anything slightly unusual and she ticks all the boxes for unusual. Rock-chick-fairy: not my type at all. But there is something about this girl with her pert arse, long legs and shy but confident edge.

It hits me, as I place our drinks on the table and she smiles up at me, why I'm finding myself inexplicably drawn to this girl, it's because she's like nothing I've ever seen before. The women in the city have a hard edge; they are primed and glossed a showcase that has been carefully constructed.

Jade is just Jade and not afraid to show it.

She sips her cider and licks her lips smiling at me. "Thanks. It's been a while since I shared a pint with anyone – apart from Bob." I love her smile. It lights up her face, she looks a little unapproachable until she smiles with her eyes lit up and not just a slight twitch of her lips. I have the feeling she doesn't smile that often in public.

Bob is up on his feet again, his nose in my crutch as he senses I have a treat for him. Jade watches me unwrap the beef jerky and I wait for her approval before giving it to him. She nods and grins as he takes it eagerly. I've made a new friend in her dog at least.

I take a swig of my beer and smile as the refreshing tartness of the drink slips down my throat. The beer is very good here. "What do you do all by yourself on your boat all day, Jade?" I ask her searching inside my shorts pocket for my Marlboro. I turn to face her, slipping one leg over the seat so that I'm straddling the bench-like seat. She is still facing the canal but turns her body slightly towards me. Good. I tap my cigarette on the packet. "Do you mind if I smoke?" I ask her before lighting up. Good manners are never a bad thing you know.

She smiles. "Not at all." She reaches for the packet and pinches one, grinning at me. I'm grinning back as I lean forward with my lighter as she places it in between her red lips. I hold the flame steady, inches from her, as she sucks on the cigarette.

Just watching the way she sucks on her smoke gives me another headrush and I've no doubt my pupils have dilated as if I've just come up on some nice little pill. She blows the smoke up over her head and looks me straight in the eyes as I light my own. "I write, that's my job. I read, I walk Bob, I sleep and I watch the world go by."

I pull on my cigarette, watching her watching me. Something is unfurling between us but I'm not sure what it is right now. I love a good mystery and this girl is certainly a mystery to me right now. "Very cool," I answer, searching my brain for something else to say as my body strains to get closer to her. She looks away again taking another sip of her cider.

"And what do you do, City Boy?" she asks, the edge of sarcasm in her voice irrefutable. I love that she has chosen to distance herself from me by giving me this nickname, it gives her power over me.

"I'm in finance." I reply without hesitation. I never tell people outside of work what I do, it just freaks them out, makes them uncomfortable, as if I'm going to psychoanalyse them. Which of course I do. Every time.

"Figures," she says with a slightly amused snort. I have her now. The lie has given me the advantage. I can be whatever I want to be with this girl and she will be none the wiser.

"What sort of things do you write?"

"Articles, astrology, that kind of thing," she answers me vaguely. Bob has finished his jerky and resumed his horizontal position at her feet.

She has my attention now. "Astrology?" I ask with a small smile. I know nothing about that world. Flaky bullshit if you ask me.

She turns to me fully, her face lighting up now as if she is about to reveal something interesting. "Yeah, I map people's astrology charts, help them see their life's path." I'm grinning at her response. She really is quirky, this sexy girl.

"How old are you?" I ask brazenly.

She takes another drag of her cigarette and smiles at me slyly. "What difference does it make?"

I laugh at the way she counter-attacks my question. "None. Just curious."

I like this gentle banter, this 'getting to know you' routine. I don't usually have to work so hard. But then usually it's a sexual pounce and whomever I'm pouncing on knows it and is up for it.

"I'm twenty-two," she says waiting for my reaction. I nod slowly still smiling. Giving nothing away. She's also much younger than I would normally be interested in. Women that young are all giggles, make-up and drama. Hard fucking work. Unless you are just banging them.

She swings her leg over the bench and straddles it, in the same way I am, facing me directly. I slow my erratic breathing as I catch a quick glimpse of her red underwear.

"And how old are you, Jax?" She's holding her cigarette in the air away from her face, holding the cider in the other hand like a double defence mechanism. She takes a sip of it and makes a show of licking the edge of the glass somewhat suggestively before swallowing slowly. God, I like this girl.

Placing the glass back down she narrows her eyes at me. Like a challenge.

"Thirty-four," I say waiting for her own reaction to the fact I'm quite a few years older than her.

She nods, smiling. "You look younger."

I shrug, noting that her left leg is bouncing a little now like she is nervous or excited. I take all these things in. "Thanks, I guess." We continue to stare at each other for a moment smoking our cigarettes in silence. I take one last slow drag on mine and then stub it out, she does the same, mirroring me perfectly.

A very good sign indeed.

I take a gamble and reach for her wrist, lifting it to inspect her many bangles and bracelets. She flinches a little when I first touch her and I loosen my grip so that she doesn't get too skittish. "I like these, very pretty." They jangle as I lift her arm. She blushes a little. Sweet.

"I make them," she says, her eyes downcast as if a little embarrassed.

I raise a brow. "You do? A girl of many talents then. A writer and bracelet maker, I'm impressed." I release her wrist gently; she watches my fingers uncurl from around her and shivers a little. The crack is there, I can see it. She is letting me in, slowly. "Perhaps you could make me one while I'm here." She looks up at me again and I can see the cogs whirring once more, trying to decipher my unbreakable code.

"Sure," she replies. She swings her leg back over the bench seat and faces the canal again. I've pushed her too hard. She is creating a barrier again.

I reach down to stroke her dog who opens one eye and wags his tail in a slow thump as I do. We sit in silence for a moment, sipping our pints. But it isn't an uncomfortable silence. We have said what we needed to say. She has discovered how old I am (the truth), what I do for a living (a bullshit) and asserted her independence and authority over me. She has stated her intentions, which at present are just one of a casual interest with perhaps a friendship while I'm here in the countryside for the summer.

I've already made my mind up that I'm not leaving *The Water Witch* until I've found out more about this girl. She intrigues me and, of course, has pressed all my horny buttons. In a strange way, she is acting like a mirror, reflecting my usual aloof character. Holding the world at arm's length so it can't see the true personality hiding deep within.

After finishing our drinks, we walk back to my boat slowly. She asks me a few non-intrusive questions, how am I liking the boat so far? Do I like to fish? Simple questions to make an easy conversation. I know she wants to ask me what the fuck a city boy like me is doing on my own on a boat in Wiltshire. I leave her with the thoughts and the questions she would really like to ask for another time.

I like that she hasn't given me the Spanish Inquisition. She values privacy and I know to remember that. I ask if she would like me to walk her to her boat, which I've still not seen. She smiles at me knowingly and shakes her head. "I'm good thanks."

We leave it at that and, for the second time that day, I watch her sexy arse slink down the towpath in the dark. I go inside my boat and strip off, head to the bedroom and knock one out while thinking of all the dirty and dark things I would like to do to her.

I have to say that day one of 'taking time out to think' has turned out a lot better than I expected.

Chapter Seven

I wake to find the sun shining in through the double doors. I'd left the doors open last night and now the flimsy curtains are moving back and forth in the light breeze.

It was spectacularly hot last night; I woke a couple of times stark naked and sprawled out across the massive bed. I check the clock beside the bed: it tells me it's half past eleven. I've slept late, something I never do. I slept well. Really well. The boat is like a cocoon that swallows you up and cradles you like a mother would, rocking you back and forth gently like a soothing lullaby.

I stretch out languorously, take note of my morning wood and decide to take a shower, then go for a run. There is bugger all else here to do. I wonder if I could hire some fishing equipment from somewhere. I might as well try something new.

The water is warm today, heated up nicely compared to the freezing heart-starter I experienced when I first got here. I tie up my laces and decide I'll run in the opposite direction of the pub. No coincidence that Jade and her boat are in that direction. None at all.

I open the double doors that lead out to the back of the boat and the gangplank. A small bag is hanging on the tiller. I walk towards it frowning. There is no note but, as I tip out the contents that land in my hand with a small jingle, I smile. Jade has made me a bracelet. It is black and tan, woven into a plait, with an intricate tie on one end.

Two charms are hanging in the middle: one, interwoven in the string, which is coin-shaped but has the head of a lion stamped onto it, the other a silver letter 'J' which hangs down on a tiny silver loop. I am intrigued that she chose the lion-headed coin. I am a Leo after all.

My smile grows wider and I look around as if I may just find her standing watching me from the bank somewhere. But she is nowhere to be seen. My only company is a group of ducks who are quacking at each other. Noisy bastards.

After fastening the bracelet to my right wrist, I take off at a gentle jog, enjoying the sun on my face and the way my legs are stretching nicely as I open my stride. It takes virtually no time at all before I see another boat. She is just around the bend from me, ridiculously close to my new home. I stop and look for any signs of life.

The boat is shut tight, secured with a padlock and the window shutters are closed. It's a long barge, sleek and slim, not a widebeam like *The Water Witch*. I grin as I see the name at the bow, painted in a gold colour in fancy writing: *The Water Nymph*. It suits her and the picture of the nubile woman, her upper body breaking up through a pool of water like some creature from a fantasy novel, makes me grin. The artwork looks very similar to the sexy witch on the front of my boat. I wonder if she painted them both.

She is obviously out so I head off down the towpath, jogging a little faster now to get my heart rate up and burn off some of the testosterone which seems to be pumping in full force today. My dick took a while to stand down in the shower today, even after I beat it into submission. It seems he is very happy to be here as well.

I run for half an hour then head back feeling more than a little hungry. The scenery here is beautiful. I've never been one for the countryside but, as I take in the green fields, the lush canal bank and its wildlife, I can see why people would be drawn to it.

I return to *The Witch* sweating like a pig and am grateful I left the shutters open on the canal side. I take another shower, careful not to use too much water. The sound of the tank rumbling when I switch it on reminds me of some great beast that is grumbling, I'm disturbing its sleep.

I slip on the same shorts I wore last night but a clean vest. I don't want to be a total skank. I'm rubbing my hair dry thinking about Jade and how good it felt to receive a gift from her when I hear my phone ringing. I know it's Ash before I even answer it.

"Hey fucker," he greets me as I pick up. "Ready to come home and book that yacht yet?"

I place the phone under my ear and hold it with my shoulder as I start to unload bacon and eggs from the small fridge. "No, I'm staying Ash. I like it here."

He snorts down the phone at me. It's Sunday, so he is most likely bored after a night out or hasn't gone to bed yet. "You must be bored out of your skull," he says. I can hear him moving around and the sound of music in the background, other people chatting but I can't make out whether they are male or female.

"It's very liberating," I quip back. He laughs. I can hear the voices a little clearer now, he must have walked back into his living room after grabbing a drink. He has female company, possibly Jo. Who the fuck knows who else he may have dragged home last night? He's a glutton for punishment and he tends to invite them all back then gets stuck when they don't want to leave.

I have strict rules with that kind of thing. I'm very picky with who gets to see my pad.

"You're a fucking idiot and will be home by Wednesday," he pauses mid-rant; I can hear him lighting a cigarette. "I also miss you and your beautiful dick. And it's boring without you."

I laugh flipping some bacon into a pan and clicking on the gas. "Darling, you will always be bored. And absence makes the heart grow fonder – especially for my dick."

He chuckles. "Look, I've got company, Jax. Just wanted to check that you hadn't sunk the boat and drowned in the night. I do miss you. Ring me when you've stopped dicking around with this 'I need to really think about what to do with my money' bullshit and we can start having some real fun." He pauses, only for a second, before continuing his dramatic dialogue. "Met this super funky guy at the bar last night. A tattoo artist covered in them like a goddamn Adonis. And he's hung like a fucking donkey. You should meet him."

I'm laughing as I flip my bacon. "Is he there now?" I ask. Ash takes another suck on his smoke; I hear him inhale then breathe out loudly.

"No, he left an hour ago. I only have Jo and Miss Redhead to play with now and they're probably leaving soon. Then I'll be all on my own again."

I fill the kettle with water and place it on the hob next to my sizzling bacon. I need coffee and fast. "Stop being a baby, get some sleep Ash and let me have this time to do what I want to do for once." He lets out a loud humph, clearly not impressed with my flippant answer to his current predicament.

"Fuck you, prick," he spits at me then hangs up. I smile knowing that whatever insults Ash throws at me, he does it with love and, quite honestly, he hasn't seen me behave in this way before, taking off like this. Okay, he knows I've just won the lottery and need to digest that fact but the Jax he knows would have taken a month off to blow coke up his nose and dance the fandango with whoever was up for it with no other thoughts than to rock my socks off.

Even I am a little amused by my strange behaviour.

It's as if I was drawn to this place despite my lottery win. I glance at the bracelet on my wrist as I continue to make my brunch and coffee and can't help smiling again. Perhaps *The Water Witch* cast a spell on me from afar and pulled me here so that I could meet this very strange and special young woman called Jade. I snort at my own thoughts. Even I am beginning to believe in some strange twist of fate with all this, even with the fact that I have achieved a million-in-one opportunity that most people only ever dream of: winning the lottery.

With this thought on my mind, I eat, gulp down two cups of black coffee and then check for any messages on my phone. An unknown number has called and when I listen to the message left, I'm amused to discover it's from the lottery guy asking when I would like to book his financial advisor. They are insisting I do this before they wire me the money. I text him back and say I have my own financial advisor who will be assisting me and give him details of the private bank account that I have.

Won't they shit a brick when they see twenty-five million pounds arrive in my account?

I have been advised the money will take approximately three days to reach me once I have given them the account details. I intend to do my own research with what banks I will then divide the money between and whether they will be abroad or in this country.

I have absolutely no intention in having some stuck-up prick from the lottery belittle me and tell me what I should do with my winnings. I worked the stocks for long enough to know about banking.

It's just a game, like everything else in life, and I intend to play this well.

Chapter Eight

I spend the next two hours thinking about what banks I'll approach, writing down a list of questions to ask with regards to what type of interest they provide et cetera, et cetera. The top banks will no doubt want me to make an appointment before they will even speak to me about this type of information. I have a broker who I work with, he's a good bloke but, on this occasion, I won't use him to spread my new wealth across the board.

I want no one other than Ash to know I have this money. Oh, and of course the guy at the lottery. I signed the paperwork the day he came to see me stating I wanted complete privacy, he made no comment on this. I sussed him immediately. A man that ironically secretly disliked lucky people – and definitely people like me who were young enough to enjoy the spectacular windfall of a lottery win. The poor bastard probably pissed someone royally off in a previous life to land this job. All the things he hated the most in his face regularly. I tried to hide the smirk on my face when he finished signing the paperwork with me. I was rich; he wasn't. Tough titty, go and find another job, man.

I have selected three banks on my list and called leaving messages asking for appointments by the time I've finished deciding who I should trust with my new wealth. I don't want to leave all my eggs in one basket. Cautious, that's me now. I make sure to leave my mobile number and the contact at the lottery for verification of my wealth for the banks to check and to contact me on, seeing as I'm not working for a few more weeks.

I'm not sure *if* I will return to my job yet. I know I will become bored and probably end up killing myself quickly if I do nothing but party with all this money. But I'm not sure I want to return to the role of shrink again when, potentially, I have the world at my fingertips.

I think briefly of my mother and father. I am an only child. I would like to send them some money but I'm not sure how to go about it. It would give me peace of mind to know they don't have to worry about their retirement now. I'm not sure my father would even accept it. His 'faggot' son – who is not actually a faggot but something, in his opinion, even weirder and fucked-up – sending him money would not go down well with him.

Mum would be tickled pink with the money. She wouldn't have to keep working part-time at Marks & Spencer and would be able to book herself a cruise with all the other old crusties. You see, although I'm no longer in contact with my family, it doesn't mean I have no clue as to what they are doing with their lives. I have my ways. I'm not a completely insensitive bastard; I do keep an eye on them from a distance.

I decide to walk to the pub and ask about the fishing equipment. I've nothing better to do apart from smoke my next big fatty and watch the ducks. The guy behind the bar looks at me like I'm some sort of village idiot when I ask him the question. "No man. No idea where you could get fishing gear from. You could ask some of the other boaties if they will lend you theirs if you like," he says scratching his head.

I smile at him politely and leave without buying anything. I may go back later and eat something if I get bored again. I'm still not sure whether I'll get lynched by the locals if I keep popping my head in there. When Jade was with me it was easier to go in and order a couple of pints.

I consider wandering down to see if she is home yet but my gut is telling me not to push her. Let her come to me. It's frustrating as fuck. Eventually, I decide to just chill with a spliff on the roof again after making myself a light dinner of beans and toast. I happily munch on junk food after two spliffs and a can of Red Bull. I know, my diet is not the best, God knows how I stay in such good shape. Probably all the running and sex; both good for burning the calories, or so they say.

I watch the sun go down and look up at the sky as it turns an inky black above me. I see a few shooting stars, which scares the shit out of me as I'm pretty stoned by now. After seeing all the crop circle shit in The Barge Inn, I wonder if aliens are really going to land next to me and give me an anal probe.

I'm laughing like a sick fuck when I think how much I would probably like that. Something different for a change. I think about my life in general, sitting on top of the boat and listen to the wildlife around me croaking, buzzing and clicking like a National Geographic programme.

So far, my life has been an amazing journey full of fun, shit, frolics and the odd good beating. I have lived a very full life and now I have been given something almost incomprehensible to make it even more wonderful.

I'm very good at helping people work out problems in their life. I find it simple to find solutions to what they cannot see is right in front of them. But this problem – the one where I have suddenly come into an obscene amount of money overnight – I cannot seem to solve.

I cannot see what I am going to do with all this money.

I could give some of it to charity. No, screw that. They don't really use the money for the actual people that need it. I know that. I could help businesses. That would require some input on my behalf and I really can't be bothered right now. I could become a recluse and walk around naked growing a beard down to my waist and eating coconuts on some private beach on a private island I have brought all for myself. Where would be the fun in that?

I could take Ash and me on the adventure of a lifetime, we could move around the globe hitting all the bars, clubs and people we could on the way. This option would only result in the death of both of us. We would self-combust from gluttony and wickedness within a year. I need some help with this and sitting here on a boat in the middle of nowhere at present is coming up with zilch.

The only thing I've done since I've been here is to spend some time alone getting stoned, rather than being with Ash and getting stoned. I watch another shooting star glide across the dark sky and then it hits me. That's not the only thing I've done since I arrived. I've done something I've never done before. I've wanted something I cannot really have. I've started to feel something I've never really felt. Emotions for a girl I know very little about.

It fascinates me and scares the shit out of me, simultaneously.

I jump back off the roof, almost slipping into the canal after my stargazing, stumble down into the boat and crash around a bit before flopping onto the bed. I can't even be bothered to undress. I lie there looking up at the ceiling for a while, in a nice state of stoned-ness. I see images in my mind of that dark-haired girl walking towards me naked, her finger poised in front of her in a gesture of 'come hither'. She beckons me even now, like a phantom in the night, her eyes shining and her lips tilted in a smug knowing smile.

I drift off to sleep knowing that I'm fucked. Well and truly.

The next two days go by without any sign whatsoever of Jade. It's as if I dreamt her. She was not real. Each day I run past her boat it is padlocked and silent; the painted girl on the side of *The Nymph* smiles at me with a wicked knowing smile. "No chance, not even slightly," she says to me when I pass her. I think she may be right.

Jade has simply disappeared. I feel a little put out. Let down. Disappointed.

I was just starting to enjoy the chase, the 'getting to know you' thing that normal people do. But she did make me a bracelet and that must have meant something. I find myself looking at it a lot. What am I turning into? Some lovesick pubescent? I carry on regardless.

I'm pleased to hear that my money is finally being wired to my Lloyds account and should be sitting there on Monday next week. I try to make a mental note to ring my bank and give them a heads up. Right at this moment, I don't feel like speaking to anyone.

I've received daily calls from Ash giving me abuse and telling me to get my sweet arse back to London. I have humoured him so far, telling him I'm fine, enjoying the peace and quiet and am in no hurry to return to the chaotic hustle of the city.

In fact, that is true. I've started to find a rhythm in this place, I'm loving the boat and its connection to nature. I've become a water gypsy; outside all the time, during the day, during the night. I'm also smoking an obscene amount of weed but I am finding a clarity I have not had for a long time. Without my usual distractions, I'm discovering there's a part of me that relishes the slower pace of life here. It's giving me a chance to see the world with new eyes, enjoy the extra time to explore the beauty of what is around me, instead of missing it as I rush through each day on a schedule ruled by work and my desire to fill every damned second with something other than simply being still.

Time rolls by. Several days blur together, filled with nothing but a sense of freedom, as I do very little except relax into this new environment, enjoying the fact that no one is currently demanding my attention. I must be getting low on water by now and my initial food supply has now gone. I cannot believe I have been here a week tomorrow. I have survived this on my own without another living soul. I have only been to the pub twice for food and fags. I know I am secretly waiting for the return of the mysterious Jade.

Chapter Nine

Saturday morning, I am up early as I crashed around ten o'clock last night after a tequila binge. Sad but true, I know. I am looking through the cupboards trying to find something, anything, I can eat when I stumble across what looks like pieces of fishing line and hooks in a dusty corner, hidden at the back.

I remember reading that the canal has an abundance of crayfish that like to hide in the shadowy mud banks. I find a tin of Spam at the back of the cupboard. Jackpot. I eat some of the Spam for breakfast with a beer (a fabulous combination) and then decide to forgo my usual run and try a spot of crayfish fishing. I roll myself a fatty, taking note that I'm running low despite the considerable amount I brought with me and then head out of the boat in search of the perfect spot. I remember doing this as a kid with my Dad, before I grew up and he decided I was a sexual fuck-up and beat the shit out of me. It was fun – the fishing, not the beating.

In no time, I have five lines set up and am sitting under the shade of a big willow tree on the bank in a handy little nook with my spliff. I've zoned out, tuned into my music that is turned up fairly loud, happy in my own little world of imagining how I can cook and devour my crayfish when I start to experience that weird tingly feeling of being observed. I can't ignore it. As much as I want to. I'm really not in the mood to start chatting to some walker interested in what I've caught. Especially with a big spliff in my hand.

I reluctantly look up and find myself face-to-face with the particularly delicious rock-chick-fairy that had decided, until that moment, to disappear on me. She grins at me and says something, although I have no idea what until I pull the buds from my ears.

"Is that a spliff?" she asks me, pointing to the offending object in my fingers.

"Hello, Jade," I say shifting my position so that I can look at her properly.

The tinny sound of my music playing in the background catches her attention. "What are you listening to?" she says with, what sounds like, amusement in her voice.

I laugh. "That's two questions, without a hello first."

She crouches down and then I see Bob sitting behind her, his tongue hanging out. He looks like someone has given him a really bad bath and is covered in bits of green scum that resemble seaweed.

"Hello, Jax. Is that a spliff and what are you listening to?" she repeats with a twinkle in her eyes.

"Yes, it is. Would you like some? I'm listening to some drum and bass," I say, with an equal amount of cheekiness to my tone as she just dished out. She reaches forward as I pass her the spliff.

"I'd love some, thank you. And I didn't plug you as a drum and bass kinda guy."

I'm watching her like a hawk, trying to contain the excitement in my brain – and in my pants – that she is here again and talking to me as if she didn't just disappear without a trace for the whole week. I'm literally seeing fireworks exploding behind my eyes at the thrill of being so close to her again. She smells delicious, like a fruity cocktail with a hint of vanilla. The first time we met she had a slight aroma of wood smoke and something heady, like patchouli or some such hippy shit clinging to her. She looks polished like she has been at a spa; her face and hair are sparkly clean.

Her hair is braided again, tied up in a funky twist on top of her head with the spiky Mohawk sticking out in a mad display that would only work on someone so beautiful. The new and improved Jade. Not that she didn't look good before. Now she looks utterly edible and extremely tasty; I could lick all of her from top to bottom right now. If only.

She tilts her head at me as she takes a long slow drag on my joint. My balls stir and rise, as if in a salute to her sexiness. I'm feeling hot, despite the shade of the tree, and conclude that I really have lost my fucking mind over this girl. I have been patiently waiting for her to return and now she is here, looking at me and waiting for my response while I just grin like a bloody idiot.

"What kind of music did you think I'd like?" I finally ask, curious about her answer.

She takes one more hit on the joint before passing it back to me. "Not that type of music, that's for sure."

I smile and quirk a brow ignoring her jibe. "Where have you been, Jade?" I ask, narrowing my eyes as I drag on the joint and the smoke filters up into my face.

"Shopping, visiting a friend. Stuff."

I nod trying to act cool while my brain goes into overdrive. A friend? Does she have a boyfriend? Fuck.

As if she reads my mind, she sits down next to me on the canal bank. "I've a girlfriend in Devizes. I go to her place to use the internet if I need to email some of my work. She also lets me wallow in her bath when I need a good wash and brush up. It's probably the only thing I miss living on my boat. A good soak in the tub. "

I'm still smiling at her trying not to look too relieved that she hasn't been away all week shagging some prick that I would instantly want to kill if I ever met him. "You smell good," I say and instantly regret it as she laughs at me.

"I didn't before?"

I shake my head and laugh. Loudly. The spliff is already taking effect. She laughs with me. "No. No that's not what I meant," I stutter as I try to stop laughing.

Bob takes this as his cue to come and greet me. He sticks his tongue in my ear and gives me a good licking. I'm usually happy to have someone lick me clean but this guy has the worst breath ever. Jade pulls him off me still laughing. "I brought you some food. I thought you might be getting low on your stock by now."

I blink at her, the surprise evident on my face. "You did?" She looks at my wrist fleetingly, I see she has clocked I'm wearing her bracelet.

"Yeah sure, I needed to do some shopping, so it wasn't a problem to grab some for you. But I'll need your help to bring it down to the boat from the pub's car park. My friend dropped me off and I've left it all in the pub kitchen for now. They know me, help me out from time to time if I have deliveries sent here."

Ah, now there's the answer to my problem for future supplies. I will make a note to call my dope dealer and get him to send one of his cronies down with another half an ounce. I'm going to need it, just to calm my nerves down after seeing Jade again.

"Thanks, that's really kind of you. Just let me know how much I owe you," I say with a genuine smile of thanks.

She nods looking down at the fishing lines with a wry smile. "Caught anything yet?"

I push myself up and look down into the murky water, I can see activity below. Lots of the greedy buggers are there already tugging at the Spam. Brainless bastards that are about to be lunch.

"Looks like I have." She helps me pull up the lines and

we both laugh our heads off when Jade points out I've brought nothing with me to put them in and we have to throw them back in. My thoughts of a delicious crayfish lunch disappearing fast into the depths of the murky canal bed once more.

Chapter Ten

We walk to the pub to collect the food, Bob running alongside us with his seaweed coat flying out in all directions. "He jumped in the canal when we got back," Jade says when I mention the unruly state of his dreadlocks.

"Did you have to fish him back out with a hook?" I joke.

"He's a Hungarian puli, intelligent and fast. He knows how to get in and out of the canal without any trouble at all," she says with a disgruntled expression on her face. I am still smiling at her; she is cute when she chastises me.

"Unlike me then."

She looks at me with laughter in her eyes. Real laughter. "Did you fall in?"

I nudge her shoulder playfully as we walk. "Who said anything about falling in?"

She nudges me back. "Idiot."

We reach the pub and I wait outside with Bob while she goes in to collect the shopping. She reappears with a guy who is carrying quite a few bags and looking very happy to be standing next to her. I narrow my eyes at him my fists clenching by my sides. He disappears around the back of the pub and returns with a sack trolley which he then helps Jade load while I stand with Bob and continue to give him the stink eye.

I am sulking. Like a fucking imbecile.

I snap out of it when she turns to me and grins. "Think you could use some of that muscle and pull this along to the boats?" I take the handle of the trolley and then raise my free arm and flex my bicep in an Arnold Schwarzenegger style muscle show.

"Of course, my dear, no problem." She laughs at me again and we head back to our boats.

This girl I am quickly beginning to realise is most likely the long-lost soulmate I've been searching for. She has brought me absolutely everything I could possibly need to restock my kitchen. Even down to junk food and more beers. She is my own personal shopping angel. I give her the cash to cover the cost of the food and ask her if she wants to stay for lunch, seeing as I now have shitloads of food. Her own shopping is still sitting on the sack trolley.

"I should really get my own food back in the boat and in the fridge." I'm just about to pout when she adds. "But I'll come back down after I've unloaded it."

My dick is doing its own little victory dance at that. "I can help you unload if you like."

She smiles at me, already leaving. "I'm fine. I'll be back."

I know she will be fine. Of course, she will. Miss 'I can do anything and everything I want, no problem at all'.

Fuck, I like her. Too much. "Don't be too long, I'm gonna cook us up a barbecue missy and you ain't gonna wanna miss it," I say in my best southern drawl. She turns her head one last time, her pert arse sticking up as she climbs up the steps.

"Can't wait."

I'm practically dribbling by the time she steps off *The Witch.*

I get busy organising the food and lighting the small barbecue when she leaves. I'm keen to impress her when she returns and find myself smiling as I carry out tasks that would usually have me groaning in frustration. I tidy up the kitchen, wiping down the counter-tops after washing up. I don't want her to think I'm a total slob if she wanders into the boat again. The contents of my duffle bag are thrown across the bed as I try to find a decent shirt to wear.

I give myself a mental slap as I stand looking at the pile of T-shirts like a teenage boy trying to impress his first date before grabbing one that isn't completely covered in wrinkles and at least clean. I brush my teeth and apply some deodorant, running my fingers through my hair, tying it back with slightly shaky hands. I'm acting like an idiot and she's only coming for lunch.

True to her word, Jade returns quickly and helps me finish preparing the food sizzling on the grill. We are sitting on my roof in two deckchairs eating burgers and chicken, licking our fingers as ketchup dribbles down them and laughing. Bob is sitting on the deck below us, flat out like a messy blanket and catching z's in the afternoon sun. I couldn't be happier. I'm like a pig in shit. Wallowing in a big warm pool of mud and testosterone-filled goo.

I'm buzzing to be in her company again. She is witty, warm and interesting. And she smells delicious. I hand her a napkin and take a swig of my cold beer. We have talked about everything and nothing in the last hour, mostly about music, films, what we like and don't like.

Some of what I tell her is true but not everything. I'm not ready to reveal who I really am to her and I make sure I steer the topics away from anything too dangerous if I feel she is about to discover something dastardly about me. Did I say I was a good liar? Yes, I did.

"Thank you for the bracelet by the way," I say handing her a beer from the cooler. She flips it open spraying a little at me and laughing.

"Sorry! I didn't mean to do that," she apologies as I jump back with shock as the beer begins to soak into my shorts.

I laugh and wipe at my crutch that is now looking a little

wet. “It’s okay.”

She looks me in the eye again and smiles. “You like it?”

I raise my wrist and showcase it for her. “I love it. Especially the lion and the ‘J’. Very creative of you.” She is smiling her eyes downcast now as if she is embarrassed at my response.

“Why the lion, Jade?” I ask. She looks up at me her eyes sparkling again. I’m starting to think she is part fairy.

“You’re a Leo, right?”

I grin wiping beer from my mouth after I take a swig. “I am.”

She grins. “Thought so.”

I chuckle reaching for my cigarettes and offer her one. She takes it and produces her own lighter this time from her shorts pocket. It has a skull casing and is covered in black and gold glitter. Funky like her. I watch her light her cigarette and take the flame to my own as she leans forward. I get a sneaky peek down her top as she leans into me and a semi threatens to rise in my shorts.

“How can you tell something like that so quickly after meeting me?” I say, trying not to squirm too much as I feel my semi try to take control.

She blows smoke up into the air and looks out over the canal. “It’s a gift. I can usually tell pretty quickly what birth sign someone is.”

I know she is being serious and I don’t laugh, even though I want to. “Wow, that must come in handy when deciding whether you want to actually speak to them or not!”

She laughs still looking out across the canal. The sun is high in the sky but we are sheltered slightly here by the willow tree. A breeze catches her hair and ruffles it for a second making her look even more ethereal than usual. “I don’t usually speak to Leos,” she says frivolously.

I sit up in my deckchair and look suitably insulted. “And

why not, may I ask."

She turns to face me her lips twitching with another smile. "Because they're usually loud-mouthed, pompous pricks."

I burst out laughing and she joins me bending over and holding her stomach as she continues to laugh at her own joke. "Do we have any good traits at all?"

She gradually regains her breath and looks up at me, still bending over, her hair flopping over her forehead from the Mohawk. She stares at me for a moment, her tongue slipping out to moisten her top lip. The unconscious action makes me shift uncomfortably in my deckchair. She's killing me with all the little sexual actions she's making that she's not even aware of.

"Of course. They're loyal, fun-loving and make extremely good lovers."

I watch her intensely as she straightens up, still looking at me. It's as if the air around us has been stolen from my lungs. Everything remains still. Motionless. I am suspended in her gaze. Locked into the vibration of attraction growing heavily between us. The fact that she said what she said in a soft whisper has only added to the tension growing in my shorts. Fuck me. She really is flirting with me and I'm loving it.

"I agree with all of those things, especially the last one," I say with a sly smile on my lips. She bites her bottom lip and continues to look at me with such intensity in her eyes I think she may just grab my head and stick her tongue down my throat.

I wish.

She blinks and the magic pulsing between us disappears.

"I can help you move *The Witch* when you need to fill her up with water if you like." She completely changes the subject and thank God she did. My dick is shouting at me to make a move on her, even though it would be completely inappropriate given the amount of time we have spent together.

Flirting or not, she is not ready for me yet. What is surprising me the most out of all this, is I am not ready for her yet. I would normally have fucked her within the first hour of meeting her and discarded her instantly with a smile and a pat on the backside.

There's nothing condescending about me. No, I'm usually just a prick. But this time I don't want to be a prick. Not with Jade. Ever.

She is waiting for me to answer, smoking her cigarette casually as if the last moment of flirting was a figment of my imagination. I'm beginning to wonder if she is a witch and has cast a spell on me, making me doubt my own mental stability. Not that I was very stable before. "That would be wonderful. I'm sure it would've taken me an entire day to work it out on my own."

She turns to face me and stubs out her cigarette. "It takes a couple of hours to get to the nearest water point from here." She crosses her long legs and tips her head back stretching her arms back giving me a superb view of her lush tits.

"Okay. Tomorrow would be a good day to head out I guess," I say watching her muscles flex and bend as she resumes her sitting position again.

I'm hypnotised by this girl. Totally gone.

Chapter Eleven

We tidy up the lunch dishes together and take Bob for a walk along the canal bank. We walk in silence for a while, nodding and smiling at a few people that walk past us on their weekend day out. As we head back late in the afternoon, she surprises me when we stop beside *The Water Nymph*.

"Would you like to have supper with me later?" she asks me as she picks at a piece of corn plucked from one of the fields. She is shredding little pieces of it off into her hand as she stares down at the ground.

I reach for her hand and take the piece of corn. I sense she is using it as a distraction to avoid my eyes and drop it to the floor. I want her to look at me when I give her my answer, so she knows just how thrilled I am at her invitation. Smiling at her, I pet Bob, who is sitting on my foot and looking up at me as if I still have beef jerky in my pocket. He obviously sees me as a treat supplier now.

"Sure, that would be nice."

I'm getting all the right signals off this girl, although it feels like she's still a little wary of me. But it makes the chase all the more exciting.

She eventually looks at me, a slight tilt to her lips and a blush on her cheeks. "Cool. Shall we say around eight?"

I nod and take this as my cue to leave her for a while. It must be around six now and the day has been hot and I need to freshen up. I start to walk away, backwards and still grinning at her. She grins back. "See you later, Fairy Girl,"

I say. She frowns a little at the nickname. I turn and walk away before she can say anything more feeling like the sun and moon have just risen in perfect orbit around my world sending me sparkling stars as a gift.

I'm stoked. Pathetic, I know.

I return to *The Witch* and shower as quickly as possible. The tank is making an even stranger grumbling noise. I don't bother to wash my hair but tie the top section back with a band and decide what I'm going to wear. Most of the clothes I brought with me in my duffel bag are totally inappropriate for this little adventure.

I have lived in the same pair of shorts for the last week. I end up picking out a pair of old jeans that have faded to a light blue and have holes in the knees and an old band T-shirt I've had since I was eighteen with *Metallica* printed across the front. Yes, I was a metalhead at one point in my life. Hence the need to keep my hair a little longer.

As I shave I stare at myself in the mirror and see that I'm still grinning. Ash would laugh his arse off at me right now: I'm acting like a lovesick idiot sprucing himself up for someone that I have absolutely no right to fuck around with. I need to touch base with him. I'm not sure if I want to discuss Jade with him yet, she is my new, naughty little secret. But I do want to catch up with him. I'm missing the demanding bastard, as much as I hate to admit it.

I splash on some aftershave, just a dash of Calvin Klein, nothing too heavy. I check the clock beside the bed, it's half past seven. I grab the tequila and my cigarettes and step onto the front deck. A couple of shots should steady my nerves before I head down to *The Water Nymph* for the evening. I've not been on a date since I was sixteen.

My stomach is doing weird little flips as I settle into my deckchair, the bottle of tequila sitting next to me. I light a cigarette and watch my favourite swan float up to the boat.

He cranes his neck up at me waiting for a titbit. Over the last week, I have shared some of my bread with this bad boy and now he seems to visit me at this time each evening, waiting for some more.

"Nothing for you tonight, you greedy bastard," I say, laughing as I smoke. He gets the message and glides away in search of some other sucker. I take a long swig straight from the tequila bottle and grimace at the bitter sharp taste as it burns a trail down my throat.

"Fuck!" I spit out, laughing. It instantly gives me a little buzz. Like doing a line of coke, it hits me straight in the head and gets me focussed. I need to stay cool tonight, nothing too pushy with Jade or she will send me packing, I'm sure. I realise, as I wait for the time to walk down to her boat, that I came here to think about what to do with my money. All I can think about now is a dark-haired girl and how to get her underneath me. I am one sad fuck.

I call Ash. "When are you fucking coming home, Jax? I need you," he whines at me when he picks up. No greeting, straight into the guilt trip.

"Ash, seriously, stop moaning at me. I've been gone a week, you baby." He sounds a little sad, which is not like him at all. I pause, thinking this through. "Look, why don't you come down here and visit me for a couple of days next weekend." I can hear him thinking about this tempting offer and what it may result in, although he's making me sweat a little first.

"Okay. Send me the address and I'll get a taxi down. You're paying for it, prick."

I laugh. "Of course, sweetness. You'll enjoy it and the weather's been awesome here, you might even get a tan. I have." I've developed the best tan I've ever had in the last week, my eyes are popping out icy blue in my head due to my colour. Even I have to admit I look pretty damn good with a tan.

Ash groans. "Oh, fuck you, you gorgeous tanned beach bum bastard." He's laughing now. I light another cigarette.

"Don't bring any fancy clothes, you won't need them. I'll text you the address. It'll be fun." He pauses, I hear him flick on the kettle.

"Have you decided what you're going to do with the money yet?"

"No, still thinking."

"Okay, well, I'm going out with the tattoo guy tonight, so I won't be thinking about you at all later. Have fun doing fuck all on the canal tonight, loser." I smile at his brashness.

I love him and his wicked tongue so very much. "See you next weekend, gorgeous," I say.

He snorts. "Love you not." He sighs before hanging up.

Anyone listening to our conversations would think that we absolutely hate each other. It's just the way we roll. I check my phone, it's now nearly eight. I dash back into the boat, stash the tequila and grab a few beers; I don't have any wine. I grab my weed bag and stuff it into my back pocket, along with my fags.

I'm ready baby. Here I come.

Chapter Twelve

I'm greeted by a much cleaner looking Bob, who comes dashing up to me as I walk towards *The Water Nymph*. I scratch his head as he wags his tail with his paws on my thighs. I can see Jade on the stern of the boat, she has her back to me and is busy fluffing pillows by the looks of it. I'm smiling already.

I walk towards her and hear music. It sounds like some sort of ambient chill-out stuff. She turns to face me as I reach the gangplank. Her hair is now in one long fishtail braid, trailing down the side of her neck and onto her chest; her Mohawk now flattened so that she has a cute little fringe. She is wearing long silver earrings that catch the light as she turns her head.

She still has her biker boots on but now a fresh pair of denim shorts, with slashes in the front, and a pale pink top that shows off her spectacular shoulders like a naughty gypsy. I smile at her and she returns the smile, somewhat shyly. She has lined her eyes with a smoky grey eyeliner and her lips are bright red. She looks fabulous.

"Hey," she says a little breathlessly.

"Hey, Fairy Girl," I say back still standing on the bank with Bob now sitting on my foot again.

"Come on in, City Boy," she says with a grin, gesturing for me to come onto her boat. I don't need a second invitation.

She is back to using her nickname for me, a way to tease me, no doubt. I walk up the plank carefully. Her boat is a lot smaller than *The Witch* and I can see it sway a little as I put my weight onto the wooden plank. *The Water Nymph* is like a fairy garden mixed with a dash of hippy heaven. Large floor cushions on a rug at the stern of the boat create a low seating area around a small wooden table that looks like it has seen better days, but it fits in perfectly with the Moroccan theme she has rocking tonight.

There is just enough room for us to sit here outside while the evening is still light and warm. Some candles on top of the boat glitter in different coloured holders like fireflies dancing in the breeze. They will look pretty when it gets dark, I imagine, adding to the ambient sense of floating in a magical world filled with sprites. I can smell incense. I already feel relaxed and at ease here. I stand, waiting for her next move. She is looking at me with an intense expression, taking in my appearance. Her pupils are dilated a little and her breathing is a little fast. I like the fact that she seems affected by my presence in such a way. I did make a bit of an effort after all.

"I brought some beer," I say breaking the silence. I hold them up and she grins, instantly snapping out of her long stare.

"Perfect, I'll put them in the cooler. I have some wine, too, if you want that instead."

I nod. I like wine on occasion, but it goes straight to my head. I will need to be careful if we end up drinking a bottle together, it makes my tongue loose and I don't want to spill too many secrets tonight. I want her to do most of the talking while I watch her wonderful lush lips moving.

Bob pushes past me and curls himself up on a blanket tucked under the tiller. Clearly his place of residence. "Have a seat," she says gesturing to the floor cushions as she takes the beers from me. Her fingers brush against mine briefly sending invisible sparks across my skin. She seems to sense the rush of energy between us and her pupils dilate even more. I continue to grin at her saying nothing.

This is the most fun I've had in ages, the sexual spark between us just waiting to be lit like a bush fire. She disappears into the boat. I watch her go, licking my lips hungrily as I see her lovely legs stretch out down the steps. I take out my weed and cigarettes placing them on the low table before I sit down, I don't want to squash those babies. I light up a fag and sit back against the railing. I scan her boat taking everything in. There are strings of unlit fairy lights around the railing. It's all very feminine and funky.

She reappears with two bottles in her hands. Condensation drips off the outside of the bottle of white. "White or red?" she asks with a tilt to her head.

"White," I say, knowing I am less likely to get drunk and sloppy on this choice of wine. She nods and vanishes again. I can hear glasses clinking and catch an aroma of food; it smells delicious but I'm not sure what it is. She pops back up again with the wine and two glasses, she has uncorked it and placed it in an ice bucket. The perfect host. I watch her move around as I smoke. She places the glasses on the low table and begins to pour for us. She does it expertly, even twisting the bottle a little at the end so that it doesn't drip. Perhaps she was a waitress once.

"Supper is ready but I thought we could have a glass of wine first," she says, her eyes scanning my face for approval. I nod, taking the glass she offers me. She sits next to me – close but not touching –cross-legged. She seems to have no problem folding herself gracefully like this, she must be flexible. I run through a few naughty scenarios thinking of that in two seconds flat.

I am sprawled out, with my legs in front of me splayed, one leg bent. She is watching me again, trying to work me out, or possibly just appreciating the view. "Smells good, can't wait to taste it," I say.

She sips her wine and smiles. "Chilli tonight, with a touch of dark chocolate," I feel like groaning at the way she says dark chocolate as if it's an aphrodisiac I really don't need.

"Sounds fabulous."

She grins, reaching for my cigarettes. "May I?" I nod, she's a real fag thief but I don't give a fuck. She could have whatever she wanted from me. Take it all. I don't care. We sit and smoke for a moment, sipping at our wine. "You've caught the sun well this week," she notes, her eyes glistening dark blue.

I smile at her. "Yeah, the weather's been amazing. Couldn't have asked for better."

She smiles, she has an olive skin tone that is already tanned from living outdoors, I guess.

"You've been lucky this week and the weather's supposed to stay hot for another week or so," she pauses taking a drag on her cigarette. "We might get a storm later in the week, though."

I nod watching her finger flick the ash delicately into the ashtray on the table. "I love storms," I say. I really do. I have always enjoyed the shift in energy when the thunder and lightning rolls into the city. Charged. Powerful.

I wonder what it will be like to hear the rain on the roof of the boat and feel the electricity in the air around here. I imagine it will be quite spectacular and instantly imagine fucking Jade outside while the storm rages around us. I shift position slightly as my dick responds to this thought. She laughs, her eyes flashing with amusement. I'm not sure if she is aware of my discomfort or if she is laughing at my comment.

"Me too, you can feel the change in the air, it's exhilarating, isn't it?"

I blink at her as she repeats my thoughts. Without the fucking naked, that is. "It is."

We sit in our easy silence for a while sipping at the wine. It's as if our limited conversation is always enough, we are comfortable just being around each other. Bob is snoring, which makes me laugh. Jade unfolds herself. "I'll dish up, won't be a minute."

"Do you want some help?"

"I'm fine." Of course, she is.

She returns with a tray holding two bowls of chilli and rice; it smells awesome. There is a definite kick of something else in this chilli and it is most certainly acting as an aphrodisiac. I wonder if she has put another ingredient, apart from dark chocolate, in it – some witchy-herb that is making me even more captivated by her.

We eat and drink, chatting again about the weather and what I've been up to all week, which is basically nothing except chilling out and running. I find out from her that she was indeed once a waitress and worked in London for a while in a few restaurants. She is a little reserved about the details and I wonder if it was perhaps not a great time in her life. She has a brother and her family live in Somerset. She is obviously close to them and they visit her on occasion. It seems they totally accept her unusual lifestyle. She tells me a little more about her work, she has regular contracts with a few magazines that she writes articles for about astrology and, of course, her clients that ask for charts.

I ask her more about this. I am now genuinely interested in the subject when she explains to me that there is quite a lot of mathematics involved in working out people's charts. It sounds pretty damn complicated actually, lots of details involved with suns and moons rising and exact dates and times to pinpoint the exact positions of the planets. I find myself being drawn into it all as she explains in detail. She's clearly not just a pretty face.

"I could plot your chart for you, if you know your time of birth and give me the location of where you were born," she says to me once the meal is cleared away and we are lounging back on the cushions. The sun begins to slip back down over the horizon.

I grin at her. "And find out all my dark and dirty secrets?" I say with a growl.

She laughs. "I wouldn't judge."

I believe her. I think she already knows more about me than she is letting on. She seems so much older than her twenty-two years of age. Like an old soul. We are so easy around each other that I feel like I may have met her in some other lifetime. The only other person I feel this comfortable with is Ash.

"Maybe then, sometime," I say with a small smile. She nods at me saying nothing more. Not pushing me. I like that.

Chapter Thirteen

We are both lying back, looking up at the stars that are starting to pop out of the perfectly clear, dark sky. We pass a spliff back and forth. I'm slightly buzzing from the wine but not in a dangerous way; I feel relaxed, happy. Something is uncurling in my stomach again, something I have not felt before. Contentment.

She turns her head to me as the fairy lights switch on, illuminating us both in a soft glow. She smiles at me. "Do you dance?"

I laugh at the question. "Sometimes."

She licks her bottom lip as if wary of what she is about to say. "I dance … with poi. Would you like to see me dance?"

I shiver at the thought. "Yes, fucking please," I say without hesitation, nodding my head like an enthusiastic bobblehead on the dashboard of a car.

She laughs at my eager response, throwing her head back revealing her slim neck and a tiny gold necklace sitting delicately in the dip of her throat. It has a single star on the chain, which catches the light and sparkles for a split second. Just like her entire aura seems to be doing in this moment.

She stands up and I watch her like a kid in a candy shop pumped up on too much sugar. She disappears again and Bob gets up and pads over to me flopping down against my thigh so I can stroke him. He is warm and soft; I dig my fingers into his dreadlocks and sigh. My entire body is vibrating while I wait for her. The thought of watching her move that incredible body of hers in any type of gyration is ramping me up into a frenzy.

Jade reappears wearing a beanie hat that covers her head completely with just the braid over her shoulder. In her hands, she has two long strings with balls on the end. I'm very confused and have no idea what poi are or what she is about to do with them. She winks at me and I push myself up to get a better look at her. She begins to pull out an oblong-shaped can of, what looks like, paraffin oil from a box at the side of the stern.

She walks off the gangplank and stands on the towpath and places the can beside her. She opens it up and dips the two balls into it leaving it for a moment while she adjusts the beanie hat. She looks like a grunge kid. Cute and sexy. I turn to face her properly, crossing my legs as Bob shifts beside me also waiting for the show.

She has turned the music up a little and I hear that it is now playing the same drum and bass music I had on this morning. She pulls out her lighter after lifting the balls out of the can and lights one of them. Flames instantly rush up in a whoosh making me feel a little worried for her safety. She grins at me and touches the other ball to the one that is alight so that they are both now burning brightly.

I watch, mesmerised, as she begins to swing them in a loop by her sides. My mouth opens slightly and I am instantly entranced watching her move those sexy hips and swinging the ropes, creating a Catherine wheel around her body.

She is dancing with fire. Literally.

I can feel myself being dragged towards her, mesmerised by the spectacular display she is creating. She is beautiful and sexy and can dance like a motherfucker. It's as if the demon inside of me is drawn to this creature; she has created the hell-fire it desires and it is desperate to touch it. I have never seen anything quite so hypnotic in my life. I am bewitched. That is what she must be: a beautiful, wonderful, dancing witch. I watch her and know that I'm falling hard – falling fast – for this strange, amazing creature. I am truly dazzled. In the most wonderful way possible.

The flames fizzle out after a while. It seems like I've been trapped in a time warp watching her. She places the poi back beside the can and walks back onto the boat taking off her beanie, her face is flushed and she looks excited. I am very excited. I cannot move. She looks down at me smiling.

"Did you like it?" My mouth is open. She laughs. "The poi … did you like it?" she prompts me as I continue to just gawp at her.

I grin at her. "Very much."

She sits down beside me and I try to regain my coolness. "You looked amazing, Jade. It was beautiful." She is staring at me, so close again but not touching. I reach for her hand and slowly tip it over, running my finger across her palm. She shivers in response. "*You* are beautiful," I whisper, my voice wavering slightly. She looks down at my finger against her palm and then shakes herself a little pulling her hand back gently.

"Thank you," she replies with a shy smile.

I feel like I may have overstepped the mark again and pull back reaching for my wine glass and taking a sip. "I should get going," I say, wanting to make her feel like I'm not about to jump her.

She looks back up at me her eyes growing wide. "No, it's fine, you don't need to leave. Stay."

I try to contain my excitement and I simply nod, saying nothing. She disappears into the boat again. My heart is beating erratically and I decide to roll another joint just so I have something to do with my hands. When she reappears, she has pulled on some loose hippy pants and a T-shirt. She is barefoot now.

I make a bold move and lie back down on the cushions with one arm lifted out to the side indicating she should slide in beside me. She eyes me warily for a second then sits down beside me, then lies down, curling herself into the side of my body, just as I hoped she would. I wrap my arm around her shoulder and pull her into my chest. She is wonderfully warm and smells faintly of the paraffin.

She sighs, placing her hand on my stomach, her head on my chest. The joint is left discarded in my other hand for a moment as I try to regulate my breathing. We lie like this for a while, saying nothing. She begins to stroke my stomach, her fingers brushing against me in small circles. I try desperately to think of something nasty so that I don't get a hard-on.

"I think I'm beginning to like your company, City Boy," she whispers.

I chuckle as she confesses. "Well, that's a good thing."

We lie on the back of her boat, silently smoking the joint. She remains tucked into my side, her head on my chest. We finish the joint and I stroke her hair, feeling like I am diving headfirst into a pool of undiluted pleasure. Bob, however, decides we are getting too close and begins to fuss around us, stuffing his nose into my crutch again. Jade laughs and sits up staring down at me.

"I should get to bed. Thank you for a lovely evening, Jax." I take this as my cue to leave.

I sigh heavily knowing that we have made good progress tonight and I would fuck it up if I tried to kiss her. Even though it's exactly what I want to do. Desperately.

I sit up and run my hand over my face. "Yeah, it's getting late," I pause reaching for her face, I stroke her cheek gently and am surprised when she nestles into my palm. My dick is practically pulsing now. "I've had an amazing night, Jade. Thank you for everything."

She surprises me even more by turning her head and placing a small, soft kiss on the palm of my hand. I have no idea how to react to that intimate gesture.

She pushes herself away from me and stands. I follow suit and stand in front of her just waiting for her next move. She looks up at me and touches my waist, gently, her hands are warm and wonderful on the waistband of my jeans. "See you tomorrow, City Boy."

Before I can respond in any way, she pushes away from me and turns her back on me. I watch her turn just as she reaches the steps that descend into her boat. She is grinning at me mischievously.

"Sleep well."

I think it will be a while before I can slip into the world of dreamland but know that, when I do, it will be her that I will be dreaming of.

Chapter Fourteen

I wake up the next morning with a thick head from all the wine and smoking. The sun is shining. Again. There's a familiar ache in my balls and I know I'll have to sort out my morning wood before anything else. I'm surprised I'm not blind.

Jade was in my dreams last night. Dancing with fire, the flames like serpents wrapping around her naked body, writhing and teasing me as she swirled and gyrated with it. I woke twice in the night covered in sweat with a massive hard-on. Damn my cock and its persistent demands.

I hope that I can at least wash one last time before we go to the water point. My reflection in the bathroom mirror is grinning back at me, knowing that I will see her again today and that I will, at last, get to take this baby out onto the canal. The water shudders and groans and comes to an abrupt stop just as I finish washing all the important bits – and after shooting my load visualising Jade bending over in front of me, showing me her pert arse.

The boat rocks and I hear someone step onto the stern just as I finish pulling on a clean pair of shorts and a T-shirt.

"Hey, City Boy, ready to go?" Jade shouts down the boat at me. She is dressed in her short shorts, again wearing a ripped tank top and her biker boots. Her hair is loose today; her Mohawk sticking up with gel. She is wearing no makeup but looks like she is glowing. I want to eat her for breakfast.

"Ready as I'll ever be," I say as she disappears again like

a figment of my imagination.

Bob sits patiently on the large deck at the stern of *The Witch*, his nose twitching at the slight breeze. He wags his tail at me and accepts my petting for a moment as Jade turns the key to start the big black beast up. "I'll untie the ropes, Jax. You wait here."

I salute her and say, "Aye, aye captain." Ironically, I'm suddenly incapable of remembering what I'm supposed to be doing; all my reading of how to steer the boat vacating my brain as I watch her jump up and down off *The Witch* untying the ropes. I think it may have something to do with the way her shorts rise even higher on her arse cheeks each time she bends over. The boat is shuddering slightly with the hum of the engine under my feet and I lean against the tiller as she jumps on after untying the last rope.

"Ready?" She flashes me another beautiful smile. I nod and she slides up beside me taking the throttle and pushing it forward, her other hand resting lightly on the tiller. I hope she can't see my legs shaking. I'm shivering with excitement and a small dash of nerves. I'm very grateful she is helping me with my first trip out on this sexy lady.

Jade manoeuvres *The Witch* out of its mooring like a seasoned professional. I am delighted at how smooth the flow of the boat is as we move across to the middle of the canal and begin to make our way in the direction of the pub. Bob flops down with his head on his paws as if this is just another walk in the park for him.

I move out of the way a little as Jade sits her bum against the steel railing around the stern, she props her boots up on the lower rail and sits back, relaxed and steering with one hand. I am in awe of this girl. She is steering twenty tonnes of widebeam barge like it's absolutely nothing. "Do you want a coffee?" I ask. My stomach is rumbling and I need some caffeine.

"Sure. Black, two sugars please."

The gentle breeze is blowing her hair back over her shoulders and she reminds me of a pirate, sitting so at ease on the railing and holding the tiller gently in her delicate hand. I get busy making us the coffee and grab a banana to get rid of the hunger pains. I'd had no time to cook a proper breakfast. I didn't think she would be knocking on my door so early. I watch the canal bank glide past the kitchenette window and put the kettle on, heaping coffee into two cups. The feel of the engine under my feet is oddly comforting and the gentle, almost silent, movement of the boat as it slips like the white swan through the water is making me sigh with happiness. I step back up with two steaming coffees, Jade is still sitting pretty in her driving position. She takes the coffee from me and steps down from the railing.

"Would you like to steer for a while?"

I'm terrified I'll screw it up but show nothing but an air of confidence as I smile and say, "Sure, why not? It's my boat."

She laughs at my comment and sips her coffee, letting go of the tiller and handing it to me. "Just watch ahead for any bends or curves in the canal, try to keep her as straight as possible, you need to move over to the right if another boat comes. It's the complete opposite to driving a car, you push the tiller in the opposite direction you want the boat to head to. So, push right to steer left and left to steer right." She pauses her eyes flashing with amusement. "Got it?"

I nod. "Got it."

"Don't look so terrified, Jax," she chuckles. "I'm here to help you if you screw up."

She can read me like a book. Not so cool. But I smile back at her, even more determined now to get this right. I can feel the boat respond to my slightest touch, it's like a living, breathing entity and it knows I'm frightened of it. I close my eyes for a second, tuning into my inner confidence.

"I can do this, I can do this," I repeat like a mantra in my head.

Half an hour later and I'm getting the hang of it. I am now a fully-fledged water gypsy; I have lost my canal boat steering virginity and it wasn't even painful. Jade helps me out a couple of times when I start to veer off slightly and, so far, I've managed not to hit anything or totally screw up. She stands behind me with her hand on top of mine a couple of times helping me to steer correctly and I feel the flush of her touch all the way up my arm and straight down into my dick.

She still smells like tropical fruits and vanilla; her body is radiating heat behind me as she remains just inches from my back. I imagine her hands running down my spine, slipping her fingers into the back of my shorts. I resist the urge to step back into her.

A boat is heading in our direction and I panic for a second. She chuckles and steps closer to me, pressing her body into my back, just as I had just imagined – but without her hand down my shorts. She rests her hand on top of mine again and keeps it there, using her other hand to ease down on the throttle slightly. We cross paths with the other boat perfectly, she waves at the people standing on their deck and they wave back.

I'm vibrating like a tuning fork.

When they pass by us completely, she steps back away from me and then glides smoothly around in front of me. She is now facing me as I look straight ahead concentration etched on my face. "You're doing really well, City Boy," she says looking a little smug. I smile at her.

"Would you light me a cigarette?" I nod towards my packet of Marlboro sitting on the roof. She takes two out of the packet, sticking one in her own mouth, lights it, sucking it a couple of times and blowing the smoke out. She grins at me devilishly then lights her own using my cigarette as the lighter. She passes it to me and I take it using the opportunity to brush my thumb under her wrist lightly as she does. Her eyes widen a little at the contact but she says nothing.

She turns her back to me and leans against the roof, looking ahead and puffing on her smoke. I'm having trouble keeping my attention on what I'm supposed to be doing. The cheeks of her arse are peeking out of her shorts again as she reaches up on her tiptoes to look out over the roof of the boat. Like two perfect peaches.

With her back to me, I take the opportunity to really look at her. Well, perv really. She has the most beautifully slim calves and fabulous thighs; her skin is a delicious olive-brown and looks as if it has been shaved to a silky-smooth finish. I'm visualising licking her legs from top to bottom while I try desperately to keep my eyes on the horizon. I smoke my cigarette trying to keep calm.

She is either a terrible tease or has no idea that, right now, she's sending me into a head spin.

Chapter Fifteen

We arrive at the water point after another hour of chugging. She tells me this is the correct 'boatie' term for sailing a canal barge. It makes sense, the sound of the engine is like a constant chug, chug, chug, chug; the rhythm of a healthy heartbeat.

I'm loving this: loving the feeling of being so free, of moving so slowly without caring about how long it will take to reach the destination. In fact, it all seems to be over far too quickly and soon Jade is jumping off with the ropes like a nimble acrobat when we arrive at a place called Pewsey.

There are many boats moored here and there seems to be a fair amount of people milling around, some boat owners and other people walking along the canal path. Some stop and stare as we tie *The Water Witch* up at the water point. They seem to be admiring both the boat and us. We must look like a couple; we are certainly at ease with each other and could be in a steady relationship. How far from the truth that is right now.

Jade is at the front of the boat sorting out the water. She watches me wander up after I switch the engine off. "Do you need to empty the toilet, Jax?"

She nods her head over her shoulder where I see a small brick building. She is grinning at me again like she knows I am not relishing the thought of emptying my own piss and shit into a hole.

We complete our respective tasks, her filling the water

tank and me dealing with the unsavoury job of depositing my waste into a drain that smells like a communal toilet at a festival. Jade then helps me to untie the ropes again, showing me how to loosen and tie an effective knot quickly so that I have this information for the future. It's always handy to know how to tie a new knot in my world.

We set off again to another point in the canal which, Jade tells me, is a big enough turning point to manoeuvre *The Witch* into facing in the right direction again. Like an expert, she turns the boat and, for the second time today, I am thanking my lucky stars she is helping me with this. There is no way in hell that I could have done this alone. We are heading back to Honey Street by late afternoon. Jade sits on the roof for a while as I steer, looking serene and happy. Bob sits on my feet as usual and keeps me company while I ogle his owner like a horny teenager.

She makes me a sandwich at some point and feeds it to me laughing as I try to keep my eyes on the canal. She is a major tease and I love it. We laugh and talk about the area; she gives me some of the history of the region and tells me about the white horse in the hill opposite The Barge Inn and some of the stories of crop circles and sightings across Wiltshire. It seems this place is a Mecca for the weird and wonderful; Avebury and Stonehenge are not far away.

Jade knows a lot about these sites as well and I am enthralled by the number of facts she knows. My clever little fairy. I am starting to see her as mine now – even though I haven't even really touched her. I don't want to give her up. I don't want anyone else to experience what I am experiencing with her. The connection slowly growing between us. I want to *own* her. I swallow hard on that thought.

We are back at my mooring all too soon. But the sun is still shining and I'm feeling a lot more confident with my ability at sailing *The Water Witch*. We have had a few beers during our little trip out today but eaten very little. I suggest I take her to dinner at the pub as a way of thanking her for her help. She agrees and we wander down with Bob at our side as the sun starts to slip down the horizon. It's still hot and we are both grateful to head inside this evening, out of the sun. She taps my nose playfully as we sit down with a pint of cider each after ordering our meal.

"Looking a little red here my friend," she says chuckling.

"Yeah, I can feel it."

She sips her pint and leans back in her chair next to me. "I have some aloe vera on my boat, I can give you a piece if you like."

I turn to face her, watching her face for a reaction as I say, "Only if you rub me down with it." She flushes instantly and I grin like the devil himself. I couldn't help myself.

She fiddles with some of the bracelets on her wrist and I know she is feeling uncomfortable again at my blatant flirting. "What's happening here, Jax?" she says avoiding eye contact.

I shift in my seat. Here we go. "We're enjoying a pint and having dinner, Jade," I say nonchalantly.

She looks up into my eyes and stares at me biting her bottom lip again. God, I want to devour that fucking mouth. "You know what I mean, City Boy."

I place my hand carefully on top of hers and hold it gently, rubbing my thumb across her knuckles. "I'm not entirely sure right now, to be honest."

She removes her hand from mine then shocks me by linking her fingers through my own and squeezing it gently, briefly, before releasing it. "Neither am I."

We are both silent for a moment then our food arrives, breaking the awkwardness. We tuck in, Bob sticking his nose up from under the table for little titbits I feed him when Jade is not looking. I have the sick feeling she may be falling for me and not in the way I would like her too. I did not see the signs. She has hidden her vulnerability so well with her sassy banter and confident body language.

I need to tread very, very carefully from now on. For both our sakes.

We finish our meal and decide to go outside for a cigarette and to finish our pints. The cloying smoke from other people enjoying their after-dinner nicotine fix at their table is starting to make my eyes sting.

The sun has set and it's dark again. The pub is pretty busy tonight and we sit in the corner furthest away from other people; we both want to stay in our own private little bubble. I can see her shivering slightly. The temperature has dropped considerably despite the heat of the day. Perhaps the predicted storm is coming sooner than expected.

"Come here, you're cold," I say opening my legs and sliding her to me. My legs are straddling the bench seat and she turns to do the same so that her back is to my front. I wrap my arms around her and nestle my face into her neck, breathing her in. She sighs and goes limp in my arms. I can feel every inch of her body pressing into me as I rub my hands up and down her arms to warm her up. It's just a lame excuse to get closer to her. I'm tempted to run my tongue up her neck and into her ear but I don't. Fuck knows why. I really, really want to.

"We should head back, Jax. I need to feed Bob and change my clothes."

My nose is still nestled into her hair and I grunt in response. I don't want to let her go. I can feel my dick start to harden but understand that she is probably right. I might just stab her in the back if I'm not careful. I loosen my hold and she instantly pushes herself up and away from me. I watch her, a little forlorn at the loss of her touch, as she stands up and puts Bob on his lead.

“Thank you for the meal.”

“No problem,” I take a deep breath. She doesn’t resist as I wrap my fingers inside her own, leading her away from the pub.

We walk back holding hands. It feels good – normal. We reach *The Water Witch* and she releases my hand one finger at a time. I step back and put my hands in my pockets. I smile at her warmly. “I’ve had another amazing day with you Jade, thanks for your help.”

She looks down at her feet, scuffing the floor with her boot. I’m waiting for her to look up and say goodbye. I’m completely thrown when she not only looks up but reaches up with her hands and places them on my cheeks, she steps closer and pulls my head down.

I swallow hard knowing that this is it – this is the moment I have been waiting for.

She is staring at me and biting her lip again. I keep my hands in my pockets not wanting to scare her off. Her pupils are so dilated her eyes are almost entirely black. I’m beginning to think she’s either scared shitless or highly aroused at the thought of what she’s about to commit to. I hope it’s the latter. I can see her clearly in the light of the full moon overhead and she looks so beautifully vulnerable, as she hesitates for a moment, I want to scream out in frustration.

“*You* are amazing,” she whispers, then reaches up and kisses me resolutely on the lips. The sensation of her soft, warm lips on mine sends me into a back-flip. Fuck it. I take my hands out of my pockets and grab the waistband of her shorts pulling her to me. She groans as I slide my tongue inside her mouth and kiss her properly.

We kiss like we have always been joined at the mouth like this. Totally in synch; completely in rhythm with each other. I have never enjoyed a kiss quite so much. It is soft and sensual, deliriously so. I pull her closer. She must be able to feel my hard-on by now, it's jutting like a goddamn flagpole into her stomach.

She is making soft whimpering noises and I'm about to self-combust if she doesn't stop, it takes all my self-control not to rip her clothes off and fuck her here on the towpath. Just as I release her mouth and start to trail feather light kisses across the sensitive flesh on her neck, she pushes me away. Gently but firmly.

She is gasping for air and looking at me like I am some sort of dangerous animal. I am. A very dangerous animal. And for the first time since we met, I can see it in her eyes. She can see me, really see me.

"Good night, Jax," she whispers and turns tugging Bob along with her.

I am left standing with my dick pressing hard against my shorts struggling to breathe. Holy fucking shit. We are in deep trouble now. I walk, in a daze, back inside the boat, grab the tequila and head back out onto the roof with every intention of getting shit-faced.

I pushed too hard. I screwed up. I've frightened her off with just one kiss. A kiss that wasn't even at full throttle. The part of me that knew she would bolt immediately if I unleashed myself on her fully kept me restrained. Fat lot of good that did me. I open the deckchair facing it out over the canal and the field opposite. The moon is so bright tonight I can see everything in a wash of silver-grey. Magical.

A few ducks swim past and quack at me as if they are just as pissed off with me as I am with myself. I take a massive slug of the tequila and grimace as it hits me hard, like a bullet to the head. I light a cigarette and suck on it. My heart is racing and my dick is still hard. The taste of her is still in my mouth, despite the tequila doing its best to erase the memory. I know that getting wasted won't help me right now but it's the only thing I can do to stop me from striding up that canal path, jumping on her boat, pulling her into my arms and ravishing her.

She is the most intoxicating drug I've ever tried. And, believe me, I've tried a few. I'm addicted and I don't want to quit. Not this. This feeling of pure lust, emotion, happiness and just … *feeling*. I haven't really felt anything for a very long time. Sure, I think I do, especially when I'm working, drinking, smoking, fucking. But now I can see it was all just one boring slide show on repeat.

I felt nothing. I was jogging along nicely in a world of pretend.

Of course, I knew I was pretending a lot of things to a lot of people. But I had absolutely no idea – until five minutes ago – that I was pretending to myself. Jade has just broken the illusion big time. Winning the lottery brought me to this place. That should be a good thing but now I am in an even worse position than I was before.

A week ago, I was happy being a complete bastard who revelled in listening to people's shit just so I could fix it and find some amusement in life. I loved my life, my independence, my non-committal sex life, my flat. Now I'm not so sure.

I think of Ash and what he would say to me right now if he saw me sitting up here like a loser, pining over the fact a girl pushed me away before I could even get to second base. He would be crying with laughter, pissing his designer pants. He would tell me to "snap the fuck out of it" and get on with spending my millions of pounds.

Christ. I am royally fucked. I need to get a grip and fast. I take another slug of tequila and it burns twice as much second time around as it slides down my throat. I smoke my cigarette and flick it into the canal like a complete dick that has no care for the beauty around me. I feel like punching something or breaking something. I want to get rid of this fucking hard-on. I need to calm down, my leg is twitching and I'm like a racehorse that needs to break out of its paddock and run, run, run.

The only problem is the direction I want to run in now seems like it's out of bounds.

"Fuck!" I shout, before slamming the tequila bottle down on top of the roof and standing up scowling up at the moon. "And fuck you, universe. Fuck you for making me the one-in-a-million twat. Thank you very much."

The ducks quack at me again, looking up at me as if I am indeed a fucking twat making such a lot of noise so late in the evening. "Bollocks," I grumble and head back into the boat for my bag of weed.

If I'm going to get shit-faced, I might as well do it properly.

Chapter Sixteen

After bingeing all night on tequila and weed, I pass out. I smoked until I couldn't see and ended up having to crawl to the bedroom at the front of the boat. I have no memory of what happened after that. Childish and unnecessary, I know.

I wake fully clothed, laying on my front, my hair in my face and my leg dangling off the bed like a spare part. I feel like utter shit and, for a moment, have absolutely no idea where the hell I am. My head is pounding so hard I can hardly open my eyes. I'm groaning in self-pity, finally managing to get into a vertical position, which just makes my head pound even more. There's some big, hairy man in my brain, knocking it to pieces with a sledgehammer.

I stumble to the toilet, take a piss and then head to the kitchen to see if I'd even thought about bringing any pain killers with me. I sincerely hope I did. I'm a mess and I deserve it. It's a little overcast today, thankfully; I don't think I could have handled another day of blazing sunshine, not with this mother of all hangovers.

I find some paracetamol and gulp them down with a pint of water. My stomach is doing somersaults; I'm very rarely sick with a hangover and just put it down to the fact that I'm still feeling uneasy about whether Jade will ever speak to me again. I put the kettle on, still stumbling about like an idiot trying to make coffee and decide to stick my head out to get some fresh air for a moment.

Kill or cure.

There's one remaining cigarette in my packet, grabbing it, I stagger out of the boat. I stand there for a moment, my eyes narrowing at the light. Taking a drag on my cigarette I spot a small bag hanging off the tiller. My heart does a little flip as I reach for it. Inside are several strips of aloe vera and a small note. My hands are shaking as I unfold it. Holding the cigarette in my mouth my fingers fumble annoyingly with the piece of paper. I seem to have lost all co-ordination today.

I'm sorry I ran. I'm just not ready. Not yet. J x

I feel like my heart is about to explode in my chest. I haven't blown it. Not completely. She has offered me an olive branch. I overreacted. I flipped out unnecessarily. I still have a chance.

Not yet.

I hear the kettle whistling and take another drag on my cigarette, feeling like I have at last just won the jackpot. The real jackpot. Not twenty-five million pounds. At that moment, I'm hit by the simplicity of it all. You can have all the money in the world but have nothing at all if you have no one to share it with. And just like that, Jade has solved one of my problems. I came here to have solitude and time to think about what to do with my money. Now I know what I want to do with it: I want to share it with someone I can truly love.

I sit and drink my coffee. My mind is spinning as I think about Jade and I think about Ash and how I feel about them both in two totally different ways. I've loved Ash since the day I met him: he accepted who I was and gave me the freedom to be that person. But the kind of love I have for him is not the type of love you can share day to day, living together like a married couple would. It's unique and possibly dangerous for the both of us, as it comes with as many negatives as it does positives.

Jade, however, is someone I can imagine having in my life daily, permanently, with no negative side effects. I have only known her for a very short time but she has found a way into my dark, broken heart, like the exact piece of the puzzle I was looking for. Ash would never want to settle into a relationship with me as a partner, he is far too free and independent for that. Besides, I am not gay. I am bisexual and I crave satisfaction from both sides of the fence. There's the problem. I know Jade is not like me or Ash.

She makes me feel complete in many ways – she makes me feel alive – and now that I have had my blindfold removed, I want that feeling. But she would never be able to accept my sexual urges for men. And they will never go away; believe me, I've tried. I really have. I tried to have relationships at the beginning with just one girl or just one man. It never ever worked.

I gave in, eventually, and Ash was the one who helped me accept that I am just not like everyone else or other bisexual people who are happy with just one partner at a time. It is something I cannot change. I will always have that need to satisfy the craving, to sink into the black hole of decadence. Enjoying the freedom of multiple partners of both sexes. Relationships, without the emotion or commitment. It feels like a disease. Something that crawls under my skin and creates an itch that I just cannot scratch hard enough. I am a selfish prick. I want it all.

I want a woman that I can hold in my bed, make love to and feel safe and wanted with. I also want to suck dick and fuck hard whenever I feel the urge to do so. Which is often. I am back to my biggest problem again. I can't have it all. Even with the millions of pounds in my bank account.

Feeling happier that Jade is still in the picture – but frustrated that I will never really be able to 'have it all' – I make myself something to eat which seems to help with the headache.

My thoughts wander to the money from my lottery win that should now be sitting in my bank account, smiling at me. I wonder what it will look like to see such a long line of numbers on my statement. I'm sure it will seem unreal. Like a joke. I'm staring at the floor deep in that thought when my phone rings. I don't recognise the number.

"Doyle," I say, cursing silently under my breath when I find my cigarette packet is empty.

"Ah. Mr Doyle, I'm glad I've managed to reach you. My name is Mr Sinclair; I am the manager of Lloyds Bank in Notting Hill. It has been brought to my attention that a large amount of money has been deposited into your account today, courtesy of the lottery and I am calling to congratulate you and invite you in for a meeting with our financial advisors whenever you are free next." I smile. It didn't take them long to pounce did it. "We would really like to help you invest your money properly and feel it would be best to sit down in person to do this."

I imagine Mr Sinclair is sitting there, in his designer suit, sweating profusely. I bet he's clucking with the need to see me in person, manipulate and cajole me into making commitments with them so that he can make a big, fat commission from whatever account he persuades me to put my money into. Well, fuck you, Mr Sinclair.

I take a sip of my coffee.

"Thank you, Mr Sinclair, for taking time out of your busy schedule to contact me today. It is much appreciated," I say in the syrupiest voice I can muster. I hear him shift in his chair, almost see him holding his breath. "But I'm currently out of town so won't be able to make it into the Notting Hill branch any time soon. I'm also in the process of selecting various banks and investment options with the help of my own financial advisor, so I thank you for your call, but am in no need of your services other than to keep my twenty-five million safe within your system until I choose to move it."

Silence.

He is trying desperately trying to think of ways he can persuade me to rethink this decision. I wait for him to speak. "I'm sure you have a lot to think about at the moment, Mr Doyle, but I'm confident we can help manage and grow the value of your newfound wealth."

Greedy bastard. A sly smile slips onto my lips as I take another sip of my coffee and walk back to the bedroom in search of a hidden packet of cigarettes stashed in the bottom of my duffel bag. "I'm sure you are, Mr Sinclair. I will speak to you when *I* am ready, not the other way around. Have a good day." I cut him off before he can speak again. I am feeling much better already. I am in control here. I have all the power. It could just go to my head. I pull the duffel bag, still stuffed with clothes, out from under my giant bed and rummage through it, trying to find some more cigarettes. Nothing. Bollocks.

I'm still laughing to myself about my conversation with Mr Sinclair when I walk into the pub and ask for change so that I can buy a few packets from the machine. I glance at the clock behind the bar, it's only just opening time and the pub is still quiet. The bartender gives me my change and I buy three packets of Marlboro Lights before heading back out. He is the same guy that helped Jade load her shopping onto the sack trolley and he is giving me a very disgruntled look. Fuck him. I really want to see her. I want to walk down to her boat and check that she is okay, but I can't. I have to play this just right. Give her the time she needs – and I need, for that fact – to figure this all out.

I go back to *The Witch* and change into my running gear;

it might just help me to remove the last remnants of my nasty hangover if I run it off.

Chapter Seventeen

I text my dope dealer and ask him to send me another ounce of his best purple haze. I know it will cost me a fortune but he knows I'm good for the cash. Even more so now, I think with a laugh. I tell him to send his best man down in a taxi and give him the address of The Barge Inn, giving strict instructions that the guy needs to wait in the taxi and call me so that I can come down and collect. I'm not about to do a drug deal in there. Even I'm not that stupid.

We do this in code of course. Drug dealer's code. I am fluent in this language.

We text back and forth a couple of times, agreeing on a date and time. My bag of haze will arrive tomorrow at eight o'clock. Or thereabouts. You can never be exact with drug delivery times, that's just the way it is. I know Ash will most likely arrive with a bag full of snow on Saturday. I'm not that bothered about stuffing my nose in the white stuff. I'm buzzing on a totally different drug today. Money and the game of chase. I'm now chasing something I really want.

And, for the first time in my life, I'm having to work hard for it.

I take my bank card and my driver's licence with me in the pocket of my running shorts so that I can pick up cash in Pewsey, both for my big bag of weed and to cover Ash and my expenses for the week. I know it won't take me very long to run there as I trace the route we followed yesterday on the boat.

God, was it only yesterday that we were laughing in the sun, flirting and teasing each other before that explosive kiss? It feels like longer. I'm craving her touch – and her taste – again like my next fix of heroin. But I am strong. I will resist. For now.

I arrive in Pewsey shortly after – my headache gone. The bank clerk gives me a strange look when I ask for two thousand pounds in cash. I guess it's probably because I am sweating like a pig in running gear. She checks my ID then taps into her computer, her eyes widening when she sees my balance. I'm just glad I could find a Lloyds branch in this little town, otherwise I would have had to make several separate withdrawals over the next two days. Her hands shake when she begins to count out the cash. I give her my best panty-dropping smile as she hands it to me in a white envelope. I leave the bank and run back the way I came, the money stuffed into the waistband under my T-shirt. It will probably be wet with sweat by the time I get back but I don't give a shit. I can dry it out on the roof of the boat.

I'm feeling good and dandy by the time I've showered and changed. I take my phone, my fags and a pint of lemonade – yes, lemonade! – back up to the roof and resume my favourite position. I ring Ash at work. It is Monday, after all, and he should be back from lunch by now, sitting at his desk making calls and generally charming the shit out of everyone so that he, too, can make a big fat commission from some mug who wants to book their next temp or full-time staff member.

He is, of course, an excellent salesman. He answers his direct line after three rings. "Ashley Spencer, how may I help you?"

I'm grinning as I light my next Marlboro. "Ah, Mr Spencer, you can help me by sucking my big fat dick. That'll do nicely for starters."

Ash snorts. “Baby, you can’t afford my sucking rate, you know that.”

I laugh at his quip. “So how did your date with ‘tattoo man’ go, Ash?” I ask, genuinely interested.

“Oh, you know, the usual. I was too much for him, he doesn’t want to see me again, blah blah blah.”

I laugh. “Oh, honey, I know how much you hate rejection,” I say sarcastically, taking a drag on my cigarette. “Plenty more fish in the sea though, eh?”

He is tapping on his keyboard now; I can hear the tip-tap in the background and other people talking around him. “What do you want, Jax? Are you actually bored now, or do you just want to piss me off with the fact that you no longer have to work for a living?”

I smile. “Meow, Ash. Look, I’m just calling to let you know that my stash is in the bank officially and the sharks are sniffing. I want you to keep my little secret a top secret now. No accidentally letting it slip out to whoever you are slipping into next. I’m serious. I want to go through some options with you when you get here at the weekend … in fact, see if you can take Friday off and come down a day earlier. I need to talk to you face-to-face.”

He’s interested now, I can tell as he has stopped tapping into his computer.

“What’s happened down there, Jax? Tell me now and stop fucking around.” I can just imagine him tipping back in his overly expensive orthopaedic chair and tapping his manicured finger on his lip.

“Nothing’s happened, I just want to talk to you in person about some ideas I have. And I miss you.”

Now he laughs. “You actually miss me now do you, eh? Well, that’s a bloody miracle, I thought you couldn’t give a flying fuck that I’m still sitting here at work while you smoke yourself into oblivion in the middle of nowhere.”

He really is such a diva. I fell in love with Ash because he feels no need to hide behind a cool exterior like I do. He demonstrates fully to the world his every wish, need and desire. I've always admired that part of him. This part of his character essentially fills the missing gaps of my own. It's always worked perfectly for me. I also love the way he can rub some people up the wrong way. My sadistic streak adores that part of him.

"Just let me know if you can make it down on Friday, you beautiful, outrageous prick."

"Of course, I can make it Friday, I can do whatever I like," he snorts at me.

"Good. Now get on with your job for once and let me continue with doing nothing," I snap back at him.

I hang up before he can throw me another insult. I really do want to see him. I am now ready to tell him about Jade; I want to see if he thinks I can make this work somehow. Despite his possessiveness over me, he would want nothing more than for me to be happy. *I* want to be happy. And I want to give him five million pounds so that *he* can be happy. I will, of course, drip-feed it to him so that he doesn't kill himself within a month.

Still smiling, my mind wanders to one incident where he fully demonstrated his claim over me. He literally grabbed me by the crutch and pulled me from my barstool, leaving the guy chatting me up with a scowl on his face as he marched me off to the toilet, proceeded to give me an eye-rolling blow job and then left without another word. This usually happens in one way or another when he decides I've not paid him enough attention. He's happy to share but only under his terms. Like a dog pissing on a lamp post. An 'I've been here first, just so you know' kind of thing.

I spend the rest of the afternoon and evening chilling out on the boat, I cook and read for a while. Something I haven't done for a very long time. I listen to the messages left on my mobile phone and am happy to find that several banks have come back to me with invitations to see them. I make a few more calls to check the stock market and move some of my money around just for the fun of it; only a few thousand to see what will happen.

I feel superhuman just knowing I can do whatever the hell I like now. I have been worrying about something that is not actually a real problem. Life is whatever you want it to be, regardless of how much money you have. Rich or poor, it's what you do with your life that makes the difference.

It is fear that stops us from moving forward and I'm lucky enough to know that now. It is fear of the unknown that keeps us locked up in our world of misery. If we have no fear, we have no restrictions. I no longer fear who I am or what I will do. I am trusting that I can, at last, be the man I have always wanted to be. A good man. An honest man. A man that no longer hides behind a false façade.

I can live on a boat in the middle of nowhere if I like and be free. It wouldn't even cost a lot of money. I know I'm perhaps being unrealistic in so many ways. But right now, sitting on this boat, in this place, I give myself a moment to just believe it can be possible. If I have learnt anything by being in this place, it is that I can change if I want to. Jade has shown me that. She has shown me that life can be as complicated or as simple as I want it to be. She has no fear of living on her own, living a life that she has chosen doing something she loves.

I have never really loved my job. It was just something I was good at that gave me good money. The city gave me the excuse to behave in the way I did. It provided me with the toys I wanted to play with. It took me into its belly and kept me warm and safe in the idea that I could lie and cheat my way through life with no consequences. But now I can see the consequence was a sad and empty soul, with no real meaning. I was walking through my life like a fucked-up zombie, devouring flesh along the way.

I have been empty for a long, long time. Even with Ash, who has provided me with a sense of love in the only way he could. But even he has not been able to touch my soul as Jade has. To open my eyes to what life has to offer. The simplicity of life. The simplicity of nature.

As I close my eyes that night in my big soft bed and feel the gentle slide of the boat as it moves on the water, I am content and happy. She has shown me that I can be happy. And I am determined to make it so. With or without her.

I just hope she can, or will want to, fit in somewhere in this giant, fucked-up puzzle that I call my life.

Chapter Eighteen

The next three days I spend getting back into my routine of running, chilling and reading. A new thriller holds my attention for longer than I expected. Now that I have the time to read, it is something I am finding pleasantly soothing. It feels good to enjoy the world of words again.

But I've not seen any sign of Jade at all.

I have deliberately avoided her end of the canal. Maybe I heard her cycle past one day when I was in the shower. In fact, I swear I felt her as she went past with Bob running at her side. I am giving her the time she needs to process what happened between us the last time I saw her. She knows I am here for the summer.

A quick phone call to my practice letting Hilary know that I won't be back for another two weeks has at least given me some more breathing space. The decision to finish working at my practice in Harley Street, giving a months' notice to my existing clients has been made and feels right. I no longer want to pretend to be something I'm not: respectable and professional.

I just want to be me. But a better version of me.

The purple haze arrived on Tuesday, as scheduled, the guy turning up at nine and completing the deal in the back of the car park with the meter still running in the taxi. He was more than happy with the more than generous tip I gave him for his troubles. Being permanently stoned has opened another wave of my consciousness. I have laughed at nothing and cried a couple of times too, reliving some of my past.

This time alone has allowed me to use my psychologist skills on myself and analyse why I chose to distance myself emotionally from people. Why I found it easier to become aloof with partners rather than admit my soul craves stimulation and variety from both sexes. My bisexuality had become a tainted secret rather than something to be cherished as part of me.

My fear of judgement kept me chained to a revolving line of sexual partners without the connection necessary to fill the empty void in my heart. It all makes complete sense now. Avoiding my own deep-set trauma had become normal. Until now.

Truly, I have made peace with my bisexuality. I thought I had before, but I hadn't, I just fucked my way through it. I have now faced it head on, accepted the beauty of my unique soul that requires more variety and stimulation than your average person. It is not something to be ashamed of or treated like a dirty secret. Working with clients and helping them to see that no matter what they desire, or how they conduct their lives it should be done with a sense of love for themselves and others, is now something I must apply to my own life.

Thankfully, I have never contracted a sexual disease in all my years of screwing around. I've always tried to be careful but there were occasions in the past when this wasn't the case. Usually, if drugs were involved. Protection was the last thing on my mind in those moments. There were a few near misses, especially with Ash. His track record hasn't been great. I'm determined to change that reckless behaviour now. I intend to move forward without having to use sex as a weapon. I am going to treat myself and others with the respect we both deserve.

Ash will arrive tomorrow, and I am both excited and nervous about seeing him and telling him how liberated I am now feeling. I am healing at last.

The weather has changed and I can feel the storm that Jade predicted brewing somewhere close. The air is charged. It is so stiflingly close that I am sweating, even though I am only in my shorts, sitting barefoot on the roof again. I am smoking a spliff – no surprises there – and just watching the skyline as it changes to a dark ominous purple in the distance. It is getting darker, dusk is approaching. My body tingles in anticipation, the heightened effect of being stoned adding to the buzz.

My beers sit in a bucket of ice next to me and I have my packet of Marlboro Lights, an ashtray and an umbrella to hand. Yep, I'm ready. I lean back in the deckchair, which is moulded to the exact shape of my butt now and wait for the show.

I smile to myself as the first bolt of lightning hits the sky in the distance. A roll of thunder follows shortly after, adding to my growing excitement. I wonder where Jade is and if she, too, is sitting on her boat with Bob, looking out over the fields and waiting for the storm to creep closer.

As if she is psychic and tuned into the fact, I am thinking about her, I hear the sound of someone stepping up onto the gangplank and know, without turning my head, it's her. I have been waiting for her for almost a week to reappear. She certainly likes her space and takes her time. I like that very much, even though I want her to be sitting next to me every minute of every day right now.

Bob's claws tip-tap on the metal stern as they both step up onto *The Witch*. "Hey, City Boy," she calls to me and I turn my head and smile. "Fancy some company?" she asks, holding up another bottle of white wine dripping with condensation.

Seriously, I love this girl.

I grin at her and wave her over. "Sure thing, Fairy Girl, come on up. The show's just about to start." She beams up at me before crouching down to murmur to Bob. I hear them both go down inside my boat for a moment. She appears again and hops up onto the roof, pulling up the spare deckchair I have in one hand, the wine in another, no wine glasses so I presume we will be necking it straight out of the bottle. Classy. I watch her walk towards me with that slow sexy swing to her hips that has my head spinning and my dick singing.

She is wearing a short denim miniskirt, her biker boots, of course, and a crop top that clings to her chest nicely, revealing a belly ring and a small silvery scar on her lower stomach. The ring sparkles at me as she moves, a dangling diamanté star attached to a bar. I like it a lot; it adds to her funky style. Her hair is in two braids over her shoulders, her Mohawk flat again creating the pretty fringe that softens her look a little. Her eyes are dark and huge as if she is just as excited as I am at the impending storm brewing on the horizon. She unfolds the deckchair and flops into it, sticking the wine bottle into my bucket of ice. She crosses her long legs and studies me for a moment, a slight smile on her face. "You look good, City Boy."

I smile at her and nod. "I feel good."

Her eyes are roaming my face as if she is seeing something new in my features. "No. You look really good. Somethings changed for you since I saw you last. A good thing."

How very perceptive of her. I pass her the spliff and she takes it smiling. "I've sorted a few things out since I saw you last."

She takes a long drag on the spliff narrowing her eyes sexily at me as she does. "I'm thrilled for you," she says as she passes it back. I catch an edge of sarcasm in her voice.

I was probably like a wind-up toy when we first met, all coiled and ready to explode into a furious mess of springs and widgets that had been tightened so much they were stuck together by sheer force of will. "And how are you, Jade?" I ask her as she looks ahead again out over the fields which are now rustling with a breeze that is picking up as the storm grows closer.

"Good. Really good."

I watch her as she looks out across the horizon, she looks relaxed and happy. She has clearly made peace with the fact we almost detonated during our first kiss. We are back to that easy friendship I have come to love since spending time with her. Good. I knew she would process it in her own way and come back to me when she was ready. This much I have learnt from my time spent with her. She is complex but simple. She reaches for the wine bottle and takes a swig straight from it.

She turns and faces me again, smiling as she passes the bottle to me. I take my own swig and grin at her. She takes another hit from my joint and then passes it back to me. We do this for a while in silence. Enjoying the buzz of the alcohol and weed in the easy compatible silence we have now developed.

Another flash of lightning appears, this time a nice big fork that hits the ground and crackles loudly. She gasps and leans forward so that her elbows are on her knees. The thunder follows booming across the horizon, making the boat rumble. I laugh. I place the wine back in the bucket and sit back in my deckchair. "Is Bob okay down there?"

She sits back up and faces me again. "He's fine, I fed him a tiny piece of hashish with his dinner tonight, it calms him down and knocks him out. He'll be sleeping like a baby by now and snoring like a pig throughout the whole thing."

I throw my head back and laugh. Damn, she makes me

laugh so much. So unpredictable. "A stoner dog! How very amusing."

She is grinning at me with that mischievous look. "It's easier for him that way and I get to watch the storm without having to worry about him."

I nod and take another hit on the joint which is making my legs feel completely unattached to my body. "I was hoping you'd be around to see it," I say.

She turns to face the fields again, her knee bouncing a little making her legs jostle. Something she does when she is a little nervous it seems. "I wanted to watch it with you," she says, her voice soft and sweet. I'm grinning so much my cheeks hurt. Possibly another side effect of the joint.

"I'm glad you did."

Chapter Nineteen

We sit in silence watching the storm playing out like a movie before us, our own jungle TV for the evening. There is no rain yet, it seems to be more of an electrical storm, but the breeze has picked up and is lifting some of the humidity.

I am still sitting here with no T-shirt on but can't be bothered to get up out of my chair to put one on. I don't think it's bothering Jade too much. In fact, as I watch the storm, I catch her sneaking a peek at me out of my peripheral vision. It makes me smile inside and out.

We finish the joint and drink the wine, passing the bottle back and forth. We are in no rush and I am just content to sit quietly with her, watching nature do her best to scare the shit out of everyone. Everyone but Jade and me. We are loving it. The sky lights up so brightly at one point it makes us both jump up and out of our deckchairs like a firework was lit underneath them. We both laugh in shock. The storm is getting really close and we are sitting on a metal boat floating in water.

Paranoia from my stoned state raises its head and sends a shiver of fear down my spine. What if we get hit and are shrivelled up to charcoal in one fatal blast? All they would find would be two deckchairs and a bucket of beers next to our black and twisted skeletons. I start having a laughing fit so badly that Jade joins in unaware of my thoughts and we are both doubled over as our stomachs groan with the pressure.

Then the rain comes.

It's as if someone has just turned on a switch in the sky and it starts to pelt down like a damn monsoon. Big, fat, warm raindrops cascade out of the sky, straight down like a massive bucket of water has been tipped upside down directly above us. Jade lets out a squeal and, before I can even reach for the umbrella, she is up on her feet and heading down to find shelter in the boat. I grab my cigarettes and run after her, slipping in the process and landing on my arse. She is laughing her head off as she slips down onto the engine compartment reaching up to help me as I get drenched.

I jump down beside her and she looks up at me, smiling like this is the best thing in the world. Getting soaked to the skin in a thunderstorm with me on my boat. It *is* the best thing in the world.

We stand, just staring at each other for a very long time and getting soaked by the rain before my brain computes that she is shivering. I grab her shoulders and push her down inside the boat so that she is now in the kitchen. The thunder is so loud I know the storm is directly overhead. I can feel the electrical charge in the air, the absolute power of the storm raging around us. The rain is falling so hard I can barely hear anything as it drums like a thousand crazy drummers at a Metallica concert on the roof of *The Witch*.

It is just as I imagined it would be here in this place. Amazing.

"Wait here." She nods as her teeth begin to chatter.

Bob is flat out on his blanket, fast asleep as if nothing is happening around him. He looks so content it makes me laugh again. I leave Jade shivering in the kitchen, dripping wet and looking like a kitten someone has just tried to drown and run to the bathroom and grab two large towels. I wrap one towel around my shoulders and the other around her as she continues to stand there grinning at me. I rub her arms vigorously to help her dry and then wrap my arms around her to warm her up a little. I am hotter than a tropical forest. Just being with her has made my body flare up like a goddamn bonfire.

I am literally steaming; my skin is so hot, feverish even.

She stops shivering and presses her head into my chest. I just hold her like that for a moment, resting my chin on the top of her head. It feels so perfectly right to be doing this. I can feel her heart beating erratically against mine, which seems to be doing the same. It is as if we are plugged into the electrical current of the storm and it is powering us up. Eventually, she starts to move and I loosen my hold on her as she looks up at me and smiles. "That was fun," she whispers.

I nod and smile down at her, wanting desperately to kiss her again but knowing it would be a mistake if I made the first move. She needs to guide me on this path. Open the door to the roller coaster and invite me on before we can take the ride together.

The rain suddenly stops its vicious onslaught and subsides to a gentle pitter-patter on the roof, the thunder rumbles again but not as loud. It is passing over us, moving on. "Do you want a change of clothes?" I ask as she takes the towel and tries, unsuccessful, to pat her braids dry.

"Might be a good idea, I think even my underwear is wet." I groan inwardly at that thought.

"I'll find you something. Might be a bit big but better than sitting in wet undies, eh?"

She laughs as I leave her standing in the kitchen and she bends down to stroke Bob. I go into the bedroom to find her something to wear. I strip out of my wet shorts and put on a vest top and some jogging bottoms, they are really old and soft. My comfort pants. I pull out a T-shirt and a pair of boxer briefs for Jade. I rarely wear underwear but brought some just in case. She can wear them as shorts. Everything else would just swamp her.

I go back out to find her peeling off her crop top, revealing her bra, the towel now wrapped around her waist. I see her denim skirt and a tiny bright pink thong on the floor next to her. My dick jumps up wanting a closer look now that she is almost naked. She smiles, then looks at the floor as if she is embarrassed. I know she isn't really, it's a cute little trick women do when they want to seduce you. I hand her the T-shirt and boxers. "Feel free to change here or in the bedroom, wherever you like."

She laughs and looks at me with that sparkle in her eyes again. She leaves me in the living area and disappears into the bedroom. I run my hand across my face in exasperation. Fuck, this girl will be the death of me.

I'm so supercharged and horny I might just fucking come in my jogging bottoms. No help required.

She returns, dressed in my T-shirt which hangs down to her mid-thighs. I can't see the boxer briefs but assume she has put them on. I hope she hasn't. I am sitting on the sofa with my legs sprawled widely. I put the kettle on while she was dressing to make us some coffee; it whistles comfortingly in the background.

She stands and stares at me for a moment, taking me in again. I see her pupils dilate a little. I pat the sofa next to me and obediently she sits, curling her legs up to the side so that she is facing me. I shift slightly so I can face her. She says nothing but smiles coyly. Her plaits are dripping a little and I reach forward and, without saying anything, untie the band at the end and begin to loosen it.

She watches me, mesmerised as my fingers unwind her beautiful ebony hair. I do the same with the other plait. We are both silent, but I note that her breathing has hitched up a notch. I am calm, in control. For once in my life, I want to take this slow and tell myself I am completely at ease, even though, inside, my body is doing the fandango.

I run my fingers through her hair and then pull it back from her shoulders so that it hangs loosely down her back. She is still watching me intently. My eyes locked on hers, I stand up slowly, my lips twisting up into a sly smile. I walk to the bathroom to retrieve another, smaller, clean dry towel and go back into the living area. I sit behind her and begin to dry her hair, rubbing it gently in the towel. She sighs and tips her head back.

Now that she is so close to me I can smell her unique scent, the mixture of vanilla, tropical fruits and incense. I throw the towel on the floor and push her hair to one side watching her shoulders rise and fall as she breathes. Her neck is beautifully slender and so tempting to take a bite from as she tilts her head to one side. Unable to restrain myself any longer, I lean towards her.

I was going to let her make the first move, but I can't wait. I'm too pumped up. I place a feather-light kiss on her neck and she moans in response. Her reaction gives me the green light I was hoping for and I begin to trail kisses up to her ear and flick my tongue inside. She leans back into me and I run my hands up and down her arms, making goosebumps rise to the surface.

"Jax," she whispers, in what sounds like a plea for help.

"It's okay, Jade. I'm not going to fuck you," I whisper back. She shudders at my statement and I flick my tongue across her ear again. "I just want to kiss you." I suck gently on the pulse that is beating erratically on her neck and then pause, my own breathing hot and heavy. "I want to kiss all of you so goddamn much it hurts," I say, my voice so deep I almost don't recognise it as my own. Before I have a chance to react, she turns her head and finds my mouth, as if my words have instantly broken any barriers that were keeping us apart.

We kiss slowly, gently, like it is the most natural thing in the world. I'm desperate to fuck her. But I won't. I can't. I need to take this slow.

She responds to me in a way that makes my head spin. She turns her whole body, breaking the kiss for a second, until I find her sitting on my lap. The heat of her body pressed against me makes me lose concentration for a second and I can't help but let out a groan.

We kiss again, it goes on and on and on as if we can't get enough of each other. The pace changing from soft and gentle to hard and fast. I lose myself in the sensation. I have never kissed anyone like this before.

It is, quite simply, mind-blowing.

Chapter Twenty

We are making out like a couple of teenagers and I'm absolutely loving it. She presses down onto my erection with her legs wrapped around me and it takes all my strength not to strip her naked and dive straight into her.

After an infinite amount of time where the world, it seems, stops spinning, I break the kiss gently and she stares at me with luminous eyes that are questioning why I have stopped. I don't know why I have stopped. I don't want this to stop. She smiles at me shyly. Both of us are breathing hard.

"You are in control, Jade," I say to reassure her. She nods and then looks down at where our bodies are joined, flat against each other. She hesitates then looks up at me again. I know she is about to slide off me and, strangely, I'm okay with that. She touches my cheek with her finger and sighs again. She shifts back and steps off me exactly as I knew she would. I'm glad. I was seconds away from jumping her.

"Would you like a cigarette?" she asks as she walks to the kitchen.

I blow out a long slow breath. "Yes fucking please."

She laughs and takes the kettle off the boil, which I had forgotten about and has been whistling its head off for God knows how long. She lights me a cigarette, brings it to me and puts it in my mouth with a sexy smile. Sashaying back to the kitchen, she lights her own cigarette and starts to make us coffee. I don't usually smoke inside *The Witch* but, tonight, I don't give a shit. I can air her out tomorrow. The spotlights in the ceiling reflecting off her ebony hair beautifully as I watch Jade making the coffee. She spoons several sugars into her cup and then sticks her cigarette in her mouth, holding it to one side with her eyes narrowed as she brings the coffees over to the sofa.

She looks so wonderfully sexy right now, I want to launch myself at her on full attack. But I don't.

She places the coffees on the floor by my feet and then turns to face me. "Ashtray?" she asks raising a brow. I look around and grab an old beer can I left on the side table placing it next to the coffee. "Sorry I didn't even ask if it's okay to smoke in here," she says looking a little chagrin.

I smile at her and pick up my coffee, blowing on it before taking a sip. She has made it black with no sugar, just the way I like it. "It's fine, I think we can get away with it for one night," I say with a smile. My dick is screaming at me, frustrated as hell that our making out did not progress further. My lips are tingling after our kiss but I do my best to show no sign of my internal struggle. It's probably the first time in my life I've just kissed someone without it turning into an immediate fuck fest.

She is watching me again, analysing me. Probably thinking I am going to accuse her of being a prick tease at some point. I'm not. I'm really enjoying the push-pull of this relationship. I like the fact that she keeps retreating; it's making the chase even more fun. Just kissing Jade – and nothing else – has turned into my new favourite thing to do. Who would have thought it? I can see the cogs whirring in her brain as she takes her coffee and holds it in her hands, the cigarette dangling from her fingers.

"Tell me what you're thinking, Jade," I say taking a drag on my own cigarette. I wouldn't normally go into therapist mode but it's just far too tempting right now.

"I'm confused," she says with a slight frown. I nod smiling at her encouragingly. I want her to tell me what she is really feeling. "I've only just met you but I feel this intense pull towards you that's making me question myself."

I try not to spit out my coffee at that confession, as I take another sip. "Okay." I pause watching her with interest as she looks away for a moment, as if she is afraid to look me in the eye. "Why are you questioning how you feel if it's a good feeling?"

She looks back at me again and I see a little fear in her eyes. This is not so good. "I don't normally allow men into my life like this. I can't allow men into my life like this."

I'm very fucking interested now. My shrink's head is switched on and I lean forward in excited anticipation. "Can I ask why not?"

She takes another drag of her cigarette puts her coffee cup down and looks at me directly. "I can't give you what you want Jax."

I take a deep breath, take another long pull on my Marlboro then push it into the beer can. I lean back slightly from her giving her space. "And what is it that you think I want, Jade?"

She blinks at me. "That's the problem. For the first time in my life, I don't know." She has me baffled now. Before I can ask another question, probe her gently she begins to talk again. "There's something about you that I can't quite work out. A sense of darkness that seems to want to push through but you won't allow it. You're hiding something from me. I don't feel at all threatened by you; in fact, I love being around you. You make me laugh, are extremely easy on the eye and seem to not give a fuck about life in general, which I admire … I know we have chemistry."

She pauses and smiles at me, biting her bottom lip briefly before continuing. I am staring at her in awe taking in every word she is saying and holding it tightly to my thumping chest. "I want to touch you, Jax, I want to let you in, but I'm not sure whether that's what you really want or can give me in return. I'm not stupid enough to think that this 'thing' we have going on will have a happy ending or that you even want that. But you've touched something in me that no one else has ever touched before. I can't explain it."

I think my mouth may have flopped open. I'm totally shocked by her brutal honesty. "I think you just did a very good job at doing exactly that," I reply.

She laughs and pushes her cigarette into the beer can before looking up at me again. "I have no idea what you're really thinking or feeling, Jax. Apart from the obvious," she says with a slight grin. "It unnerves me a little and I also seem to have no control over how my body responds to you."

Her last statement has me grinning like a sadistic madman. I know I need to give her something back, reassure her a little. "I really like you, Jade. I mean *really* like you." I pause, she is waiting for the 'but'. I don't want to hurt her, but I need to give her something here. "But I think you're right. You most likely can't give me what I really want. And I won't push you for it. I'll not willingly hurt you, Jade." I leave it at that.

It sucks hard that I have been forced to say the truth. She stares at me for a moment, processing what I have just said. I think she will most likely get up and leave me now. "Okay, I believe you," she says.

Just like that. I blink, surprised she has not hightailed it out of here. She sighs and then pushes her hand against my chest pressing me back into the sofa. I watch her as she slides around so that her back is to me again and rests against me a little awkwardly, indicating she wants me to hold her again.

I shift so that I am now lying back horizontally on the sofa and pull her down with me so that she is lying flush against my chest, her body flat against me between my legs. She raises her arms above her head and puts them around my neck pushing her fingers into my hair. In return, I wrap my arms around her and hug her against me. She fits into my body like she was made to do so. She plays with my hair and I run my fingers up and down her waist gently.

We say nothing more.

The storm has passed, and the rain has stopped. I know it's getting late. Jade lowers her arms again after a while and places them on my thighs making my dick twitch slightly. "Stay," I whisper. She doesn't respond. "Please stay, Jade. We can just sleep together here tonight; Bob is out of it anyway and I really don't relish the thought of carrying him back to your boat."

She chuckles. "Okay."

I push her up slowly and untangle myself from her. I take her hand leading her down the corridor to the bedroom. She follows me, her hand gripping mine tightly. I stop beside the bed and pull back the covers. Stepping aside I gesture that she should scoot up and onto the bed.

It's dark and I can only see her in shadow but I feel everything about her. Her heightened breathing, her scent and the way she gracefully slides up onto the massive bed and moves over towards the wall.

I take off my vest but leave my joggers on: I don't want to scare her again. She rolls onto her side so that she is facing away from me as I slip in beside her and pull her into my arms, spooning her perfectly. She fits me like the last piece of the puzzle. Her hand reaches for mine that is tucked around her waist. She links her fingers through my own and pulls me closer. I hold her tightly and nuzzle my face into her hair. She smells and feels sublime.

"Goodnight, Jax. Thank you for a wonderful evening."

I kiss her hair gently. "You are most welcome."

She relaxes into my arms and I try desperately not to stab her in the back with my persistent hard-on. She doesn't seem to mind. For a while, I lie there, listening to her breathing and find my own body start to relax. My muscles unwind and I close my eyes, taking in every single sensation that I am feeling lying in bed with her wrapped in my arms. It is just as I imagined it would feel. Blissful.

Her breathing changes quickly and her fingers loosen on mine. I know she has fallen asleep. This is what life is all about. Feeling like this. So completely and utterly relaxed; happy and content.

I eventually drift off on a magic carpet of Jade-filled visions. She is my fairy goddess. My angel of happiness. I know I've got it bad. But the one thing I do know is that she isn't going anywhere. She didn't run and she didn't question my response to her honest admission of feelings for me.

I couldn't be happier.

Chapter Twenty-One

I wake to an empty bed. I'm disappointed but knew instinctively she would be gone when I woke up. I sense this may be something she does when she needs to process a situation. It gives her control. I understand, I really do. Last night was a lot to take in for both of us.

Her scent, left on my pillows, fills my nostrils and it makes me smile. As I move, I feel something under my arm and sit up to find a note stuck to my bicep. I peel it off and read it. *I will see you later, City Boy. PS you snore louder than Bob. J x.* My smile grows just that little bit bigger and I stretch out feeling better than I ever have despite the fact I have yet another raging hard-on and didn't get my screaming orgasm last night.

The clock says it is ten o'clock. I have enough time to prepare myself for Ash's arrival. The taxi is dropping him off at The Barge Inn at around twelve. I put a rocket up my arse and head for the shower. I don't want to wash the smell of Jade off me but know I must sort myself out, in more ways than one. Ash will know I have shared my bed with someone if I don't shower. Like a bloodhound, he can literally smell it on me and, right now, I am covered in Eau d'Jade.

They will meet this weekend, possibly today if Jade's note is any indication. I was prepared for the fact that she may just do her little disappearing act again for a few more days. But last night something was different. As if she was feeling a little safer with our relationship now. Maybe that will give her the ability to spend more time with me without feeling overwhelmed. I hope so.

If Ash is not prepped first, Jade will most likely suss me – us – out instantly. I have no idea what will happen when they meet. I don't want him to act any differently around me than he usually would but I may just have to get him to tone it down a bit. I think I have no real choice in this. It is what it is. She will find out eventually if we are to remain friends.

The storm last night cleared the air completely and it is much cooler today. The sun is playing hide and seek behind a few clouds, popping in and out and casting shadows over the landscape. I make myself some breakfast and check my mobile. Ash has already sent me a text to say he is on his way. I am looking forward to seeing him. The kettle boils and I make an extra-strong coffee and take it out to the roof with my morning Marlboro. The bucket of beers is still sitting up there with the two deckchairs. I fold one away and put it back down into its box. I don't want it to be too obvious that I have had company.

I sit and drink my coffee, smoke and watch the ducks float by. I feel so at home here, more comfortable in this environment than I ever felt in my flat. I am now dreading leaving but I know I will have to leave this bubble of wonderfulness at some point. I still have a shitload of stuff to sort out. I contemplate contacting the owner of *The Witch* and making him an offer. Although I have no idea how much this boat would cost, I know I could afford it. I put that thought to one side, for now, knowing that it will probably not even be for sale. But who knows?

Just to appease his need for order and cleanliness, I tidy up a little, making a bit of an effort for Ash. I make up one of the bunk beds so that he has a comfy place to sleep. He will most likely bitch about how small it is but I intend to get him so fucked-up on my purple haze later he won't give a shit by the time we call it a night. I am not letting him sleep in my bed with me, not with Jade around. She would freak out completely if she unexpectedly popped her head in and found us both naked in the same bed. I can't do that to her just yet.

I head on up to the pub, waiting for the call from Ash to say he is here. My heart is thumping in my chest like I've sniffed some poppers as I stride up the canal path.

The pub is closed. It doesn't open until lunchtime, so the garden is empty and I am grateful for that. Just as I sit down on one of the benches and light another cigarette, a taxi pulls in. Perfect timing. I stub the cigarette out immediately and walk over to the taxi, grinning like an idiot.

I can see Ash in the front seat, his beautiful brown eyes popping out of his head as he takes in my tan and my casual attire. I'm wearing my scruffy Doc Martins with the laces undone and my faded, old Metallica T-shirt again.

He is clearly shitting a brick. The door of the taxi flings open and he is on me before I get a chance to even say hello. He clings to me like I am a life raft. "You fucking bastard. That was the longest, most boring journey I've ever had to endure in my entire life, with a man that stank of BO and picked his teeth the whole way here."

I laugh and pull him away from my body holding him at arm's length. "Well hello to you too, Ash," I say with a smile. He grabs my head and kisses me on the mouth so hard my teeth rattle. I let him. He needs it. So do I, actually.

He pulls back and I can see something like tears in his eyes. He really has missed me. I fling my arm around his neck and we saunter back to the taxi. The driver is staring at us with his mouth open as if we are both aliens with probes in our hands. I grab some cash from my back pocket and shove it into his hand. “Keep the change, mate.”

Ash snorts. “Get him to pop the trunk, Jax. I want to get as far away as possible from him, as quickly as possible.” I take the huge suitcase Ash has brought with him out of the boot and pull up the handle ready to drag it down the towpath.

The taxi takes off as if we are about to hijack it, leaving dust in its wake. Not the first time that has happened with us around. Ash looks around, eyeing the pub and the canal with distaste. “Where in the fuck are we, Jax? Have you completely lost your mind?”

I laugh and put my arm around his shoulder again. “Come on, you pussy, let’s get you a beer.” As we walk off past the pub, I wonder if anyone was watching our little reunion and grin. I hope it gave them something to talk about if they did.

Now sitting on the sofa in the living area of *The Witch*, Ash is grinning. He is wearing a baby blue shirt that has a thin pinstripe running through it, black designer jeans and Converse trainers. His shirt sleeves are rolled up slightly and his collar is undone giving him a slightly casual, edge to his city attire. His blonde hair is ruffled and scruffy like he has been running his hands through it continuously in the taxi. He most probably has. He looks gorgeous as usual. His eyes are bright and taking everything in. So far, he thinks we are in a theme park and this is one of the rides.

“This boat is fucking awesome, Jax. You need to buy it immediately,” he says, his eyes as wide as saucers. I am pouring us two beers with two tequila shots to start us off.

“I’ve considered doing just that.”

He leans back on the sofa and crosses his legs. “I’m almost understanding why you haven’t come back yet.” I take the drinks over to him and place them down on the small table beside the fire. He leans forward and claps his hands together, grinning like the devil himself.

"Right, let's get fucked," he says, licking his lips with relish. We down the tequila and start on our first beer.

I have the feeling today is going to be a very long and messy day indeed.

Chapter Twenty-Two

Ash chops up several fat lines of cocaine and jabbers on about what a terrible week he has had and how inconsiderate I have been leaving him for so long. It's probably around five in the evening now and we have been drinking since he arrived. I am anticipating Jade's arrival with a slightly worried feeling she will take one look at us and fuck off forever.

"Jax, are you even listening to me you utter prick? Why do you keep looking at the back door like you're expecting us to be raided?" he looks up for a second from his chopping. "Are we likely to get raided here?"

I laugh taking a sip of beer and lounging back as casually as I can on the sofa. "No, Ash. Highly unlikely."

He nods and bends down with a twenty rolled up in his hand. Just as the note makes it to his nose, I hear the tip-tap of Bob's little feet outside. Fuck. Ash looks up like someone just caught him screwing his sister. "What was that?" he hisses, cocking his head to one side. I'm on my feet in an instant as Jade pops her head inside, her face a picture as she sees both me and Ash inside.

She takes the whole scene in and her mouth pops open into a perfect 'O'. Busted.

"Hey, Jade," I say, smiling like I'm really, really sorry she had to see this. Ash becomes statue still, the twenty still in his hand, his head still poised over the coke.

"Is this a bad time?" she says with a slight waver to her

voice.

Ash leaps up, almost knocking the table over. "Hell no, Baby Girl. Come on in, join the party."

I am wishing that there was a hole directly underneath my feet and I could just step silently and quickly into it, completely denying the fact that I was even here. I couldn't bring myself to mention her to Ash during our catch up this afternoon or to prep him for appropriate behaviour. Awkward is not the word to describe this moment. A potential disaster comes to mind.

She completely astonishes me by smiling and stepping in, revealing her long legs and beautiful body in one graceful swoop. Ash is grinning like he just won the lottery not me. Bob follows her and he immediately jumps back a little. Ash and animals have never quite seen eye to eye.

"Ash, this is Jade. Jade, this is Ash," I mumble as my stomach rolls. I grab Bob before he reaches Ash and pet him so that he doesn't get too excited by my new visitor.

Jade walks slowly towards us and reaches out her hand for Ash to take. "Nice to meet you, Ash," she says with a smile. He ignores her hand and grabs her into a full hug, making her squeal and then laugh. He looks at me over her shoulder and licks his lips provocatively. He releases her from the hug but wraps his fingers around her forearms and grins.

She is smiling back at him and taking in the fact that he is like a supermodel wrapped in city plastic. Her eyes grow big and wide as they wander over his features, her lip catching between her teeth as he holds her. I continue to pet Bob, watching the whole interaction. This could go one of two ways.

"Well now I completely understand why Jax hasn't wanted to come home," Ash says, still grinning. He releases her and flops back down onto the sofa. Jade looks at me and blushes slightly. Ash is now watching us both with the eyes of a hawk and the grin of a vulture. "Care to partake, Baby Girl?" he says as he bends down again, completely ignoring the fact that taking cocaine in front of complete strangers is totally not PC.

"No, thanks, I'm good. Not my bag," she replies. I sigh with relief but feel very edgy that Ash will be passing me the twenty next. I'm in a bit of a conundrum with that one.

"Do you want a beer?" I ask Jade, wanting to get as far away from the table of narcotics as possible.

I practically run to the kitchen to retrieve one for her. I grab the tequila as well. I need a generous shot for what's coming next.

She sits down next to Ash and watches him with a look of amusement as he snorts two lines, one immediately after the other. "Fuck me that shit is good," Ash says dramatically, flinging his head up after line two. Jade chuckles. At least she hasn't run out of here calling the police as she goes. It seems nothing fazes her. Bob settles himself by her feet looking completely at home. I walk back with a beer for her and the tequila in my hand. I take a swig straight out of the bottle. Jade is looking up at me with a very amused look on her face. She can tell I am sweating big time over this.

"So, Jade, tell me everything about you and how you know the delectable Jax. How you met, how long you've been fucking et cetera, et cetera, et cetera," Ash says matter-of-factly. I pale instantly, even with my wonderful tan, but Jade laughs, crossing her long, bare legs slowly. She is wearing her funky little short shorts again and her biker boots.

"We're just friends," she says while trying not to laugh. She clearly found Ash's line of questioning extremely amusing. I feel like I'm going to puke.

Ash rolls his eyes at her. "No one is *just friends* with Jax, honey."

She looks at me again and I see something flash across her eyes. A look of knowing. It is as if she knows I have revealed a part of myself to her alone and that this man who knows me so well, knows me not at all. I feel my body gradually begin to relax and the colour return to my cheeks. She is taking this all so well. And she is not freaking out, not one bit. This might just work.

An hour later, Ash has declared he is taking Jade home with him on Sunday and there is nothing I can do about it. We have settled into a comfortable banter. Ash is stealing the show, of course. His gayness is overflowing today. I'm not sure if he is trying to make Jade feel that he is no threat to her whatsoever or staking his claim on me. So far, he has not touched me while she's been on the boat. I am grateful for that small mercy.

He did, however, hand me the twenty casually when Jade went to the toilet and I took the opportunity to snort my two fat lines as quickly as possible. Yep, I am that fucking predictable. I couldn't say no.

I'm buzzing like a freight train now and feeling as horny as fuck. Jade could be in deep trouble here if she stays too long. Ash is constantly touching her, admiring her bracelets and her hair, running his fingers across her thighs every now and then almost as if he is enjoying teasing the shit out of me, now he knows I have a claim to her. He keeps eyeing me slyly and pouting, running his tongue over his bottom lip suggestively when Jade turns to talk to me.

I'm trying not to punch him in the face.

After a beer and two tequila shots, Jade stands up and says she needs to get going as she has some errands to run. I breathe a sigh of relief; as much as I want her to stay, I'm glad she is leaving. Ash is so pumped up right now he may just reveal all my secrets before I even have a chance to explain what the hell is going on here. I walk her and Bob to the back of the boat. Ash waves at her as he leans back on the sofa with his legs sprawled, giving her a great view of his crutch.

"I hope to see you again very soon, Baby Girl," he purrs at her. She blows him a kiss as she leaves and Ash grins in return like the Cheshire cat. I frown at him but follow her as she heads towards the door.

"Sorry about that," I say, feeling very awkward indeed now that we are alone.

She reaches up and touches my lip with her finger, trailing it along the bottom edge teasingly making me shiver. "Don't be. Ash is fun." I snort, playfully snapping at her finger so that she pulls it back laughing. We stand staring at each other for a moment. I want to kiss her so badly it hurts. "By the way, the pub is having a little festival thing over the weekend. They do it every year. Thought you might like to come up there tomorrow night with me. They have a live band and plenty of local beer. Bring Ash with you."

I groan inwardly at the thought of subjecting the locals to Ash. "I'd love to. Not sure whether we'd end up being chucked out with Ash in tow though, Jade."

She reaches for my hand and squeezes it gently. "No pressure," she says to me in that low sexy hum I'm beginning to love. I think I may just have to marry this girl. I blink, stunned I even just thought this incomprehensible thought.

"Okay cool. Come by tomorrow night on your way and pick us up."

She grins up at me like I've just told her Elvis is not actually dead. She reaches up on her tiptoes and kisses me with warm smooth lips on the cheek. "See you tomorrow, City Boy." I watch her saunter back down the towpath with Bob at her side, wishing I could just be like a normal human and give her everything she ever wanted.

I step back into the boat to find Ash racking up again. He's going to kill us both before we even get to the pub tomorrow night. I'm not sure I really want to take him but I do want to spend some more time with Jade. He looks up grinning at me while he continues to chop like a ninja. "Spill it, Jax. Tell me everything – every fucking detail – and don't leave anything out. I'll know if you do!"

I sigh dragging my hand through my hair. Here goes. I tell him everything. We are both so coked up by this point, it's impossible not to. He listens intently, his eyes wired and his leg tapping like a cartoon character. "You are royally fucked, my friend," he declares when I finish.

I'm pacing the boat like a crazy person. "You don't have to fucking tell me that Ash. I already know."

He laughs and throws an empty beer can at me. "Look, Jax, you have to tell her. Give it to her straight. She seems like a really cool girl and deserves to know the truth. I think she'll take it. She seems open-minded enough."

I continue to pace, wanting to punch something. "Yeah, thank God she is fucking open-minded with you here acting like bloody Scarface." He rolls over laughing at that. His legs in the air like an upturned beetle. I feel a smile begin to slip onto my face; I can't be mad at him for long. He's stating the truth. I do need to tell her everything but I just don't want to ruin what we have.

I also still desperately want to fuck her. No, that's not true. I want to make love to her. Oh God, I'm so totally fucked. I know that this possibility will disappear like a virgin's cherry on prom night once she finds out who I really am. How I *really* live my life.

Ash jumps up and strides over to me. He pulls me into his arms and holds me for a moment, pressing my head into his neck so that he can whisper into my ear. "Jax. You *have* to tell her. I can see something has changed in you." He strokes my neck with his thumb as he holds me. "That hard shell you've always had wrapped around you seems to be cracking a little. Your expression softened whenever you looked at her. Don't destroy whatever it is you've started to feel by lying. I want you to be happy. It looks like she makes you happy. I've never seen you act like this over anyone before, but it will all just be a waste of time if you don't tell her who you really are. You have nothing to lose."

I pull away from him gently, looking into his beautiful soulful brown eyes. "I have everything to lose Ash."

He stares at me for a second his eyes, scanning me intently, before he then pulls me to him and kisses me. His lips are familiar and his tongue feels the same as it always does. It is comforting and it is safe. But it is not Jade.

I let him kiss me, his hands wandering up my back as he grabs the fabric of my T-shirt possessively. I kiss him harder and we tussle with each other battling for supremacy. Just like we always do. I win and pull him into the bedroom. It's dark outside now. I hadn't even registered the day had slipped by we have been getting so wasted. I slam the door of the bedroom shut, kicking it with my foot and take my frustration out on him.

He loves every single minute of it.

Chapter Twenty-Three

I wake to the smell of bacon wafting into the bedroom. I'm glad I didn't wake up to find Ash draped over me. He's a lover of morning sex and, if he'd instigated it, I doubt I would have refused him. The irony is I'm feeling much better now I've finally managed to orgasm without masturbating but somewhat guilty that I did it with Ash. Several times.

My head is thick and my nose is blocked thanks to all of last night's snow. Bad, bad, bad. I hadn't even thought about the white stuff until Ash appeared. I'm beginning to see how much of a bad influence he is on me and that I was absolutely right to drip-feed him my gift of money, which I have yet to tell him about.

I pull on my joggers and wander down the boat into the kitchen scratching my balls, which are, thankfully, not so heavy now. Ash, bare-chested, is standing at the hob, flipping bacon. He still manages to take my breath away every time I see him. He is astonishingly beautiful.

"Morning, shithead," he says with a smile. Beautiful but gross I conclude. I slide onto one of the barstools opposite and watch him flip the bacon. I'm grateful he is wearing pyjama bottoms. They hang low on his hips, showcasing the perfect 'V' and the best set of abdominal muscles I have ever seen. Even better than mine, and they are pretty damn fine. He looks at me from beneath his thick dark lashes and grins. "Feeling better?" he asks, his tone oozing smugness.

Despite my obvious need to take the next step with Jade,

Ash still has the upper hand over me. I reach for my pack of Marlboro and light one up, blowing the smoke into his face. The 'no smoking on the boat' rule has completely gone out of the window. I will pay the extra cleaning bill. He waves his hand dramatically in front of his face coughing. "I feel like shit," I grumble.

He doesn't need to know I feel physically soothed after he encouraged me to release all my pent-up testosterone on him last night. If I admit that he will continue to rub my nose in it. He grins and slides me a cup of coffee continuing to move the bacon around with his other hand.

"Drink this and shut up. I've made you pancakes to go with your bacon."

I drag on my cigarette and lean back on the barstool. It always amazes me how wonderful he looks even after a heavy night on booze and coke. It's as if he puts himself into an invisible rejuvenating machine overnight and pops out looking totally gorgeous again, without even breaking into a sweat. On the other hand, I probably look as bad as I feel.

"What exciting things are we going to do today then, Mr Misery Guts?" he asks as he bends down to retrieve the pancakes from the oven. My stomach grumbles loudly.

"I intend to do absolutely fuck all," I say, sipping my coffee. He pouts at me and begins to dish up two plates of pancakes and bacon. I have no idea if I have maple syrup or not. Knowing Ash, he has brought some with him. "But tonight, Jade's going to take us to the pub … there's some festival thing going on that she wanted to take me to."

His eyes light up as he does, indeed, produce a bottle of maple syrup out of thin air and squeezes it liberally over the plate of grease and sugar. "Fabulous. I can't wait."

I stub out my cigarette in the ashtray that has appeared from outside and grab my plate pulling it towards me with a slight scowl on my face. "That's what I'm afraid of."

He clicks off the burner and moves around to join me at the counter, sliding his perfect arse onto the barstool next to me. "I'll play nicely, Jax. I promise not to fuck this up for you," he says with a grin. I stick my fork into a piece of bacon and shove it into my mouth.

"Impossible promise, Ash," I mumble as I chew.

He nudges me playfully with his shoulder. "You're so adorable in the mornings, Jax."

I ignore his jab and continue munching my breakfast. I may be a grumpy bastard today for all the wrong reasons. But I know that by the time I've digested this meal I will have other things to think about.

We spend the rest of the day chilling out on the roof, talking and smoking my newly arrived purple haze. I am drinking water and lemonade alternately while Ash drinks from his bottle of fancy sparkling water. No wonder his case was so damn heavy, he brought at least five bottles of the stuff with him. We are in a nice state of numbness by late afternoon and my mood has improved considerably, so we switch over to smoking cigarettes and eating junk food to try and remain semi-human before Jade arrives.

"I want to give you some of my money, Ash," I say to him as he lounges back in his deckchair with his eyes closed and a smile on his face while soaking up the sun.

He opens one eye and swivels his head to look at me. His expression is like a lazy cat as he throws me a sly smile. "You do?"

"Of course, what sort of friend would I be if I didn't?" I state, acutely aware he will be waiting for me to reveal exactly how much I'm prepared to give. "I'm going to gift you five million. I'll pay off the mortgage on your flat and then give you the rest in a monthly allowance."

The deckchair creaks as he sits up and leans towards me his eyes narrowing and a little kink appearing between his brows. "A monthly allowance?" he repeats.

I try not to laugh or roll my eyes at him. Only Ash would question the allowance issue, not the total amount. "Yes. A monthly allowance. You can work part-time to keep yourself occupied. I have no doubt you'd kill yourself very quickly if you had too much money at your disposal and I want you around for a long time," I say with a thin smile.

"So, you don't trust me to manage my own money then?" he says with a pout.

"We both know it's better that way, Ash."

His eyes become glassy with tears as he nods slowly. "Sure. Whatever. It's your money. You know best."

I shake my head with a smile and lean back in my own chair.

"Thank you," he says reaching for my hand and squeezing it.

"You're welcome," I say as he lets go of my hand and reaches for my packet of cigarettes. The sound of him sniffling makes me turn to face him again as he lights his smoke. "Why are you crying?" I ask with amusement.

"Why do you think, you shithead?" he sniffs, wiping a rogue tear from his cheek and turning his face away as he puffs on the cigarette.

"It's just money, Ash. I haven't proposed for fuck's sake."

"It's a lot of money, Jax, and I am grateful. You didn't need to give me any."

Seeing him come undone gives me an immense sense of satisfaction. He really is grateful and I'm glad he feels overwhelmed by my gift. I could have given him more but he won't need it. I'll always take care of him. This is just a token that allows him to feel I do in fact trust him to have his own wealth in his bank account. "No, I didn't. But it's yours. Prove to me you can manage it properly. That will make me even happier."

Rolling his eyes, he sucks in a breath and then shakes himself. “Well, now we’ve got that awkward conversation out of the way what are you going to do about Jade?” he says as he flops back into his chair looking up at the sky.

Taking a deep breath and then letting it out on a sigh I shake my head slowly. “No bloody idea.”

The smoke from his cigarette wafts over to my face and I close my eyes again trying to come up with a solution and finding nothing but more confusion swimming around in my brain. “Just be straight with her Jax. Stop being a pussy.”

I let out a humph. “Yep. Be ‘straight’ with her. Very funny. Ha ha.”

He laughs at my quip but says nothing more. It seems that even he has no miracle plan, other than for me to tell her upfront that I am already in a relationship with him while chasing her tail and that my bisexuality is something she will have to accept if she wants a piece of me.

The thought of explaining this all to her makes me feel sick. In the past, I’ve kept my sexuality a secret for good reason. Being gay comes with difficulties; laws are changing slowly but bisexuality is still somewhat the awkward cousin. Not many people understand the concept of how someone could be attracted to both sexes. The fact I like to switch between the two frequently is even more confusing. Even to the gay community.

There are a lot of people walking up the canal path today and I can feel them all staring at us. I’m not sure if it’s because of the way we look or if they are just admiring the boat. Probably both. The sun is out in full force again but thankfully it’s not too hot.

Ash has dressed down a little today, he is super casual in his shorts and T-shirt but considers it classy to add designer flip-flops to the ensemble. I am wearing a black vest and board shorts, they are my only clean pair of shorts left. I had not anticipated that the weather would continue to be so good here. The tan I have gained is off the scale now and I really do look like an Australian beach bum. I have tied the top section of my hair back as it is getting quite long now. Ash has told me he likes it longer: it gives him something to grab onto. I beg to differ. I like to do the grabbing.

Ash decides it's time to do another cheeky line before Jade arrives. It is nearly eight. We haven't eaten much today except breakfast and crap. I know that as soon as Mr Snow hits my system, I will not eat another thing until tomorrow but, right now, sitting with my best boy, I don't give a shit.

We go back inside and shut all the windows of the boat so that we don't give anyone passing by a reason to call the police. I feel like my head is about to explode after my second line – the stuff Ash gets is top class – and as the initial shock settles, I feel a surge of power run through my veins and I am now wide awake and raring to go. Supercharged like a fighter jet racing across the sky.

I check out my reflection in the mirror as I brush my teeth. I look okay, not too freaky, my pupils are a little wider than normal but it's not totally obvious I'm flying high. Ash looks super cool and totally unaffected, as normal.

I shower after Ash and change into jeans again, my old faded blue ones with the holes in the knees, my Doc Martins and a fresh T-shirt that I found in the bottom of my duffel, which has a picture of Jimi Hendrix on it. I must have been drunk when I shoved *that* in my bag. I think it will fit in well at the pub.

Ash dresses in suitably grungy combat trousers and a black T-shirt that shows off all his muscles in the right places. He throws a couple of beaded necklaces around his neck and gels his hair, making it spike up all over the place. He looks good enough to eat and I know he will have his tongue down someone's throat by the end of the evening. I just hope it isn't mine – again.

We wait in the living area for Jade to arrive, a bottle of champagne Ash had brought with him sits open (I think he has brought more food and drink in his case than clothes). I am hyped, ready to see her and am desperate to touch her again. I am twitching like a man with tourettes and Ash grins at me as he sips his champagne from a wine glass; he bitched about the lack of flutes on the boat but seems to have forgiven me now.

He has that naughty glint in his eye I know all too well and I know Jade is in for a good show tonight. He has promised me he will behave.

We will see.

Chapter Twenty-Four

Jade arrives at nine just as it is starting to get a little darker. I hear her step onto the boat and my heart lurches in my chest. She sticks her head down into the boat and waves. My eyes nearly pop out of my head. She looks amazing. Transformed from the girl I am usually presented with.

"Hey, Baby Girl," Ash shouts, the glint in his eye growing even more evident as he takes in her appearance as she steps under the spotlights in the kitchen area. I am speechless.

Jade is wearing a dress. It has long, flowing sleeves and is very short. It clinches at her waist with a thick black belt and flows out like a skater's skirt at the bottom, just covering her arse cheeks. The off-the-shoulder neckline shows off her beautiful collar bones. What makes me stare is the colour. Bright red and sexy.

Her hair is intricately braided down both sides of her head and flows down her back with what looks like pieces of silver thread woven into the braids. The top is twisted and spiked with little clips that are tiny red roses. She looks like a Viking princess, with a rock chick edge. Of course, she is wearing her trusty biker boots. I wonder whether she is wearing that little pink thong again. Or nothing at all.

She grins at me as I continue to stare at her like a horny teenage boy. "Hi guys," she says, raising a brow in my direction.

Ash is looking at me like I am the worst host in the world as I just stand and stare at her. I am most likely dribbling.

"Would you like a glass of champers, Jade?" he asks as I continue to stare like a dumb motherfucker. She smiles and walks towards him, stopping in front of me briefly and planting a kiss on my cheek.

"Yes, please Ash."

Just that slightest touch to my skin makes my dick twitch, despite the amount of cocaine I have snorted. I watch her walk past and sit down next to Ash on the sofa where she crosses those long olive legs like a ballet dancer. I try not to stare at her crutch as she sits. I am a desperate pervert when it comes to this girl.

"Lost your tongue, City Boy?" she says to me as she takes the glass of champagne Ash has just poured for her.

He laughs loudly. "God, I love this girl," he says, slapping his thigh. I'm glad he finds my inability to move, speak or function so funny.

I eventually find my voice. "You look stunning, Jade." My voice is thick and low, which makes Ash laugh even more.

"For God's sake, sit down Jax before you ejaculate in your jeans," he says with a chuckle. I give him the finger in response which makes Jade smile even more before I sit down next to her.

Ash moves up slightly so that he can turn and face us. He is giving me the space I need to make a move on her, mark her as mine and mine alone for the evening. I press my thigh against hers and throw my arm over the back of the sofa behind her. She sips her champagne, a small moan of approval humming in her throat as she does making both Ash and I stare at her again.

She is the best filling in any guy-sandwich you could ever ask for. Shame it will never happen. I wouldn't allow it, especially not with Ash. It's obvious she has absolutely no idea of the effect she is having on both of us right now. It is potentially very dangerous. But also, extremely appealing. She savours her champagne before turning to face me again. "Thank you for the compliment, Jax." She pauses and looks me up and down with a sly smile on her lips. "You look very edible tonight."

She turns to Ash before I can comment. "You also look good enough to eat, Ash."

He is leaning back away from her slightly, just watching her with a tilt to his lips that says 'and I would love nothing more than to eat you up my darling'. I see the flicker of realisation pass across her expression and know that she is now totally picking up on his vibe. As confusing as that may be at present. "Well thank you, beautiful. We made the effort especially for you."

She leans forward and picks up my Marlboro packet opening it up and helping herself. She lights one with a funky skull-shaped lighter, which was tucked into her boot, passes it to me then lights one for herself. Ash raises a brow watching her as she does. The boldness of this girl is beyond beautiful.

I take a long drag on the cigarette and smile at her. She didn't offer one to Ash, which makes me feel a little smug. He hasn't charmed her enough to knock me off the top running position in winning her over. Like an old married couple now, she knows exactly what I want and when I want it. Apart from the fucking, which I want right now but can't have.

"Where's Bob tonight?" I ask her, reaching for my glass of champagne.

"He's on *The Nymph*, cuddled up with a pig's ear and his blanket. Too many people make him hyper and uncontrollable."

Ash snorts a laugh and reaches for my cigarettes. "Like someone else we both know."

She watches Ash light his cigarette and lean back

casually. She laughs at his comment. "Oh, I can imagine." I shake my head at the pair of them but smile.

Jade smiles at him and leans back into my arm that is still on the back of the sofa behind her. "Have you managed to smoke that whole bag of haze Jax has yet?" She uncrosses her long legs and then folds them over again as if she knows I just want to see up her skirt.

Ash follows her movements like a snake about to strike. I take the opportunity to stroke her neck with the tips of my fingers lightly. She shivers a little at my touch and I know she feels it all the way down to her funky boots as she moves her head a little as if she is a cat nuzzling into the petting.

Ash is taking all of this in with amusement. "Not yet but we are working on it," Ash replies.

The three of us sit on the sofa sipping our champagne and smoking in a weird kind of standoff. Ash waggles his eyebrows at me as Jade shifts a little closer to me making her dress rise higher. The tension is growing by the second and feels like a ticking time bomb about to detonate.

I'm getting twitchy and know that either Ash or I will do something stupid if we don't get up off this sofa and down to the pub. "Shall we get going then?" I say stubbing my cigarette out in the ashtray. Jade still has her glass of champagne in her hand but turns to me and smiles, licking her lips seductively as she does.

"Definitely," she replies with a soft purr in her voice. The air is practically vibrating with the sexual tension between the three of us. Like a highly flammable liquid just waiting to be lit. I'm glad I put my cigarette out.

Ash chuckles his eyes sparkling like two pieces of jet. "Right," he says jumping up like a jack-in-the-box. "Let's go and scare the crap out of the locals."

I groan running my hand over my face. What the fuck have I done?

Chapter Twenty-Five

We are standing at the packed bar of The Barge Inn waiting for our drinks. The place is heaving and I can hear music coming from the field out the back, which is now full with people, tents and a small stage where a rock band are banging out some old covers of Led Zeppelin songs.

I sense that every single man in here already hates me and Ash and have their eyes glued to Jade's beautiful legs. The frequent side-eyes we are receiving are giving me the impression we stand out far too much in this crowd and we may be more competition than they are happy to deal with. Having such a beautiful woman as Jade in our company only adding to the disgruntled egos flying around in this situation.

I want to kill them all. My alpha instinct is beating in my chest, ready to demonstrate she is not up for grabs, ready to defend her if necessary. I sense also that Ash and I are attracting a lot of female attention. Especially Ash, who is already on the prowl. I'm not sure the women in this area are really ready for him but they are all pouting and preening themselves around him. If only they knew how much of a handful he is. It may just be their worst nightmare if they end up catching his eye.

I am standing directly behind Jade with my arms either side of her on the bar, caging her in and protecting her arse from any wandering hands. She leans back against me just slightly. Ash is leaning casually with one arm on the bar, the other in his pocket like he owns the place.

He smiles at a young guy that pushes up to the bar beside him with a glint in his eyes. The guy gives him a nod but has no idea that while he stands and waits patiently for the barman, Ash is currently imagining various pornographic scenes involving his cock in the young guy's mouth – and other orifices.

I have the feeling I may end up with a black eye and a thick lip tonight if we don't find a quiet spot somewhere in the dark. Ash is cocky at the best of times and has no problem demonstrating this. If he oversteps the mark with someone and causes a scene, I'll have to step in, and I have no doubt the men giving us surly looks would take great pleasure in putting us both in our places. No one likes strangers with pretty faces pissing all over their territory. It's the rule of the jungle and I have no intention of getting into a fight tonight.

I'm beginning to think this is a very bad idea when, thankfully, our drinks arrive and we can leave the cramped bar and head out to the music outside. Jade nods her head to the music as we walk out swinging her hips a little making her skirt swish. I follow her, watching the way her waist twists just slightly and her arse cheeks lift as she moves. It's exquisite torture.

We stand off to the side to watch the band play. I'm jostled twice by guys that are clearly trying to piss me off. By the time we find a nice little spot to chill in, my hand is covered in cider. Bastards.

Ash is grinning like he is enjoying the whole push and shove routine. I know he just likes fucking people off with his perfect looks and cocky strut. Jade seems oblivious to everything that is going on around us. I have already scanned the area twice looking for escape routes if it all kicks off.

I place my cider on a table behind me and reach for my cigarettes. I need something to calm me down. I light one for Jade and pass it to her just as she did for me earlier. She smiles and takes it from me, sipping her cider. Ash grabs the packet from me and steals one too. I will need to buy another packet at this rate. I place my free arm around Jade's shoulder and pull her to me so that I can talk to her over the music. "You okay?"

She turns her face and looks up at me her eyes sparkling. "Are you?" she teases.

I laugh as she throws the question back at me and nod. She can sense my discomfort. It is rolling off me in waves. I now have two people to keep an eye on tonight and one of them I know will, no doubt, be causing more problems than the other. I slip my arm down and rest my hand on her waist while we smoke and watch the band. They are, actually, very good.

Ash is surveying the area, clearly on the lookout for his next victim. His expression is one of extreme calm and coolness but I know he is champing at the bit to get in the mosh pit and take a bite out of someone. The mini-festival has been going on all day and it is obvious there are a lot of very drunk people here. The women seem to be drunker than the men and quite a few are dancing or, more to the point, staggering around in front of the stage like crazed go-go girls.

I see Ash hone in on two young women that are dancing like it should be some pop group on the stage, not a rock cover band. They have the sultry hip flick down to perfection. He places his pint next to me and clicks his fingers in front of my face. "I'm off to strut. See you in a while, my beautiful friends."

Jade laughs as he turns around dramatically and heads straight to the two women wiggling their backsides, his cigarette dangling from his mouth like he is James Dean. I can't help but smile. Jade turns around fully to face me still doing her little hip swing as she holds her pint and cigarette. I keep my hand on her waist loving the way she moves under my touch.

She takes one more sip of her pint then puts it on the table behind me just as the band start to play 'Whole Lotta Love'. I love this song. I watch every movement she makes, smiling at her with pleasure. She takes a long slow drag on her cigarette then drops it to the floor and twists her boot over it. I extinguish mine and then flick the butt over into the bush beside me. Ready for action. She bites her bottom lip and then lifts her arms up to my neck hanging her hands over my shoulders. I place both my hands on her waist and pull her into me.

She grins slyly, rotating her hips into my groin. I sigh heavily, knowing that this is heading in one direction only and it may just be a little too dangerous for her despite her current bravado. I lower my head down. "Are you sure you want to play this game with me, Jade?" I whisper into her ear. She continues to gyrate against me making my dick jump.

"It's not a game, Jax."

I nod my head and move my hips in time with hers sliding my hands down onto her arse cheeks where I squeeze them gently. Okay then, the game is on. Her pupils widen and she grins at me as I keep up with her rhythm of slow teasing circles. She asked me once before if I dance. Yes, I do. And I do it very well. Her expression shifts from a sultry tease to concentration as she tries to outwit me with a few little hip moves that could, perhaps, faze the average guy. But I keep in synch with her and she moves her hands down to my arms and grips my biceps holding on as we continue to dance like there is no one else around us. We are lost in our own world of intense teasing. I am enjoying it immensely.

We dance like this for a while, our eyes locked together, our bodies moving as if we have practised this routine many times before. We are creating quite a stir, I can tell. I can see people watching us in my peripheral vision and know that we must look like we are about to tear each other's clothes off and get down to it up against the table.

When we first arrived, I was concerned about the unwanted attention. My need to avoid conflict with the locals was high on my priority list. Now, I don't give a damn. I want everyone to know she is mine and mine alone. Let them think what they want. I'm having fun and prepared for the consequences, if any, of this little display we are putting on for everyone.

In a slow slide up the sides of her waist, I move my hands up from her gorgeous arse cheeks and brush the soft underbelly of her breasts with my thumbs, before trailing them back down again. She takes a small step back from me and I take the opportunity to spin her around by the waist, then instantly pull her back flush to my chest. She spins perfectly without stumbling and I place my hands flat on her stomach pressing my hard-on into her back. She leans her head back and lifts her arms up again stretching up and pushing her fingers into my hair. I'm vibrating like a wild stallion about to mount his mare. She is looking up at me with those big blue eyes, giving me the come-on, daring me to do something I wouldn't normally do with her in front of all these people.

I grin at her and bend my head down and place an open-mouthed kiss on her neck, sucking on the skin and running my tongue over the soft flesh. She squirms against me and I know she is getting close to her exhibition limits. I want to make her squirm more and spin her back around before she can react.

Holding her leg at the back of her knee, I grab her left thigh and lift it up so that she is exposing more of her body than she may just be comfortable with. She is tight against me, standing on one leg as I steady her with my other hand on her waist and pull her left leg up around my own waist. She clings to my arms, staring up at me, her mouth slightly open as if she is confused for a second and thinks I'm going to drop her just for the fun of it.

I tilt my head to one side and hold her like that just staring silently at her for a moment. She stares back. The look of defiance and fire glowing in her eyes is all the confirmation I need to make my next move without another moment's hesitation. I go in for the kill. Guns blazing.

I kiss her like my life depends on it. Devouring her mouth just the way I have wanted to since the day I met her. I hold nothing back. She groans against my lips, pressing herself into my groin like I'm a flagpole she is about to climb. The kiss is messy and ferocious, full of lust and aggression, we are both quickly losing any control we may have had when we began this primitive form of seduction. We are definitely putting on too much of a show, even for this fucked-up, drunken crowd.

"Get a room," some guy laughs, knocking my shoulder as he walks past us and making me drop her leg to the floor and release her mouth abruptly. I instantly switch into attack mode. She staggers back from me, breathing heavily; her eyes glistening and her lips wet from my saliva.

I'm still holding her by the waist but looking over her shoulder now at the guy who just bumped past us. He has his back to us now and I begin to relax slightly. The coke has evidently made me very edgy. She begins to laugh and pushes my chest to get my attention again.

"Down boy." She punches me on the arm.

As I regain some clarity, my breathing steadies. No one

is really paying us any attention. I'm just paranoid as hell and on the defensive when it comes to this sexy girl in my arms. The crowd, it seems, are more interested now in Ash, who is dancing with the two young women like a gyrating sex-machine. They are absolutely loving it and I don't blame them. That guy can dance like the devil himself.

I look down at Jade and smile apologetically, knowing my eyes are most likely glazed over with a mixture of lust and need. She trails her hand down to my hard-on and squeezes it gently making me jump. "I think we need to take a step out for a moment," she says with a teasing smile. I nod, saying nothing.

Quickly adjusting my hard-on, I grab her hand and my pint and drag her away from the field, back out to the garden at the front of the pub where there are fewer people. She jogs along behind me giggling.

I'm like a mad man on a mission, my heart thumping in my chest and my dick straining against my jeans. I need to calm the fuck down again. She just pressed all my buttons and played with the fire demon that wants to come out and brand her soul. I'm resisting the urge to drag her back to *The Witch* and fuck her senseless.

Instead, I find an empty bench seat furthest away from any wandering drunks in the corner of the garden. I pull her down onto my lap aggressively and she laughs louder as I crash my cider down on to the table, sloshing most of the contents in the process. She is struggling to pull away from me like a wild cat, laughing her head off at the same time. I growl at her and she laughs even more.

"Jax! Stop it, you're going to make me piss myself!"

I note she doesn't say piss her pants. My dick grows harder at the thought that she isn't wearing any underwear at all. I let go of her and she stumbles forward clutching her stomach as she laughs. I slump back against the table my legs wide open my body heaving. Fuck. I really need to get a grip. The cocktail of cocaine and adrenaline has turned me crazy.

Jade turns around and stops laughing when she sees I am slumped in defeat and discomfort against the table.

"You're fucking killing me, Jade," I say, looking up at her with fire in my eyes.

She steps back towards me, into the gap between my legs and places her hands on my shoulders gently giving them a squeeze. "I'm sorry, I just got a little carried away. I didn't mean to tease you so much."

I place my hands on the back of her thighs and press my forehead into her chest, breathing in her scent like a starved man. "Yes, you did."

She pulls my head closer into her chest and pushes her fingers into my hair again making me moan. "City Boy, you need to start dealing with what you dish out," she says with a wry chuckle.

She's right. I started all this two weeks ago when I recklessly started the whole slow tease. I need to finish it. I also need to slow this down a little. I need to have the talk with her before we do something we can't move back from. She pushes back again and looks down at me lifting my chin with her finger and staring at me like I am the most precious thing to her in the world. I'm lost for a moment in the dark blue depths of her eyes. "I really am sorry I pushed you so much," she whispers.

I smile at her and pull her closer sliding my hands up under her skirt and placing my palms flat on her bare arse cheeks. She gasps a little but doesn't stop me. I slide one hand up and underneath her and suck in a breath when I find that she is in fact *sans* underwear.

Fuck it with the going slow.

Her mouth opens slightly and she tips her head back,

her eyes rolling shut as I slip a finger down underneath her, then slowly up and inside her. I can't stop myself. I hold it there, savouring her warmth and silkiness as she clenches her thighs together in a vain attempt to either make me let her go or pull me in further. I growl low in my throat. "You're playing with fire, Jade."

I slip my finger back out again and then make a show of raising it up to my mouth, placing it inside and sucking it slowly. She is watching me again, her eyes wide, her breathing erratic. She tastes like vanilla ice cream. Sweet and oh so bad for you.

"I know," she whispers so quietly I almost don't hear her.

I lean back slightly still holding her peach-shaped arse cheek with my other hand. "I think I left my cigarettes on the other table," I say nonchalantly with a dark smile on my lips. She laughs and steps away from me. I note she is a tad unsteady on her feet after my finger dip.

"I'll go and get them," she says before quickly turning and walking away with her hips swinging and her braids swaying sexily. I watch her go, my chest heaving and my balls squirming like it's a bag full of snakes. I tip my head back and look up at the sky, which is twinkling with a thousand stars.

I know right then and there that I have finally crossed the line and there is no going back from it. I'm screwed.

Chapter Twenty-Six

She returns with her pint and my cigarettes. I've managed to calm my raging hard-on and compose myself enough to not draw any further attention our way. She sits down next to me and takes a sip of her cider; her face is flushed and her chest glistening with a little sweat. I take the Marlboro packet from her and light one up.

She watches me intently. "I just saw Ash kissing one of those girls at the back of the pub," she says and looks a little confused.

"It doesn't normally take him long to find his next victim," I say taking a deep inhale of my smoke.

She sips her pint again and crosses her legs, this time giving me a wonderful flash of her naked pussy. I lick my lips trying desperately not to get another hard-on. "I thought he was gay," she says her eyes reflecting her perplexity.

Oh, here we go. I turn to face her straddling the bench again and take her pint from her hand. I take a long, large swig and put it back down on the table. She takes the cigarette from me and takes a drag on it as if in defiance. I look down at the floor for a second, running my hand over my face, trying to think carefully about what I'm going to say next.

"He's a man with many tastes, Jade."

She hands me back my cigarette and I take it from her placing my hand on my thigh as it burns slowly and sends a wisp of smoke up between us. She is looking at me with curiosity, not quite sure what I am trying to say. I wait for the penny to drop. I wait for the questions that will come from her when it does.

She shivers, then makes a noise in the back of her throat that sounds like she is purring. I look up at her and she grins. "He's bisexual?" I nod slowly feeling like my whole world is about to implode. "Ah, that makes more sense," she says with a nod.

I'm waiting for her to ask me. Waiting for the bomb to explode. She tilts her head examining me like I am some strange science project. Her eyes wander across my features, as if this is the first time, she has ever met me. I can feel the tension in my chest pushing up towards my throat, it's beginning to choke me I'm so wound up. She reaches tentatively forward and brushes her fingers across my cheek.

"That's it, isn't it, Jax? That's the secret … the darkness I can see in you."

Her palm is on my cheek and it feels warm and soft, so wonderfully comforting. I turn my head and nestle into it closing my eyes tightly. She is going to walk away. Run away and I will never, ever see her again. She sighs, leaning forward so that her face is so close to mine that I can feel her warm breath on my lips.

"Your beautiful darkness, Jax."

Everything around us becomes still and I feel my heart stutter in my chest. She knows. She really knows. I feel like I cannot breathe. I am drowning in my own fear.

She takes the cigarette from my hand and throws it on the floor, I still have my eyes closed but I hear her movements and feel her touch as if I'm looking right at her. She places her hand under my chin and lifts it slowly, making me face her again. "Open your eyes, Jax," she whispers.

I'm shaking now, my entire body is shivering with the fear of what I will see in her eyes when I do open them. When

I do, she is staring at me, the most beautiful expression on her face and her lips tilted up into a smile that would make an angel weep.

"I don't care if that's what you are too, Jax. I honestly don't care."

Before I can even respond she kisses me on the lips, a gentle closed mouth kiss that makes me moan in relief. I kiss her back tentatively, gently, like she is the most breakable thing I will ever own. I don't want to break this, destroy it with my truth.

The ugly truth of who I am: I'm a man like Ash, who takes what he likes, whenever he feels like it, without remorse. I'm reeling with the shock that she has not slapped me and spat in my face for keeping this perhaps shocking revelation hidden from her. She is kissing me like I am worthy of this kiss. Worthy of the affection, the attention. The love.

I cannot get my head around what is happening right now.

"Jax, stop tongue-fucking Jade and get me another drink will you?" Ash says, right beside me. And just like that, my moment of bliss is shattered.

I let go of Jade and look up at him with a scowl. He has his arm around the neck of the girl Jade must have seen him devouring earlier. The other one is nowhere to be seen, obviously getting jealous and taking off in search of another plaything. I'm amazed he doesn't have the pair of them tucked under each arm. He really is trying hard to behave.

I take a twenty out of my pocket and shove it into the waistband of his combat trousers. "Get your own bloody drink. And get me and Jade one while you're at it."

He pouts and pulls the note out of his trousers, the girl giggling as he does. "Why are you so fucking grumpy all of a sudden?" He clearly misses the fact that I am in the middle of the most important revelation of my life.

"I'd love another cider, Ash," Jade says sweetly. He glances at her, a frown on his face. She blinks her long black eyelashes at him and he tilts his head, his expression changing quickly as it clicks in his brain what's really happening here.

"Of course, Baby Girl. Be back in a jiffy." He swings the girl around so quickly she almost falls over and marches back towards the pub. On a mission to get away from me as quickly as possible. A very wise thing to do, indeed, right now.

I take Jade's hand and turn it over, tracing a circle in her palm. "We need to talk Jade."

She watches me trace patterns on her palm and folds her fingers inward clasping my hand gently. "I know."

I look up into her beautiful eyes and feel like my soul is so wide open and bare to her right now, it might just break into a million tiny pieces at her feet. "But not here," I say.

She nods and turns around so that we are both straddling the bench and I can wrap my arms around her waist. She leans back into me and strokes my forearms softly, sending shivers up my spine. "When you're ready, City Boy," she whispers as if it's the most normal thing in the world to just find out that the man you are falling for, is more complicated than a Rubik's cube.

Ash returns with a tray of drinks and we resume our gentle banter. He drapes his plaything for the night across his lap and teases her relentlessly with his sharp wit and the flick of his tongue in her ear. She is clueless about what he is and what is in store for her if she allows Ash to continue in his pursuit of pleasure. He will be banging her so hard later she won't be able to walk for a week after. I'm not selfish enough to deny him the use of my boat tonight if he wishes to indulge.

We stay at the pub for another hour, until it starts to get

cold. I'm starting to feel like I need to smoke a joint, now that the coke has left my system. Ash is looking at me as if he desperately wants to pull me to one side and force me to reveal what happened earlier with Jade. It's killing him, not getting all the juicy gossip. He will have to wait until tomorrow. I need to get Jade back to her boat and chill the fuck out.

We wander back down the towpath in the dark, leaving the drunks and misfits behind us. I take Jade's hand and grasp it, gently threading my fingers through hers. Ash and his girl are stumbling ahead of us, laughing and giggling. Jade is silent beside me but I can see that she is smiling. I'm still reeling at what has happened between us tonight.

We reach *The Water Witch* and I open her up, switching the lights on and starting up the engine so that there will be some hot water for the morning and power for Ash tonight. Jade grabs the kettle and starts to pull out cups to make coffee. Ash has dumped his girl on the sofa and is currently making out with her, his hand up her skirt. I slide behind Jade and put my hands on her waist, nestling into her neck. She sighs and stops gathering cups for a second.

"You okay, City Boy?" she asks me as I lean against her.

"Yes. No."

She laughs at my response. "Let's make a quick coffee and then go back to mine. Leave these two to it."

I have my eyes closed and am sinking into her slowly like she is my own personal pool of pleasure. "Good idea." I release her and walk past Ash to the bedroom to retrieve some of my stash of haze. I take several condoms out of my duffel bag and stuff them into my back pocket, just in case. I take a piss and look at myself in the bathroom mirror, not recognising my reflection for a second. The Jax staring back at me looks like a different person from the one that left earlier tonight. I'm not sure who he is right now.

I splash some cold water on my face and brush my teeth. I walk back down the boat and find Jade pouring the hot water into two cups. She hasn't bothered to make any for Ash and his girl, who are now so engrossed in each other I doubt they even know we are still here.

I kick Ash on the way past making him jump in shock, his mouth emitting a loud smacking noise as their lips disconnected. "I'm going to Jade's. Don't smoke all my gear and don't fucking break anything. You should have enough power for a while but don't leave the lights on all night."

He grins up at me with slightly glassy eyes. I know he will have his nose in his bag of powder again as soon as I'm out the door. "No problem, honey," he says before turning back to the girl and shoving his tongue back down her throat.

I stride up to Jade, grab a fresh packet of cigarettes and my coffee. She is holding hers in her hands and smiling at me. "Let's get out of here." She nods in agreement and we leave to the sound of moaning and Ash saying, "Yeah baby, open up for me."

I am so out of here. I switch off the engine and slide the door of *The Witch* shut so that anyone passing by doesn't get an unexpected show. We walk down the path with our coffees in hand towards Jade's boat.

This will be the first time I will be invited to see *inside* it. I can't wait.

Chapter Twenty-Seven

Bob greets us like he has not seen us for at least a year, jumping up and down like he has springs in his legs. I take Jade's coffee and let her settle him down in her little kitchen. I stand on the steps for a moment looking around. The lights are soft and give a comforting ambience, not like the glaring spots in *The Witch*. The kitchen is so small I'm surprised we can both fit into it but everything is neat and tidy. Herbs hang from hooks around the edges making it look like an apothecary.

Once Bob settles, she gestures for me to come through into the living area. Drapes are hanging across the ceiling and big comfy cushions are scattered on the floor, a small sofa and a miniature wood burner sit against the wall. The battered carved table I saw the first time I came for dinner is in the centre. It's cosy and oh-so-Jade.

I place the coffee cups down on the table and sit on the sofa. Jade walks off, disappearing for a moment. I sit back and wait for her and take the time to look around. There are several paintings on the wall that catch my eye. Beautiful artwork of the surrounding area. I wonder if Jade was the artist. When she reappears, she is wearing a pair of hippy pants and a vest top and has taken the rose clips out of her hair, loosening her braids. She is barefoot now and looks like a wild sensual goddess.

I watch her as she settles back down crossed-legged on one of the floor cushions and reaches for a wooden box from under the table. Opening it, she pulls out some incense, lighting a stick and pushing it into a crack in the wooden panel behind her. Then she produces a small pipe from the box and hands it to me. I pull out my bag of haze and start to fill it without saying anything. I need a big hit for what is coming next.

She takes her coffee and begins to sip it silently. I light the pipe and take a hit, blowing the smoke up into the air and savouring the burn as it slips down my throat, loosening my mind in one big soft cloud of purple-coloured wonderfulness. I put the pipe back down onto the table and let my head tip back against the back of the sofa closing my eyes for a moment.

"We don't have to do this tonight, Jax," she says her tone laced with empathy. I lift my head and place my arms out wide across the back of the sofa opening my legs as I do, letting it all hang out. Her eyes widen a little and I hear her breath hitch.

"Yes, we do, Jade."

She places her coffee back onto the table and takes the pipe. I watch her take her hit and feel like my heart is going to explode, it's so full of love for her right now. She places it back on the table and then puts her hands in her lap. "Is Ash your lover?" she asks me outright.

I take a deep breath and lean forward putting my head in my hands. "Yes."

She shifts slightly. "Are you in a serious relationship with him?"

I sit up and put my elbows on my thighs staring at her. She looks so breathtakingly beautiful it hurts. "It doesn't work like that Jade."

She bites her bottom lip again. "Then tell me how it does work."

I want to just hold her, kiss her, make love to her, but I

know she wants to hear the truth first. I know I'm not going to get away with this any other way. I take my packet of Marlboro and light one up. "Okay."

She listens to me as I talk, her eyes wide, her cheeks flushed slightly. I give it to her straight. How I work; how I don't work. How complicated it is to be me. She takes it all without saying a word. I reveal myself to her in a way that I have never done with anyone else ever before. I give her the good, the bad and the ugly, disclosing the full depths of my sexuality and my behaviour. How I enjoy sex with both men and women for different reasons and that I have never wanted, or even considered, having a proper relationship with any of them. Except Ash, who is the only person I allow even remotely close to me. I explain how our unique relationship works and how strongly we are bound to each other.

She seems to take it well.

But I keep my other secret, the story of my recent change in luck and fortune to myself. This is something I'm not ready to share with her just yet. One thing at a time for her to digest seems more appropriate.

When I have finished, she nods slowly. Her coffee is finished and mine is cold. She has smoked her own cigarette while I talked, we have both taken another two hits on the pipe. I am waiting for her to speak. She stands up slowly and reaches out her hand for me. "I want to go to bed now, Jax, and I want you to make love to me."

I blink up at her, stunned for a second at her request and then take her outstretched hand. She pulls me up and I feel like I am in a dream floating, looking down on myself in some surreal parallel universe. She leads me down her boat into her bedroom and shuts the door behind us. She lifts my T-shirt up and over my head and throws it on the floor, trailing her delicate fingers across my nipple piercing as she does.

"I hope you brought some protection with you, City Boy," she says with a smile as she reaches up on her tiptoes and kisses me lightly on the cheek. I nod in response.

No further words are spoken between us, and I thank the gods above that I had the foresight to come prepared.

Chapter Twenty-Eight

I wake up the next day to find Jade still wrapped within my arms. Last night, for the first time in my life, I *made love* and I did it with this amazingly beautiful woman who is still here next to me. I smile and pull her closer to my body, revelling in the feeling of her lithe and naked body so close to mine. She moans a little as I squeeze her gently. She smells divine and I can't help running my tongue up her neck as she pushes her pert backside into my morning wood.

"Good morning," she sighs.

"It is indeed."

She rolls over and faces me, her eyes sleepy and a soft smile on her lips. Her hand pushes back my unruly hair and she looks at me like I am some kind of god she needs to worship daily. "What would you like for breakfast?" she asks.

"You." I pull her towards me roughly making her squeal.

After I take her again, she makes me breakfast. Boiled eggs with soldiers. The sex was harder, rougher this time and she seemed to like it just as much as last night when we took our time to explore each other slowly. We have found a rhythm together and it is perfect. She smiles at me as I drip egg down my chin.

"I wonder how Ash is today," she says with a grin.

"Still fucking that girl most likely," I say as she leans forward and wipes the egg off my stubble with her thumb. She laughs and leans back stretching so that her crop top rises and shows me the underbelly of her breasts.

"I can imagine he has a ferocious appetite," she says her eyes sparkling.

I snort in response. "You have no idea."

She slides gracefully out of her stretch and looks at me with a slight edge of nervousness in her eyes. "Will you tell him about us?"

I push away my empty plate and reach for the coffee she has made me. I cradle it in my hands, enjoying the warmth on my palms before answering. "He knows everything already, Jade."

She cocks her head to one side and frowns a little, creating a cute little kink in between her eyebrows. "I don't understand."

I sip my coffee, looking at her over the edge of the cup, before putting it back down again and reaching for her hand. "He will know the moment he sees us that we have slept together and that we've taken that first difficult step over the uncrossable line."

She looks at my hand as I hold hers, rubbing my thumb lightly across her knuckles. "Uncrossable, eh?" she says warily.

"Mmmh."

We still have so much ground to cover on this difficult path but right now I want nothing more than to just spend time with Jade, touching her, talking to her, and getting to know her even more. Unfortunately, I know I will need to return to *The Witch*, to check on Ash and make sure he hasn't broken anything – or ended up tying his plaything to my bed overnight. My desire to jump straight back into bed with Jade will have to wait.

Bob nudges me with his wet nose, breaking the moment. He has been sprawled out next to me while we sat on the floor in the living area eating breakfast, sleeping throughout the entire course as if we managed to knock him out cold last night on the euphoria of our joining and the effects of the haze in the pipe. I stroke him, smiling as he places his head on my thigh and looks up at me adoringly. He seems to have fallen in love with me too. For that it is what I sense now. A love between the three of us that is so unique and delicate it is held together by a single thread of hope that could easily be snipped once I leave this place and head back to the city.

I know I will have to leave her at some point and sort out my life. I still have twenty-five million pounds to deal with. And a life in a place that doesn't seem like home anymore.

"I need to walk him. Shall we head back to *The Witch* and make sure Ash hasn't sunk her," Jade says, reading my thoughts again. She is so very different from any other woman I have ever met and way beyond her twenty-two years of age. We walk back down the towpath, holding hands and throwing a stick for Bob who gallops along with an extra spring in his step. He seems very happy today. As am I. Ecstatically so.

The day is bright and dry again; the sky a beautiful canvas of blue and white with huge cumulus clouds drifting above us lazily. I feel a sense of ease I have never felt before as if I am now truly in balance with the world around me.

We arrive at *The Witch* and I am glad to see that she is still sitting in one piece against the bank, silently hiding one of the secrets of my life inside. I find Ash still asleep, in my bed, of course. The enthusiastic young girl he was indulging in is nowhere to be seen. I flick his ear, making him jump up with one eye open the other glued shut. I grin at him happy to see that today he at least looks like a normal human would after two heavy nights on the razz.

"Glad to see you're still alive, Ash," I say sitting on the bed next to him. The room smells like sex and I know I will have to change the sheets – again. In fact, I will most likely have to buy a fresh set and throw these away.

"Fuck you," he replies, scratching his head and yawning.

"Get out of my bed and put some clothes on. Jade's with me. I'll make you some coffee." He narrows his eyes and smiles at me smugly, like he already knows we have done the deed. Just as I knew he would. I leave him to dress before he can make another sarcastic comment.

Jade has already put the kettle on and is sitting on one of the breakfast stools, her back to me, stroking Bob's head as he sits next to her looking up at her with revering eyes. I know how he feels. "Ash is getting dressed," I say as I slide onto the stool next to her and place my hand on her thigh squeezing it gently.

"Alone?"

"Thankfully."

I reach for an apple in the fruit bowl on the counter and take a bite sending juice spraying out as I do. I don't remember buying any apples. Ash must have brought them with him, along with the maple syrup. He's strange that way. The kettle begins to whistle and she slides off the stool, kissing me quickly on the cheek as she does.

"Hey, Baby Girl, you look fabulous today, as always," Ash says as he appears from the bedroom and saunters across to us in his low hanging pyjama trousers and nothing else. He slides onto the seat next to me. Bob jumps up at him and he pulls his arms up into the air making a face at him.

"Thank you, Ash," Jade says, laughing at Bob who is determined to put his nose in a new crutch.

I sit back and enjoy watching Ash try to push him away with his foot so that he doesn't have to touch him. Bob quickly decides he is not going to get anything from this new man, abandons his mission and pads over to sit beside me, where he flops down and resumes his rug impersonation.

Ash looks at me, then to Jade, scanning us in only the

way that he can. I can see him processing everything like he is a Jedi Master and is downloading our new energy fields. He grins. "Good night, eh?"

Jade looks at him from beneath her lashes, smiling coyly. She slides us both a coffee and leans her hip against the counter, holding her own cup between both hands. I say nothing. "Very good," she says as she blows on her coffee before taking a sip.

Ash takes his coffee and sips it, grinning sadistically. "Fuck me, that girl was game for anything last night. And I mean *anything*. I hope she comes back today for another session."

I give him my best glare and shake my head. "Oh no, Ash. Today, you'll behave and help me tidy up the mess you created before I put you back in a taxi and send you home."

He pouts at me, then runs his hand through his messy hair. It looks like it has been grabbed and pulled all night. It most probably has. "You're no fun at all, Jax," he says, glaring back at me.

Jade laughs. "Why don't you both come back up to mine for an early supper later before you go Ash?"

Ash's eyes grow big and round and he grins salaciously. "That would be wonderful, Baby Girl."

I smile around my apple, loving how the three of us are becoming so easy around each other and the fact that Jade is accepting Ash as a big part of my life. She really has no choice in that matter.

We finish our coffees and chat for a while, nothing heavy, just chit-chat about the band that played last night and Ash's antics. He has Jade curled up laughing as he gives her a blow-by-blow account of how he persuaded his girl to let him snort cocaine from her arse. I cringe inwardly but smile when I see Jade is not offended by his crassness. She laughs it all off as one big joke. He's deadly serious.

I'm sure that's not the only place on her body he used as a table to snort his white stuff from. Jade leaves shortly after, telling me she expects us at six o'clock sharp for supper. I hold her to me standing on the stern of the boat and kiss her thoroughly before she goes.

This time, when she walks away with Bob, she turns around and blows me a kiss, a huge grin on her face as she walks backwards down the towpath. I feel part of my heart going with her. It is in her hands now and I think she knows it.

I step back inside *The Witch* and Ash is waiting for me sitting on the sofa with a cigarette in his hand and an 'I told you so' smile on his face. "Well?" he says, leaning back on the sofa with one leg crossed over the other like a camp queen.

"Well, what?" I answer, looking inside the fridge for something cold, sugary and fizzy. I find a can of soda and open it, spraying that across the counter too. This place needs a bloody good clean. I wish Ola, my Polish cleaner, was here and I could just go out for two hours and leave her to it. No such luck.

Ash takes a drag on his cigarette and blows the smoke up into the air tapping his fingers on his thigh. "Stop fucking with me, Jax. Tell me everything."

I take a few gulps of the soda and walk back around the counter, heading to the sofa. I flop down beside him and pick up my Marlboro which are now almost all gone. Figures. "I told her everything."

Ash stops his finger tapping and turns to me his face a picture of surprise. "Everything?"

"Pretty much." I nod slowly. "I left out the 'I'm now a multi-millionaire' part. Thought I'd hit her with that one after she gets to grips with the rest of my confessions."

He grins again nodding happily. "Good, good. That's

really good."

"Is it?" I turn to face him. He frowns at me for a moment and then looks up at the ceiling as if exasperated by my negative response. He looks back at me his eyes glinting in the overhead spots like two pools of dark chocolate. He really does have the most beautiful eyes.

"Of course it is, you prick. She didn't run, she's still here with you and she's invited us back round for supper. She's giving you what you want, isn't she?" He looks at me a little worried for a moment that he has read this all wrong. He hasn't. She is giving me what I want. But for how long. That's the million-dollar question, isn't it?

"I don't want to hurt her, Ash."

He takes another drag on his cigarette and then stubs it out dramatically in the ashtray. "Look, Jax. You've been handed this amazing opportunity with an amazing girl and you're analysing it far too much. Plus, you did just win the fucking lottery for God's sake. You need to just trust that this will be okay. Run with it. Take the bull by the bloody horns and stop thinking everything in life is just a big fat lie for once."

He looks pissed with me now. I know he's right. I have trust issues. Understandably. I have been given two incredible gifts by the universe and I am doubting them both despite the obvious benefits. I am a fucking idiot.

He places his hand on my thigh and squeezes it gently. "Jax. You deserve this. You really do. If I could find a girl that hot, with that many brains, balls and sass, who would accept me for who I am, I'd bloody snap her up in an instant and marry her."

I laugh at that comment. "I'm not going to marry her Ash. I hardly know her."

He pouts at me. "Oh, Jax please, for Christ sake. I've only just met her, seen the two of you together for literally only a few hours and I can see it as clear as day. The connection you've made with Jade is something special. *She* is special. You don't just throw something like this away because you're scared you might both get hurt." He takes a deep breath and then blows it back out slowly. "You've been hurt enough as it is, Jax. It's time to let someone other than me into that black heart of yours."

I sip my soda and digest what he has just said. I do have a black heart. It is dark and dangerous and has been that way for so long, I had forgotten. No. I had accepted, that it would never be light and bright ever again.

I took what I could, when I could, to survive. I did not feel; I did not love. I existed.

I stare at him taking in his beautiful handsome features that I know so well and feel my blackened heart dissolve just that little bit more. His smile is shrewd as he taps his finger against his lip.

"Now, go and take a shower you prick. You smell like a fucking hippy mixed with a heavy dose of sex."

Chapter Twenty-Nine

I have decided to spend a few more days with Jade then head back up to London. I need to sort out my shit before I can come back and spend the time I have left booked on *The Witch* relaxing.

I will go back to my flat for two days only. Two productive days of meetings with banks and to tidy up any loose ends with my practice in Harley Street. I need to hand in my resignation so that when I finish my time on *The Witch* I can work for a month before shutting the door permanently on that part of my life. At least that is one definite decision I have made since coming here.

I will no longer be *that* person: the psychologist leading a double life, with double standards. He disappeared the day I stepped onto *The Water Witch* and Jade cycled past me on her bike. I am not entirely sure what I will do next. I am very tempted to make an offer to the owner of *The Water Witch* and buy her outright. I like the boat life and I like it here in the sleepy hippy village of Honey Street. How long I will feel that way, I have no idea.

I am done with the city for a while and want to spend some serious time with Jade, getting to know her and seeing if what we have started is something we can maintain. I am not sure how she would feel about that but I will make the most of my week or so left here being proactive and finding out exactly where I stand with her.

We say goodbye to Ash later that evening after our early

supper on *The Water Nymph*. He found Jade's boat highly amusing. But he also couldn't wait to get off it; it was far too small and hippy-trippy for his liking. He was polite and respectful, despite his obvious discomfort at having to sit on the floor with Bob as we ate. Jade had put together a delicious supper of chicken parmesan and bohemian salad, decorated with nasturtium from her window basket.

This girl is not only beautiful, sassy and sexy, just as Ash had said, but she can cook like a motherfucker as well. Major bonus. He kissed us both and made us promise we would call him the very next day.

Neither of them knows that I intend to go back to the city very soon for a quick pit stop. I need to clean my clothes and bring some more appropriate ones back with me. It has just started to rain, the sky filling with murky grey clouds. It feels like a bad omen but I guess it's just that we have been lucky so far with two whole weeks of beautiful sunshine. I walk back to Jade's boat with her after we wave Ash off in his taxi and make love to her slowly, leisurely, like we have all the time in the world to do just this.

I listen to the rain tip-tapping on the roof, feeling both blissfully happy and a little unsettled.

Watching Ash drive away in the taxi tonight was like saying goodbye to an old lover and moving quickly on to a fresh shiny new one without any remorse. But that is how this thing works. This *thing* that is my life. I know in my heart Ash feels no jealousy or anger towards me for taking Jade as my lover. He knows I will return to him at some point. It will always be that way.

I just need to work out how to do this with Jade and if, indeed, she will do this with me.

Cradling her in my arms, in the dark, I think about all the things that have happened to me since I came here; all the things that are, perhaps, to come. I am looking for the ultimate dream where I can have both her and Ash in my life. I know it may never come to fruition. But, as she emits a breathy sigh and pushes back into my body, soft and warm and so very perfect, I hope for the first time in my life that I can have that dream.

Someone I can love that will love me for who I truly am. Shadow and light. Sun and moon. Yin and yang. The perfect imperfection.

We spend the next two days together as I had planned. She seems to have welcomed me into her heart – and into her bed – without any other questions and we have not discussed my bisexuality any further. Or my track record of revolving, non-monogamous relationships. It is as if she has just accepted it without any problem whatsoever. I know this is not true and it lurks like a dark shadow in the corner waiting to pounce on the pair of us and rip us to shreds. But, for now, I am enjoying spending this time with her before I do my own disappearing act back to London for a couple of days.

We take *The Witch* back up to Pewsey, refill her with water and do the nasty waste point deed. Jade helps me give her a good clean after my weekend with Ash who, despite his usual obsessive ways, made a lot of mess. She also takes me out on *The Water Nymph*, heading in the opposite direction to another section of the canal which is sublime and beautiful in a way I could never have imagined.

The canal twists and turns through this stretch of countryside like a peaceful refuge that calms my mind and my body in a way I have never felt before. We open and close many locks, finding a system between us of jumping on and off the boat as if we have always done this together.

The scenery is spectacular and the wildlife is in abundance. She points out various birds to me and tells me about the pike in the canal that are the predators of the water:

huge fish with huge teeth that eat just about everything they can find. A perfect example and reminder of the old me. The person that would devour whatever crossed his path without thinking of anything but carnal satisfaction.

The weather has settled again and we have had only one light shower making both trips easy and fun. Two days out on the canal in two completely different boats. The dark, shiny *Witch*, all mod cons and sleek sexiness and the worn and cosy *Nymph* with her soft hippy furnishings and unique scent.

I love them both and feel the difference between their unique energy. Their individual personalities and vibration. I am quickly beginning to understand that this strange way of life is like an extension to the person that lives on it. The owner and the boat are joined in a kind of psychic connection as you steer and guide them down the canal. Like riding a horse that picks up on the rider's movements and intentions. It's a living, breathing thing.

I had a car like that once, a beautiful old Mustang that I brought on a whim. She was my baby for a while and purred beneath my body as I drove her, like the wild thing she was, down the motorway and back again whenever I felt the need to get out of the city. Sadly, when it became obvious, she was more of a liability than an asset parked outside of my flat, I sold her, and I haven't had a car since. I really don't need one in London. I commute using the Underground and taxis like any other city dweller.

It is now very early on Thursday morning and Jade is still asleep. I slip out of her bed and pad out as quietly as I can towards the back of the boat and am greeted by Bob who jumps around me as I wander into the kitchen. I give him some water and fill his food bowl after stroking him for a while. He settles down and I find a piece of paper and a pen. I hate leaving her like this but hope she will understand. She has done this to me several times. I write her a note saying I need to go back to London until Saturday morning when I will return. A work-related emergency that I have no choice in. I also write down my date and time of birth and the location I was born as I am curious as to what my astrology chart may reveal to both of us if she chooses to explore it as she once offered me. I was born on the nineteenth of August and my birthday is coming up fast. I will be thirty-five this year and I haven't even thought about what I will do to celebrate it. Ash normally insists we go on an all-night bender and fuck as many people as possible.

This year the only person I want to fuck is Jade. She will be my birthday treat. I will invite her up to London for the night as it, conveniently, falls on a Saturday this year. I need to show her my life at some point, even if it is just for one weekend, before she makes her decision as to whether we stay in contact or not. The thought of not having her in my life makes my gut twist.

I am finding that I am becoming possessive over her. This is a new emotion I have not felt before. I do not want to give her up and I certainly do not like the idea of any other man being in her life. Not one fucking bit. I may expect her to share me with others in the future but I'm damned if I want her sharing her heart – or her bed – with anyone else.

The selfish bastard that I am.

Chapter Thirty

I step off *The Nymph* into the crisp, misty morning air and head back to *The Witch* where I call a cab and pack my bag. The taxi arrives at eight and I slide inside, feeling odd and out of sorts. I don't want to go but know it will make things easier if I get this out of the way and return on Saturday, where I can truly make the most of my last week here in Honey Street.

I am back in London and stepping into my flat by mid-morning. Throwing my keys into the bowl on the table by the door, I dump my duffel bag and look around at the strange place I am now in. It smells stuffy and clinical. It feels like I am in a stranger's home, breaking into a place that is not mine.

I shower and throw my dirty clothes in the washing machine. Several calls later, I've arranged meetings with three private banks over the next two days. They are *very* happy to hear from me. I read my post with disinterest and drink coffee. I feel empty. Cold. Jade has become the sun I crave, the warmth I need and I am missing it terribly.

That same afternoon I change into my sharp, charcoal grey pinstripe, three-piece suit and take another taxi to Canary Wharf for my first meeting. Sitting in the office with the manager, I switch into shark mode. The man sitting on the other side of the desk grinning at me is a great white and I know I will need to step up to swim in his ocean.

We negotiate and I sign the deal moving a large chunk

of my money straight into my new account on the spot. I do the same at the next bank and then head back to my flat feeling a little happier. I have decided to spread my newfound wealth over several accounts, one offshore and I will also keep a big stash of cash completely separately in a bank vault that I can access easily if I need to grab it quickly. Like a gangster would.

I type up my official resignation letter for my practice and email it to Hilary. She will be very confused but I will see her right. She has been a good PA to me over the last few years and deserves a big fat bonus for putting up with my shit. I don't really want to work my notice and the old Jax would have just buggered off without any second thought but I feel I need to see this through. Do it right for once. There are other people out there in this fucked-up world that rely on me.

By that evening I am sitting with a beer in hand on my sofa watching TV, some mindless bullshit that I couldn't care less about. I smoke the last of my haze and order some more; I have smoked copious amounts in the last few weeks. I don't care. It takes the edge of my need to take a taxi straight back to *The Nymph* and into the arms of Jade.

I slip into the strange bed in my flat around midnight, stoned to fuck and lonely. I am lonely for the first time in my life in a completely different way than before. I could call Ash but know it will end in something I do not want right now. What I want is most probably sitting crossed-legged on a boat in Wiltshire, plotting out my astrology chart and discovering who I truly am. I hope she finds at least a few good things in the stars about me.

Friday, I visit another bank and speak to my broker. I ask him for some advice on stocks and he is eager to help me. Of course, he is, the greedy bastard. I venture further out into the city and have lunch by myself in the food hall at Harrods, just to people watch over tapas and beer. It feels surreal and I can't wait to get the hell out of there.

I plough through the busy bustle of people like a bulldozer. They move out of my way as if I am Moses parting the sea. I know I look scary today, I have a frown on my face and my energy says 'get out of my way'. I'm blending in well again with the city vibe where everyone is on a mission to go somewhere without making eye contact. Back at my flat I call Ash.

"Hey, Jax," he says with a smile in his voice when he picks up. "Is your dick still attached or have you fucked it off with Jade yet?" He chuckles at his own joke.

"I'm back," I say taking a drag on my Marlboro. He makes a funny noise that sounds like he is choking.

"What? I thought you were staying for another week."

I stretch out on my sofa and click through the channels on my satellite box, looking for some porn to indulge in. "I'm just here for tonight, going back tomorrow."

I hear him lean back in his office chair. "Ah, I see."

I find something interesting. Two girls and a guy about to have some fun. One of the girls has black hair and blue eyes. I press play and watch it begin with the mute button on while I think about what I am going to do next. "Come over when you finish work, I'll take you out for dinner tonight," I say with my eyes fixed on the TV screen. I can imagine his cat-like grin at my words. "See you at eight."

I try desperately to climax watching the porn but find I am impotent. It seems that Jade is the only one that can excite me now. I take another shower and dress in a casual, but chic, shirt and black designer jeans. It all feels alien and itchy to me now. I want to slip into my dirty shorts and vest *sans* shoes. I leave my hair loose tonight and am amused at how long it has grown in the past few weeks. My tan is glowing, highlighting my icy blue eyes more and they sparkle at me in the bathroom spotlights as I brush my teeth. I look good but there is an emptiness in my expression today.

I know exactly why that is.

Ash arrives at eight sharp and gives me a kiss and a squeeze before popping open a bottle of Louis Roederer Cristal champagne he has brought over. I know that it cost him a pretty penny and he is spending his gift before I have even wired it into his account. Some things never change.

He is animated and excited to see me. We drink the champagne but I decline his offer of a line. He finds that highly amusing but I am not interested anymore. I have a new drug of choice. We head out to a restaurant in Soho that we frequent and settle into an easy conversation. He asks me about Jade and what we got up to after he left. I tell him how we have spent the last few days cruising on both boats.

"You're turning into a water gypsy, Jax," he says with a grin as he twirls his pasta on his fork before slipping it into his mouth in the most sensual way a person can when eating. Several men are looking at us with admiring eyes. They can look all they like. Tonight, I am not interested.

I lean back in my chair, watching him for a moment and twisting the stem of my wine glass in my hand. "Perhaps."

He grins at me again licking sauce off his lips like a Persian cat. "All you need is a three-pointed hat my friend and you can be the 'Pirate of the Canal'. I could suck you off while you wear just that and nothing else steering that sexy black boat." I laugh at that delicious thought.

We finish our meal and walk back to my flat where Ash stays the night. But we don't have sex and he doesn't push me for it. He lies next to me in the dark, his breathing soft and steady as he sleeps like a baby. I am staring at the ceiling with one arm behind my head the other resting on his waist my fingers stroking him absently like he is my pet. He feels warm, hard, beautifully masculine.

I am comfortable with Ash in a way that is so familiar to me it calms me a little after the two days of running around back in the city. He is my beautiful secret. The other one is far away at present. I fall asleep eventually to the scent of male cologne and the warmth of a man instead of tropical fruits, vanilla and a soft breast to hold.

I dream of Jade. She looks at me with those beautiful sparkling blue eyes and whispers, “what are you doing, City Boy?”

I don’t really know. I am living two lives again but in a totally different way.

Chapter Thirty-One

Heading back to Wiltshire early, I leave a note for Ash on the kitchen counter telling him I love him and that I will be back soon. I also tell him not to arrange anything too over the top for my birthday in two weeks. I doubt he will pay any attention to that at all.

I arrive back in Honey Street just before lunch, a spring in my step as I walk back down the towpath towards *The Water Witch* and my favourite blue-eyed girl, who I hope is still waiting for me around the bend on her own boat. The day is clear and warm and I am back in shorts and a T-shirt, loving the scent of nature in the air and the sound of ducks quacking on the water.

I am home again. I grin as I approach *The Witch*. She sits there looking all coy and naughty, glinting in the sunshine. She knew I would be back. I open her up and start up the engine putting on the kettle and opening all the windows again. I dump my duffel bag back in the master bedroom and it feels more like my real bedroom. More than the one I just left with the handsome Ash who is, without a doubt, still fast asleep in it.

I make a coffee and let the engine run, while I sit on the roof with my pack of Marlboro and enjoy the same view across the fields. My old friend the swan swims up and looks at me, accusing me of being neglectful and gives me a hiss as if he is swearing at me for being unfaithful to him and disappearing without a kiss goodbye.

I finish my coffee, brush my teeth again, tie my hair back and then head up to *The Water Nymph*. My stomach is doing somersaults and I am clenching my jaw like I've popped a pill and am gurning like an idiot. I reach *The Water Nymph* and sigh in relief when I see Jade sitting on the back of her boat reading. Bob spots me first and comes bounding up to me, barking. I pet him lovingly; despite the fact he has just put dirty paw prints on my clean shorts. Jade turns to face me and her face lights up.

I feel like my world has just tilted, to return once again, to the correct position on its axis. She stands up and drops her book to the floor. It lands with a clunk as she puts her hands on her hips and just waits for me to come closer.

"Hey, City Boy," she says with a smile as I step onto the gangplank making the boat tip a little. I stride across to her and pick her up, swinging her around and making her laugh. I bury my face into her neck and breathe her in. She smells delicious and looks even better. It looks like she has been to her friend's again for a good soak in her bathtub and is squeaky clean and fresh as a daisy.

She stares up at me her hands on my chest as I take her in. "Hello, Fairy Girl," I say.

Before she can speak again, I kiss her. Tenderly at first, my tongue teasing her bottom lip, my hands sliding up to her head where I push my fingers into her loose hair. She moans as I probe deeper with my tongue and take the kiss to another level. I begin to lose myself blissfully in the kiss when I feel Bob beside me, nudging my leg as if he, too, wants to get in on the action.

I release her begrudgingly and she stares up at me breathing heavily, her eyes bright and sparkling. "I missed you," I say, meaning it.

She tilts her head at me and gives me a cheeky smile. "I can tell." She scans my face as if she is looking for signs of something untoward but continues to smile. "Did you sort out the problem at work?"

I nod, hating the fact that she still has no clue I am not a city banker and have, in fact, been juggling my millions with the sharks for the last two days. I will tell her at some point but not right now. I just want to spend time with her doing what we do best. Touching each other and hiding from the world.

We retreat to the inside of her boat and spend the next hour doing just that. I take my time, travelling across every part of her body with my tongue and hands before making her orgasm twice. After we have both caught our breath again, we put some clothes back on and head back up to the front of her boat. We sit under the small veranda, lounging on soft cushions drinking beer and smoking cigarettes, with Bob beside us.

She tells me that she has completed my chart and that I should read it alone sometime, without her around. I find that very interesting. Perhaps she has discovered something dark and deadly within my chart. Not that I really believe in any of this fortune-telling stuff. But I'm curious none the less. She asks me if I saw Ash while I was back in the city and I tell her yes, we had dinner together in Soho. She asks me nothing more.

That evening she slides the astrology chart towards me and takes Bob out for a walk on her own, leaving me to digest the information. I sit and read, a spliff in my hand. It is like reading my entire life in black and white. All the details are there in glorified, brutal honesty. My personality down to a tee: my traits, my habits, they're all there in print.

What surprises me most is the fact she has stated that I will come into a great deal of abundance and material wealth at some point and that it will give me the opportunity to really live my life to the full. But only if I make the right choices and decisions on that new path and change the patterns of how I have been living up until now. It also says that I will find true love with two people in my life and that they will give me everything I need and desire, if I am honest with them and tell no lies. It does not state that these people will be in my life at the same time, just as I am hoping.

It goes on to say that I am very intelligent and able to manipulate people, dealing with most situations without any trouble whatsoever. I should pursue a career in any line of work that would help others with tough decisions and problem-solving. I am a born leader – apparently. It also states I am best suited to partners with the star signs in Aries, Gemini, Libra and Sagittarius. I smile, remembering that Ash is a Gemini.

I wonder if Jade will fit into any of the other categories. It is a lot to take in and I am absolutely amazed at how accurate her astrology reading is, considering she only knows one thing about me: my sexuality. I have lied to her about my work and told her nothing true about my life. Least of all the choices I have made or the way I live. But now she has seen it all.

She returns to *The Nymph* shortly after I finish reading the report and smiles at me shyly. Her cheeks are a little flushed, she looks excited about something. Perhaps she knows her report was spot on. I stand and pull her into my arms as she comes close, nuzzling my face into her hair.

"You seem very good at your job, Fairy Girl," I say, tickling her sides as I kiss her neck.

She squirms against me. "Well, thank you very much." She wriggles free from me trying to restrain my wandering hands. Her eyes are indicating something has roused her. Something other than my groping. She pulls on my hand and bites her bottom lip playfully. "Come with me, Jax. I want to show you something."

She leads me back off the boat and we wander down the towpath, in the opposite direction to the pub, with Bob trailing along behind us sniffing at the shrubbery and generally ambling. He has already been for a long walk with her and is no longer in a hurry. She keeps looking up at me as we walk, and I smile at her wondering what she has found.

I'm beginning to wonder where the hell she's taking me when she pulls me into what looks like an overgrown path off the towpath. I haven't spotted it before when I was out running. Dusk is approaching and it's a little darker now, the animals are settling down for the night; I hear a blackbird chirping close by. I follow her, ducking under some low hanging branches.

She tugs on my hand, eager for me to follow. We step out of the undergrowth and into a small clearing, which looks like it could have once been a garden. It is overgrown and tangled with vegetation and it takes me a moment to see what is sitting behind it. A beautiful, old cottage sits back from the clearing. It is chocolate-box perfect: white and small but it looks like it has been derelict for a while.

She grins at me and pulls me forward. In the dim blue-grey light of dusk, I see it for what it is. Magical. There is a wooden sign outside with *For Sale* printed on it with details of some local estate agent. She looks up at me and smiles.

"I'm going to buy this cottage, Jax. I've had my eye on it ever since I came to live here. No one else knows it's here. I stumbled across it once when I was walking Bob. Up until now, it has just been sitting here empty. But tonight, I saw the sign." She is looking up at me with those perfect blue eyes sparkling with a thousand thoughts spinning through them. "I have some savings and could apply for a mortgage; my work is steady, and my books have been good for a while now." She looks back at the cottage. "What do you think?"

I know what I think immediately. I will buy this ramshackle, tumbledown cottage and do it up for her. Without question. That is what I think.

"It's beautiful Jade but clearly needs a lot of work."

She starts to bite one of her fingernails as if she is a little nervous and I grin, I have never seen her like this before. She obviously really wants this place. We walk closer and she shows me around the cottage as if she has done the same inspection many times before. She probably has.

Her secret dream home has been sitting quietly hidden away from the rest of the world, just waiting for the right moment to be claimed. I ponder, while we stand looking in one of the windows at the empty rooms that are littered with old and broken furniture, that perhaps the universe sent me here for two things now. To fall in love *and* to make someone truly happy with the gift of money I can bestow upon them. I hide my own excitement at the thought of telling her I will buy it for her. I have no idea how much a place like this would cost or even how much it would take to restore it to its former glory. I am already imagining moving her in and living with her alternatively between *The Nymph* and this glorious little country cottage.

I file that thought away for now. She may not even want me in this cottage with her.

We return to *The Nymph* and settle Bob down for the night. I am taking her back to *The Water Witch* for the night. I want to sit on the roof and talk to her. I don't think I can tell her outright that I am thinking about buying the cottage and setting her up in it. Best to leave that until after I have phoned the estate agent.

But I do want to discuss my birthday with her and persuade her to come up to London with me next week. I will have to leave her again and work my notice before I can even ask her if she would like to spend more time with me.

I also think that she needs to see my life in London, experience it with me, even if it is only for one weekend, before we can decide between us if there is indeed any future for us.

I have no idea what that future would be right now.

Chapter Thirty-Two

We sit on the roof of *The Witch* with a bucket of beers between us. It is so comfortable and familiar now, just sitting together in two deckchairs looking out over the canal in the dark, the night sky above us and small creatures rustling around us.

I pass her a freshly rolled spliff and crack open another beer. It is warm and balmy tonight and we sit silently for a moment, I can hear Jade's mind whirring like an overworked clock as she thinks about the cottage.

"Do you mind if I ask you how much money you've saved?" I ask. If she believes I am still in finance, I might be able to find out some information under the guise of giving her advice. She turns to face me, her soft sensual features slightly illuminated by the large citronella candle sitting between us on the roof of the boat.

"No, I don't mind at all." She takes a long drag on the spliff and then passes it back to me. "I have thirty thousand pounds in a high-interest account."

I nearly choke on my beer. She is very young to have such a large amount of money to her name. She sees the look of shock on my face and smiles. "I had a job for a while that allowed me to put a lot of cash away."

I nod taking my own hit from the joint. She looks back out over the canal and crosses her long legs slowly. I have the feeling she is about to reveal something to me that I may not like. I can sense it in the air, sliding between us like a dark snake in the grass about to strike.

"When I was seventeen, I was diagnosed with uterine cancer … the cancer was aggressive and they operated on me and removed part of my womb. They told me that I would never be able to have children because of the damage to my uterus."

I am utterly speechless as she pauses for a moment.

"They wanted me to have chemotherapy as well, but I refused. I wasn't going to let them poison me with that shit and kill me off any quicker than life was already trying to do."

I pass her back the joint thinking that right now she needs it more than me. She pauses for a moment before revealing the parts of her life that I sense she has kept a secret from the rest of the world. "I went down a route that not even my parents know about, I did my research and contacted a few people I knew and used cannabis oil to heal myself."

I am watching her now with my heart in my throat. This beautiful young woman has already been through so much in her life and I had absolutely no idea until now. I hadn't given the small scar on her abdomen much thought when I'd first seen it as it was quite small and inconspicuous. Now I know where it came from. I feel like I cannot breathe as she continues to tell me her story.

"I still take it now. In fact, I take a tiny amount each day and it keeps me healthy and basically kept me alive when I needed it to. My life changed the day I was diagnosed; I decided from that day on, I would live each day as if it were my last and only do the things I wanted to do, with the people I wanted to do it with."

She turns and smiles at me reaching for my hand. I take it and wrap my fingers around her delicate palm. "After I recovered from the operation and the oil did its job, I went up to London and worked as a waitress during the day and then I danced at night."

I take a sip of my beer and nod slowly encouraging her to go on, to reveal the dark part of her life that I sensed. "I worked in a strip club for a year, pole dancing and earnt a great deal of cash." She grins at me flashing me her beautiful white teeth. "I was a very good dancer."

I lift her hand and kiss her knuckles. "I'm sure you were," I say drolly and release her hand.

She takes another hit on the joint and then passes it back to me again. "In a year, I managed to save enough cash to buy *The Water Nymph* and have a big enough deposit for a house, if I ever found one I liked. I came here and studied astrology, something I'd always wanted to do, then started working for various magazines that liked my work."

I am listening to her with an entirely new respect and understanding as to why she is the strong, incredible woman that she is.

"I don't regret that part of my life, it gave me the life I have now and I am grateful for the cancer in a way … it made me wake up and lose the fear that so many people have in this lifetime that stops them from doing what they really want to do."

I feel the intense urge to take her into my arms and hold her there forever. She is the most incredible person I have ever met and she is teaching me so many things. She looks at me with that same soft smile and sweetness I have come to love. "So, you see Jax, we all have secrets and we all have the chance to change them in this lifetime."

I place the joint in the ashtray and stand up. She watches me, her expression calm and in control despite what she has just told me. I stand before her and take her hand, pulling her up slowly so that she is now standing with me. I hold her face between my hands and look into her eyes. "You are the most beautiful person I have ever met, Jade. If you will have me, I am yours."

Her eyes begin to glisten. Emotion thick and palpable flows between us as I kiss her passionately and she moans in response as if I am pulling her underwater and drowning her in a pool of love.

Inside *The Water Witch*, we make love again and I kiss the scar on her belly that I had, in my selfish ignorance, dismissed before. She trembles in my arms and looks at me as if I am the only person in the world that could ever understand why she did what she did, at such a young age, and all alone. We are two kindred spirits who have been walking two different sad paths and, at last, we have found each other.

I am now, without a single doubt, completely and utterly head over heels in love with her.

The next morning, we sit and eat breakfast at the kitchen counter on *The Witch*, listening to the rain that has arrived again during the night and is drumming its own tune on the roof. "I'd like you to come up to London for my birthday Jade," I say, taking a sip of my black coffee.

She is wearing one of my T-shirts and nothing else, her long legs crossed elegantly as she sits on the stool beside me. "Okay," she says taking a bite out of a piece of toast slathered in butter and honey.

"Ash will probably arrange something completely over the top and outrageous but I want you to come up and stay with me for the weekend." She is looking at me with interest as she crunches on the toast. "You need to see that part of my life before you make the decision as to whether you wish to stay in contact with me or not."

She stops chewing her toast, swallows it and then stares at me with a small frown on her beautiful face. "Why on earth would I *not* stay in contact with you, Jax?" she asks me as if this is the most ridiculous thing, I have ever said to her yet.

"My life is not pretty, Jade. But I want you to see it for real. Experience it with me."

She digests this information and takes another bite out of her toast. I watch her tongue slip out and lick the honey off her lip and wish it were my tongue doing the licking.

"I've already told you, Jax. I don't care."

I take a deep breath and turn to face her properly placing my hand on her bare thigh, revelling in the silky smoothness of her skin. "We've been living in a bubble for the past few weeks, Jade. You've seen a part of me that others have not. I want you to see where I come from. I want you to see the other part of me that you've not experienced."

She grins at me wickedly. "You don't scare me, City Boy." I can't help but laugh.

Nothing seems to rattle this girl but I know she may think differently once she has been out with Ash, Jo, and me. When she sees the city life in the way we see it: raw, dark and deadly. While I am not intending to continue living in the way I was before, I want her to see some of my realities, my expression of my sexuality.

I know that Ash will arrange for a meal somewhere swanky, then an evening of clubbing in a place that Jade would never have been to before. A place where the naughty misfits come out to play. She needs to see it in all its technicoloured glory. Of course, I'll protect her from stepping too close to the hell-fire but I am ready to show her my true colours now.

She smiles at me mischievously and runs a finger across my jaw. "I'll ask Chloe to look after Bob for the weekend and get the train up. I'd like to see where you live, and I'd love to celebrate your birthday with you." I assume Chloe is her friend who lives in Devizes.

"I'll arrange for a taxi to pick you up and bring you."

She snorts at my suggestion. "Don't waste your money, City Boy."

I shake my head. "Oh no. You don't get to dictate that one to me, Jade. I'm not having you wandering around London looking all sexy and gorgeous with your arse cheeks hanging out of your shorts." She laughs but does not fight me on that statement.

After collecting Bob, she insists we walk him in the rain and without an umbrella resulting in us becoming totally drenched. We spend the rest of the day wrapped around each other, hiding in the warmth of *The Water Witch* having peeled each other's clothes off as if it were a wonderful playful game. Her carefree way of looking at the world and what it can give us is rubbing off on me.

I enjoyed seeing her pert nipples sticking out from under her vest top as the rain-soaked us thoroughly. I dried her somewhat roughly with one of my pristine fluffy towels, courtesy of *The Water Witch* supply cupboard, in the same way she did Bob.

She shrieked and growled at me as I trapped her in my arms and held her down like a misbehaving child. I have never laughed as much as I have in the company of Jade. She chased me with the towel flicking my naked backside, then ran away from me as I chased her back, trying not to fall over down the corridor of the boat.

I'm adolescent again, carefree and innocent. Taking the time to enjoy the simple things in life. Being in the present moment, instead of constantly thinking ahead and planning my next strategic move.

The days fly by at an alarming rate.

We live alternately between the two boats and are together constantly. I sit and watch her while she works. I smoke spliffs and smile at the concentration on her face as she plots and writes out her astrology charts.

I will buy her a new laptop when I return to the city. The one she is currently using is out of date and I want to gift her a new one so that she has access to everything she could possibly need for the work she clearly loves doing. As she works, I see that she is not only intelligent, witty and ballsy but also incredibly creative and generous.

She shows me how to make the bracelets and bangles that decorate her arms. I have not taken the one she made me off since I put it on. I intend to keep it on until it falls off. She tells me that she painted the figureheads on both *The Nymph* and *The Water Witch*, as I suspected, and she paints occasionally when she has time. It seems there is nothing this girl cannot do; I am in awe of her.

I make love to her every day, sometimes several times, alternating between moments of tenderness and an almost animal-like ferociousness. Each time with a sense of desperateness, as if I know this time will soon be over and we must make the most of it. Like a sponge, she soaks up the attention I give her and returns it to me with equal ferocity.

Sunday afternoon soon comes and my month in this unexpected paradise expires. The time has disappeared all too quickly. I close *The Water Witch* for the very last time and stand silently on the roof for a moment, not wanting to say goodbye to her before stepping off.

Jade is wrapped in my arms, my duffel bag by my feet as the taxi waits to take me back to the city – and a life I no longer want or need. She holds me tightly as if afraid to let me go. I know exactly how she feels. She has promised me that she will travel up to London the following Saturday for my birthday.

I hold her for a long time, trying to memorise how she feels, smells, and sounds for the last time until we see each other again. Eventually, when I comprehend the meter in the taxi is still ticking, I release her. She stares up at me and speaks to me telepathically, 'I love you,' she says with her beautiful, deep blue soulful eyes.

We both know this 'thing' between us is not just a thing anymore. Neither of us wants to say the words out loud in case it shatters it irrevocably. I kiss her once on the forehead and then walk towards the taxi without saying a word. She watches me walk away and I hear her call to me in her sexy sing-song voice.

"See you later, City Boy."

And then I am gone as if it were all just a dream.

Chapter Thirty-Three

The next week I spend working at my practice in Harley Street, slipping back easily into the falseness of the professional world I once thought I loved. I find myself taking more time with each client, listening more intently and giving them the help and advice, they really need, instead of being flippant and blasé about the whole thing.

Hilary looks at me as if an alien has invaded my body and taken me over. I am polite and courteous to her and she blushes and stumbles around as if the new me is making her head spin in confusion and she has forgotten how to act around me.

I spend some time walking around Hyde Park looking at it with new eyes, taking in nature and the wildlife with new respect and admiration. I cannot wait to get back to Wiltshire again and the real countryside.

The asking price for the little cottage was a mere £300,000, surprisingly low considering how much land is part of the package but will probably need at least another £100,000 to restore it. There was shock in the estate agent's voice as I made an instant cash offer and paid them an extortionate price to process the paperwork in double-quick time. I wonder if Jade has contacted them and been grieving over the fact that someone has stepped in and brought it before she could. I grin at the thought of her stomping her foot and swearing like a fisherwoman if she has. Maybe I am still an evil bastard at heart.

Talking of estate agents, I have had my flat valued; it has almost doubled in price since I bought it. It is no longer my home and I want to get rid of it. I have put it on the market and am waiting for a buyer so that I can move out and start my new life.

I want that new life to be with a certain ebony-haired girl in Wiltshire. I have already discussed this with Ash and he has told me that I "would be a stupid prick" if I didn't jump at the opportunity to live with her. She makes me happy and he can see that I have fallen for her in a way I have never done before.

It is a foregone conclusion, as far as he is concerned. I haven't even asked Jade if she would be willing yet but from the time we have spent together and the way she looked at me when I left, I would be very surprised if she turned me down now.

My furniture will have to be put in storage until the cottage is restored but I will probably sell most of it as it won't suit the little cottage in sleepy Honey Street anyway. Perhaps I am jumping the gun here but I don't give a flying fuck. If Jade does send me on my way, I will find somewhere else to live in the countryside. For I am no longer a city boy. I am a free man who wants to break away from the destructive patterns that have overshadowed my life so far.

I want to live my life without having to watch my back constantly.

I send a cheque to my mother via courier with a letter explaining that I have come into some money and would like to help her and my father with their retirement. She will likely faint when she sees the amount. I have no idea whether she will bank it but I feel happier with the thought that I have done the right thing. She lost her son the day I walked out the door. I owe her this much for all the pain I put her through that day – and every day since.

Waiting for Jade to arrive, almost a week after I left her, I feel the anticipation start to rise in my body. It snakes up my legs like a hit of heroin, filling my veins with heat and fire. I am literally shaking with excitement when I hear the buzzer.

I let her in and open my front door waiting. She steps out of the lift with a small rucksack and dress bag over her arm as if she has been here many times before. She is in her short shorts, biker boots and a Sex Pistols T-shirt. Her hair is braided, her Mohawk sticking up and her lips are painted bright red.

I almost come in my pants.

I wait for her to come to me and pick her up, throwing her legs around my waist and kissing her like I need her to breathe. She laughs against my mouth as I crush her to me. Her rucksack and dress bag now discarded on the floor.

She pushes against my chest in a feeble attempt to slow me down as I devour her. If I could climb inside her right now I would. She tastes exactly as I remember and I cannot believe how much I have missed her. She finally manages to extract herself from my lips and stares at me, grinning.

"Miss me much, City Boy?" she says, winding my hair around her fingers and tugging hard.

I growl at her, narrowing my eyes as I allow her body to slide back down my own so that her feet hit the floor. She watches me with amusement as I then grab her bags and shove her through the front door.

For the next hour, I show her exactly how much I missed her.

After, I show her around my flat with an air of indifference. This place means nothing to me now, even though she looks around with interest and says it is 'very me'. I see nothing but cold lines and emptiness in this place now. Perhaps that's how I was: cold and indifferent.

I make us some toasted sandwiches for lunch and we sit and chat about what we have been up to in our week apart, I skim over the details of my work. She tells me that Bob has missed me and was probably now sulking that he has been left behind at the 'Chloe day spa'. I can't stop looking at her, grinning like a complete idiot as she talks to me.

"What time is Ash coming to pick us up tonight?" she asks as we stretch out on my sofa together after our lunch. I am trailing my fingers up and down her arms as she lies between my legs, flat against my chest.

"Eight-ish. I still have no idea where we're going. Jo's coming with us apparently."

She turns her head and looks up at me. "I'm sure you'll like where we're going," she says with a cheeky smile.

I raise a brow. "He's been in touch with you?"

She licks her lips slowly as if she knows it makes my cock twitch every time she does. "Mmmh." She gives nothing away.

I tickle her waist making her squeal. "Plotting behind my back, eh? I think that deserves punishment young lady." She laughs and pushes me away jumping up suddenly and leaving me sprawled on the couch with another hard-on.

"No plotting, he just wanted to let me know the restaurant we are going to is fancy and he sent me something I could wear tonight. With a note, I may add, indicating it would be more appropriate than my usual 'hippy' attire." She moves her hands in an air quote motion as she says the word 'hippy'. I laugh at Ash's bluntness but am intrigued to see what he has sent her.

She stands before me with her finger on her lip looking up at the ceiling for a moment a smile on her face. "Oh, and I almost forgot." She looks back at me and bites her bottom lip shyly. "Happy thirty-fifth birthday, City Boy."

I smile up at her as she turns around and begins to

rummage through her rucksack.

I sit up and reach for my Marlboro, lighting one up as she saunters back over to me with a present in her hand. It is wrapped in shiny gold paper with a big purple bow around it. I hold my cigarette in my mouth and take it from her my hands shaking a little. It looks like a picture.

She is standing with her legs crossed, her hands in front of her in a nervous pose. I hold it in my hands for a moment and then begin to tear off the paper. I narrow my eyes as the smoke from my cigarette begins to waft into my face.

It is, indeed, a picture. It's a painting of *The Water Witch* – and it's incredible.

I place the cigarette in the ashtray beside me and hold the painting with both hands so that I can study it properly. She has captured the boat in intricate detail; it is astonishingly accurate. What stuns me the most is the person sitting on the roof in a deckchair, looking out over the rolling fields in the distance. Jade has painted me in perfect detail, with my hair tied back wearing a vest and board shorts.

She has captured me as I sit in my favourite spot, spliff in hand and a bucket of beers by my side. I feel like my heart is about to explode in my chest. It's so breathtakingly beautiful and, without a doubt, the most thoughtful gift I have ever received.

She is waiting for me to say something and fidgets a little as she stands quietly. I look up at her and smile. "Thank you, Jade. It's the most beautiful thing anyone has ever given me. I will cherish it."

She grins and uncrosses her legs. "Good, I was starting to think you hated it."

I stand up and place it on the sofa beside me pulling her into my arms. "I could never hate anything you gave me Fairy Girl," I whisper into her hair as I hold her. She sighs, perhaps with relief, and I squeeze her closer. I am dissolving quickly into a puddle of soppy goo.

It appears that I'm now the fish food, not the other way around.

Chapter Thirty-Four

Ash arrives at half seven, surprising me as I take a bottle of champagne out of the fridge. He has his own key and walks through the door as if he owns the place.

"Happy Birthday, you old bastard!" he says, throwing a Gucci bag onto my sofa along with another bottle of champagne.

Jade is in the shower and I can hear the water running as she gets ready for our night out. I grin at Ash as he sashays over to me and pulls me into his arms, giving me a hard kiss on the lips. He holds me at arm's length for a moment studying my face and grinning. "Baby Girl in the shower, eh?"

I nod and push him away before he does something else inappropriate.

"Good, get in the shower after her, you stink of sex – again – and I want to help her get ready while you spruce yourself up, bad boy. Make sure you put this shirt on," he points to the bag on my sofa, "and tie your fucking hair back tonight. You're looking like a bloody hippy again," he says as he walks into the kitchen and reaches into the cupboard for my champagne flutes. God, I love this man and his vicious tongue.

Jade appears shortly after wrapped in a towel, her hair twisted up in another small towel. She looks beautiful dripping wet and without make-up. I want to pull the towel off and lick her from head to toe.

"Hey, Ash," she says with a grin. He waves at her from the sofa with his champagne in hand his legs sprawled open as usual.

"Well, good evening, beautiful. Ready for the big night out with our birthday boy?"

She begins to rub her hair and it spills out from the towel like an oil slick, shining in my spotlights and smelling like sunshine and vanilla. "Absolutely."

I leave them to it and take my own shower listening to the pair of them laughing as they disappear into the spare bedroom. Ash can indulge in his own little fantasy with her, like she is his own life-sized doll to dress up and play with.

I dread to think what he will do to her behind the closed door but know Jade will be able to handle him. I take my time in the shower and shave, brush my teeth and tie my hair back as Ash demanded. My tan from Wiltshire still glows and, as I finish the polishing process, I catch sight of myself in the mirror: I look like one handsome bastard tonight. I grab the Gucci bag and head into my bedroom to dress.

I'm smoking and sipping my champagne wearing my new Gucci shirt and Hugo Boss jacket and trousers when the door to my spare bedroom opens and Ash reappears looking very happy with himself indeed. He has dressed suitably sharp tonight: a black shirt with a thin gold pinstripe running through it and a charcoal grey designer suit jacket and trousers. It looks like a Versace to me. His dirty blonde hair is gelled and messy, giving him that 'just got out of bed' look. His chocolate-brown eyes sparkle at me as he walks into the living room. I feel like my tongue has just flopped out of my mouth and is now sitting on the floor as I see Jade walk out behind him.

She is dressed in a floor-length, silver-grey dress. It slides down her body like a second skin, pooling around her feet delicately. It has tiny spaghetti straps which show off her slim arms, showcasing her tattoos beautifully. Her hair is clipped up in a soft swirl and pinned at the top with a complimenting silver flower. Her fringe is flat and fluffed delicately with wisps of her hair around her face. She smiles at me coyly, her eyes are a dark smoky grey, her lips ruby red. She looks like she has literally just stepped off the catwalk.

"Doesn't she look good enough to eat, Jax?" Ash says.

I am speechless. This is not the girl I have grown to love over the last month. This is something else. A goddess sent from the heavens.

"Give Jax a twirl, Baby Girl."

She complies and my dick instantly twitches as she turns around and reveals that the dress is backless and she is clearly not wearing any underwear at all. The dress is open to the base of her spine and I can see the curve of her delectable arse, just asking to be licked and stroked. I intend to do just that later.

"Holy fuck," I whisper.

Jade turns back around and smiles. "I take it you like it," she says with amusement in her voice.

Ash sniggers. "Baby Girl, he fucking loves it."

We are meeting Jo at the restaurant. I still have no idea where we are going. We slide into a sleek black limousine that Ash has arranged. We are drinking champagne and enjoying the luxury and novelty of it all. Ash proceeds to snort two lines of cocaine within five minutes of us leaving the kerb. I make a mental note to get him into a rehab programme at some point. I decline again; I no longer need it or crave it.

Jade is sitting between us like the jewel in the crown. She is positively sparkling tonight and I cannot fathom for the life of me how the fuck I got so lucky. I have two of the most beautiful people in the world sitting next to me in this car and I'm loving every second of it.

Chapter Thirty-Five

We pull up at The Dorchester and I help Jade out, enjoying the fact that she is mine to show off for the night and people are looking at us like we are superstars. Ash takes control and we are shown to our table, where Jo is waiting for us and looking suitably gorgeous in a chic red dress that exaggerates all her curves. We look like we belong here.

Jade fits in as if this is all nothing at all. The food is superb and we laugh and joke as close friends would, drinking more champagne and making the other diners stare at us with envy. Jo instantly loves Jade and they chat as if they are lifelong friends.

I catch Ash looking at me with a wicked smile on his lips, he is loving this; loving the attention we are receiving and how Jade has slipped into our world so very easily. I also know he is thinking of ways to get her out of that dress and in between us. But it's my birthday, not his, so he hasn't a chance in hell. Ever.

We leave the restaurant suitably full and slightly drunk around half eleven. I'm holding Jade's hand as we jump back into the limo and head off to our next destination, a bar in Soho for cocktails before we hit a club. She leans into me and whispers into my ear. "You look happy, City Boy." I am. Extremely happy, in fact. She slips her hand down my thigh and squeezes it crossing her legs slowly. "I can't wait to get you naked later, then I can give you your real birthday gift."

I smile at her. "I look forward to it." Ash is watching us

as he talks to Jo and his mouth quirks up as if he can hear what we are saying. He probably can.

We arrive at the bar and order cocktails, finding a booth where we can sit and drink without being jostled by the crowds. We stay until one, then stumble back out to the limo and head off again. Destination unknown – to me at least.

Ash and Jo do a couple of more cheeky lines and I can feel the energy lift again. I am high on Jade and she seems to be buzzing with her own unique vibration right now. Her eyes are bright and her lips are shining as she watches me with an expression of mixed lust and love.

We end up driving around for half an hour, a ploy, I surmise, to confuse me. We end up returning to Soho and arriving at a hip gay club that Ash loves to prowl in. I take a deep breath as we walk in and am extremely grateful to discover Ash has arranged us a VIP table as we are ushered by a very tall transvestite, carrying a clipboard, to the swanky reserved seating area. We won't have to fight the crowds for a space to sit and relax between hitting the dance floor thanks to his forward thinking.

We order more champagne and I sit back with my arms across the back of the sofa we are all squeezed onto surveying the crowd. The dance floor is packed already, full of gyrating, sweaty bodies. You can smell the pheromones in the air and it's already making Ash twitch. He is a sex addict and this is where he will most definitely get his next fix.

My eyes are starting to blur a little just as the DJ slips a mix of Kylie's latest single, 'Spinning Around' on and Jade leans into me. "Dance with me, City Boy," she whispers into my ear, flicking her tongue against the outside. It would be rude to refuse and I grin as she slips her hand down my thigh.

She leads the way and I watch her pert arse swish from side to side like a hypnotic snake about to strike. She turns around and puts her arms around my neck and begins to sway against me in time with the music. I pull her closer to me and roll my groin into her body making her throw her head back and sigh. I'm gone. Lost in the music and the sexy wild woman I am holding in my arms.

We dance as if we are having sex on the floor and don't give a damn. She slides her hands down my chest and pushes me away so that we are standing close but not touching. Then she turns around and raises her hands above her head, twisting and turning them in a tantalising display that makes me lose my concentration for a moment.

Her bare back moves fluidly, making the silver-grey dress twist and shimmer in the light. She is fucking with me and I'm loving it. My dick grows hard and I groan. Jade continues to tease me, dancing in a way that I am sure she did back in her strip club days. She is attracting a lot of attention but I watch them all like a lion, ready to pounce if any of them dare to touch her. The tune changes to a hard house beat and the bass begins to vibrate up through my legs into my groin that is doing its own dance right now.

I'm tempted to take her to the toilet and fuck her hard against the wall. But I won't. Not here. Not now. I'd rather enjoy her in the privacy of my flat later where I can take my time with her. Explore every room with her, trying every position without having to think about anyone else walking in on us. She looks up at me coyly and gestures for me to come close again. I grab her and instantly punish her with a hard kiss that makes her whimper and go limp in my arms.

I feel someone slide up behind me and place their hands on my waist and realise that Ash is pushing against my back, wanting to get in on the action. I reluctantly end the kiss and release Jade before looking over my shoulder at him. He grins at me like the predator he is.

"Can I cut in, birthday boy?" he says with a quirk of his brow.

I don't want him to take Jade away from me but I know she can handle him. And I need to adjust my dick before it springs out of my trousers. I step back from Jade and give him a hard glare. "Don't kiss her or touch her in any way that's inappropriate, Ash. If you do, I'll punch you so hard you won't be able to suck dick for a week."

Jade laughs behind me and I leave them to dance and head to the toilets. I'm smiling as I weave on slightly unsteady legs through the crowd. I'm having the best birthday ever.

I quickly deduce that I am more inebriated than I originally thought. Pissing with a hard-on is difficult enough. Pissing drunk and with a raging hard-on is even more challenging. After finally managing to relieve myself, I wash my hands, splash my face with cold water and leave the crowded toilet pushing my way past people and heading back to the dance floor to find Jade and Ash. A hand on my arm stops me.

"Jax? It's good to see you, man. It's been a while …"

I look up into the face of a guy I fucked once after a night with Ash at Heaven. The three of us had a very hazy and crazy night that, right now, I want to forget. He smiles at me and runs his hand down my arm. "You look incredible. Have you been abroad?"

I give him a quick smile, shaking my head as I try to manoeuvre my way around him. I stumble a little in my drunkenness and he grabs me laughing.

"Hey there big boy … steady," he chuckles as he pulls me out of my stagger and manages to press me back up against the wall before I have a chance to say anything. As I try to regain my balance, he discretely slides his hand between my legs and squeezes my, still semi-hard, dick.

I am momentarily stunned, unable to move. He seems to take this as a green light and, before I can react, he goes in for the kill, taking a hold of the back of my neck and pushing his fingers into my hair. In the blink of an eye, he has angled my head roughly to one side and begins to kiss me. I hold onto his biceps and try to push back against him but his tongue is in my mouth before I can even register what is happening.

He almost has me in a headlock and, if I wasn't so drunk right now, I would have punched him to the floor. I shove him away hard, trying to get a grip on the situation that has quickly spiralled out of control and see a glimpse of silver dress flash in my peripheral vision. At that moment, I know Jade has witnessed what just happened.

I glare at the guy, saying nothing and turn my back on him, leaving him against the wall with a smug smile on his face.

I am no longer smiling. I stride after Jade watching her slip through the crowd on the dance floor. Fuck. This is not good.

When I finally manage to catch up with her, she is sitting in the booth alone with her champagne in her hand. Ash and Jo are on the dance floor and I'm glad they are. This is going to be very tricky.

She smiles at me briefly before turning her head back to the dance floor as I sit down and run my hand over my face trying to sober up a little. She remains looking out over the dance floor, her legs crossed and her foot tapping in time with the music as if nothing is untoward. I slide my right arm around her shoulders and then pull her chin towards me with my free hand. She stares at me with those big blue eyes that are scanning me intently.

"I'm sorry, Jade. He's just some guy I knew once. I didn't kiss him back, he practically strangled me in a headlock," I explain feeling very uneasy.

She takes my hand and kisses my knuckles. She smiles at me. "I know."

I lean back and grab my Marlboro. "Let's take a break," I say and take her champagne glass out of her hand, setting it down on the table. She allows me to lead her back out over the dance floor where we find Ash and Jo gyrating with two guys and a girl. She puts up no resistance as I lead her out of the club so that we can smoke outside and I can talk to her without shouting over the blaring club music. I take her over to a quiet doorway and take out two cigarettes lighting one for her before lighting my own.

"It's okay, Jax. Really," she says, blowing smoke up into the air. I scan her face and try to see if she is lying. She's giving me every indication that she isn't. Her body language is relaxed and there is no underlying tension in her voice. But I feel the need to probe her more. Find out if she really is as open-minded as she seems to be suggesting.

I drag on my Marlboro greedily. "How did it make you feel to see a man kissing me like that Jade?"

She puts a hand on her hip and juts it out a little, making her look even more sexy and delicious. "Strangely aroused," she says, taking another drag.

"Aroused?" I repeat, amusement in my voice.

"Yes. And a little unnerved if I'm honest."

I look up at the sky and close my eyes for a second, this must be hard for her. She has now seen first-hand that I have a colourful history, a past where I have engaged fully with same sex interaction. Her cool response to my questioning is perhaps a shield for her real thoughts on the matter. "You've nothing to fear Jade. I've no intentions of disappearing with anyone else."

Her eyes wander across my face as she bites her lip. "Tonight, or in the future?" she whispers.

My brows quirk up in response as the insecurity bell rings loudly in my head. “Both,” I state, taking her hand and squeezing it.

“Okay.” She nods slowly digesting my statement.

“Okay.”

Her easy acceptance may not be the truth. But the fact she seems willing to trust me on this, for now at least, means a lot. It’s a good start. I thank the gods for sending me this woman. Her willingness to accept who I have been, how I have conducted my life so far is a big leap in the right direction. I look back at her and smile feeling slightly more appeased.

“Okay,” I repeat with a nod.

We finish our smokes and I slip my hand back into hers and lead her back inside the club.

Chapter Thirty-Six

The rest of the evening goes by without any further mishaps or accidental fuck-ups. Very drunk and very charged, we drop Ash and Jo off at his flat and head back to mine in the limo. They will, no doubt, be calling a few friends to come around and have some fun with them by the time I reach home. Jade walks straight to the bathroom without saying a word and I go into the kitchen and grab some water from the fridge.

I'm still drunk and feeling a little woozy. But I instantly sober up.

She walks back out completely naked, wearing just her high heels and a sexy smile. I stand, leaning against my kitchen counter and watch her as she walks towards me, slowly taking the pins out of her hair and throwing them on the floor. They ping against the tiles as she drops them. "Would you like the rest of your birthday present now, City Boy?"

I take a swig of the water, wipe my mouth with the back of my hand and pounce. Yes fucking please.

I wake the next morning to discover that Jade is deciding to have me for breakfast. I smile lazily, stretching my arms up and over my head as she strokes and sucks me like a lollipop. I return the favour and we fall back to sleep for a while, curled around each other, sated and happy to continue hiding in our comfortable bubble beneath the duvet.

Sometime later I wake again and leave her sleeping in my bed while I check out what food I have left in the fridge (virtually none) and put the kettle on. I am now another year older and a whole lot richer.

I smile to myself as I make two coffees and saunter back into the bedroom to wake Jade. She is already awake, sitting up in the bed when I go back inside. Her hair falls messily around her shoulders and her lips are plump and swollen from where I have kissed her so much since she arrived. She smiles at me and I see a real sense of happiness in her eyes.

I hand her a cup and place the other on the bedside table and slip back into bed beside her. "Thank you," she says before blowing on the coffee and sipping it delicately. I watch her with a smile on my face and brush a strand of hair away from her shoulder running my finger across her collar bone.

"Thank *you*, Fairy Girl, for a wonderful birthday."

She shivers and closes her eyes as I continue to trail my finger up and down her collar bone and across the top of her left breast. She is holding the coffee cup tightly in both hands clearly trying not to spill any as I play with her. She opens her eyes again and takes another sip.

I leave her alone for a moment and take my own cup.

"You're most welcome. I had a lovely time."

I take a gulp of my own coffee. It is scolding hot and I burn my tongue. She laughs at me as I swear and put it back down again.

Already we are like a married couple, sitting here in bed drinking coffee late on a Sunday morning. All we need now is a copy of *The Times* and Bob sitting between us and we would be picture perfect. But we are not old and we are not married. "You did very well to survive a night out with Ash and me."

She places her coffee back on the table on her side of the

bed and then turns around to face me lying on her side with her hand propping up her head. "Jo seems very nice," she comments.

I nod and pull her to me so that she is now lying on my chest. I stroke her arm and sigh. "She is."

Jade begins to twist my nipple piercing gently making my breath hitch a little. "Is she like you and Ash?" I continue to stroke her silky skin, tiny goosebumps rising as I do. I simply moan in response, enjoying the sensation of the slight pain her fingers are creating as she continues to gently tug at the piercing. She says nothing more but as I look down at her I see she is now frowning slightly.

I stare at her for a moment wondering why she is acting a little odd. My brain finally clicks with the answer. She may be wondering if I've had sex with Jo, as well as Ash.

"Ash and I take care of her. We've been friends for a few years now. Neither of us has ever had sex with her," I say to ease the troubled look beginning to show in her eyes.

She seems surprised by this and stops twisting my piercing to look up at me. Her eyes are wide and still a little smudged with makeup. She looks adorable and very young right now. "That's nice. I wish I had someone like you to protect me when I was younger."

I kiss the top of her head. "You are still young and have me to protect you now, Jade."

She snuggles into me and sighs. "How long will I have you though, Jax?" she whispers.

I sense her unease as she lies on my chest, evidently last night's little show-and-tell experience did have more of an effect on her than she let on. "For as long as you will have me."

I mean it. I have no intentions of leaving Jade. I want her in my life. Period.

She makes no further comment to that confession.

We shower and dress a little later and I take her to a café I like not far from my flat for brunch. We sit outside and watch the city people wander by, analysing them and their lives. She makes me laugh with her observations of the city folk and I am amused at how much she sees in people from just looking at them.

I am beginning to think she may just be a little psychic: she is as good as I am at guessing people's lives. We walk for a while and I show her around Notting Hill, all the wealth and all the interesting characters. She takes it all in and seems just as at ease here as she is in her sleepy village in Wiltshire.

Back in my flat, I roll us a joint. We lie on the sofa and I flick on an old black and white movie to watch while we get stoned and enjoy the last few hours of our time together.

"I'd like to come down and visit you next weekend, if that's okay, Jade?" I ask as I pass her the joint.

She chuckles. "I thought that was a foregone conclusion, City Boy."

I smile but I feel we may need to talk about how this is going to work between us. She still has no idea I am in the middle of reinventing my life.

"I'm a foregone conclusion now, am I?" I say with a smile in my voice. She sits up a little to look at me taking a drag on the spliff and then passing it back to me. I can see a shift in her expression, a slight seriousness and guess she is most likely going to surprise me again.

"I can't imagine not having you in my life now, Jax. If it means we only get to see each other on weekends and commute between our two homes, then so be it. I sense you feel the same way and I'm happy to fit around your life. I'll take what I can when I can."

I blink at her feeling a surge of overwhelming love for her. It warms my heart and my soul instantaneously. "I'll give you what I can, when I can."

She grins, seemingly totally satisfied by my response and rests her head back down on my chest. She has absolutely no idea that I intend to give her everything I can very soon.

Chapter Thirty-Seven

Jade leaves me at seven that evening; I already miss her by half past. I call Ash, he takes a while to answer but makes me smile when he does. "Hey old man, has Jade just left?"

"She's just left."

"Figures. Otherwise, I wouldn't have heard a peep out of you for another week. Are you bored already and need a handjob?"

I laugh. "No, I don't need a handjob, Ash. But yes, regrettably, I'm bored. I'm coming over and we're going to go out for dinner."

I hear him light a cigarette and take a drag. "The thought of food is making me feel sick." I can imagine him pulling a face as he talks.

"Well, if you stopped blowing snow up your nose Ash, you might just feel a little less rough and be able to eat something."

He snorts at me. "Oh right. Mr High-and-Mighty, 'I no longer need to do drugs' because I'm in love with a sexy brunette who lives on a boat." He is only teasing me but I catch an edge of something that may just resemble a touch of jealousy in his voice. I definitely need to coddle him and make him feel really special again. He really is such a diva.

To placate him, we go to his favourite French restaurant. We sit side-by-side, my hand on his thigh under the table and with expensive wine, watch the other diners. I never usually touch him as openly in a place like this but today he needs to know he is loved as well. He pouts and sulks a little at first but softens quickly and listens, with amused interest, when I tell him about my run-in with the guy who kissed me in front of Jade.

"She took it okay then?" his eyes wide as he spoons dessert into his mouth.

"Seeing it for real must have been hard for her but yes, she took it okay."

Ash takes my hand under the table squeezing in gently. "She's fucking amazing, Jax."

I nod in agreement. "She is," I nod in agreement.

He grins at me. "Do you think she'd be up for a double-tap at some point from the pair of us?"

I laugh. "I've no idea, Ash. Early days for that I think and, to be honest, I'm not sure it would be a good idea."

He looks at me as if I'm a complete idiot. "Oh, come on, Jax. Tell me you haven't visualised it in graphic detail a million times already. I know she's a sexy little kitten with claws and would make a very delicious filling in our sandwich." There's a purr in his voice.

He's right. I have played many scenes out in my mind already with the three of us. I'm just not sure it would be a good idea; it may just change the dynamics far too much between us. I'm also very hesitant to even broach the subject so soon in our relationship. I will wait to see how things develop between us, despite Ash's obvious interest to get in on the action.

He can see I'm thinking about it though and smiles again, wiping his mouth with his napkin. "She might just surprise you," he says with a devilish grin. I take a sip of my extortionately priced wine and sigh.

"She already has, Ash. Many times."

I work another week at the practice and find that I am enjoying my work a lot more and, strangely, feeling a little sad that I will be leaving. I know I am meant to do something else now and I can't live here in the city any longer with Jade so far away. I spend nearly every night with Ash chilling and we end up having sex one night when he stays over.

I started it. I wanted it. I still need him; he knows it.

I will tell Jade if she asks me. I will not lie to her; she deserves the truth if she wants to live a life with me.

I decide to hire a car to drive down to Honey Street for the weekend. As well as seeing Jade, I want to take a tour around the area and get a real feel for the place I am planning to move to. I pick a suitably over the top Range Rover. It drives most impressively, like a jumbo jet down the motorway; smooth and powerful. It's like a great black beast bullying other cars out of the way as I loom up behind them. I drive it like it's supposed to be driven, as fast as possible, without getting tugged by the police, and delight in the feeling of having a car again, even if it's only for the weekend.

I will probably buy a car when I move down to the countryside. I will need one if I want to travel between Wiltshire and the city to see Ash. I know Jade only uses her pushbike to get around and I'm not sure if she even drives but it will be handy to have something for the future.

I arrive in Honey Street on Saturday morning and can't wait to see her again. Just as I am unloading my duffel bag from the boot, I feel a wet nose push against my hand. Bob is staring up at me and it looks like he's smiling. That makes two of us.

"What the hell is that, City Boy?"

I turn around and find her walking towards me. I look at the Range Rover and grin. "It's a car, Jade."

She's wearing black and white striped stockings with the garter belt showing, her boots and ripped and torn denim short shorts and an off-the-shoulder long-sleeved top with a picture of a unicorn on it. She looks ridiculous. And hot. Ridiculously hot. Let's not forget that.

"That's not a car Jax, it's a fashion statement. And a dick extension."

I laugh. "Well, I hope my dick doesn't need too much of an ego boost."

She sidles up to me and slides her hand down onto my crutch squeezing it gently. "No, it doesn't." She says with a grin. I grab her and kiss her hard. My way of punishing her for her tease. Bob jumps up at us, jealous as always, and she breaks away from me laughing.

We walk back to *The Water Nymph* and I smile as we pass *The Water Witch*. I give her a little nod as we do. She changed my life in many ways and I will be forever grateful to her for it. We drink coffee and smoke cigarettes on the back of the boat with Bob sitting between us. "Why did you drive down this weekend?" she asks.

"I want to have a proper look around the area, I thought we could take a drive out and was hoping you'd show me around."

She looks at me with interest. "Sure, there's some cool places around you might find interesting." I am in her hands with that one.

We leave shortly after, putting Bob in the boot of the car and he instantly flops down and falls asleep. I drive, following Jade's instructions to Avebury. She wants to show me the stone circle there and says there is a haunted pub we could have lunch in.

We put Bob on his lead and walk across to the stones that stand tall and majestic against the flat topography. There's a weird shift in my chest as we walk around as if this place really does hold magic and it's pulling on my higher senses. Jade smiles up at me as I hold her hand. "You can feel it can't you?"

I look at her with an amused smile. "Feel what?"

She stops me and puts her hand on one of the stones. "The energy here, it's very faint now but you can feel it none the less."

I laugh but humour her by putting my hand on the stone next to hers. It feels cool and rough under my palm. A strange tingle like sensation travels up my fingers as we stand there silently. I frown a little. "I know you can feel it, Jax. You've a natural ability to channel."

"I have absolutely no idea what you are talking about," I retort.

The sun suddenly breaks through from a patch of clouds and lights up the area brilliantly as if a light switch has been turned on. She smiles knowingly and we continue to walk around the stones as Bob runs between them sniffing eagerly at the new smells. The air is warm and the ground is dry and hard. We have had an amazing summer so far. I sense it probably won't last much longer.

We head to The Red Lion Inn directly across from the stone circle and order lunch. I think about what Jade has just said about me being a 'natural channel' and wonder what she means. I'm completely sceptical about those types of things. My analytical brain does not want to acknowledge that there is more to the human psyche than I already know. But Jade is opening my mind to many different things now and although I'm curious and would like to probe her more on the subject, something else more important is taking precedence in my thoughts right now. We sit outside the pub and eat our lunch, drinking lager shandy and feeding Bob titbits.

"I'm moving out of the city, Jade," I say, finally blurting out what's been on my mind all day without really thinking it through properly.

She stares at me, her eyes wide, as she takes a bite from

her baguette. "You are?" But she's smiling as if she already knew. I take a deep breath and decide there and then to put all my cards on the table.

"I've put my flat on the market and handed in my notice at work. I'd like to move closer to you so that we can be together. Properly. Not just at the weekends."

She puts her baguette back down on to the plate and wipes her mouth with a napkin. I can see the cogs whirring again. She smiles. "That's a big decision to make just like that, City Boy."

I take her hand and smile at her, my mouth suddenly very dry, as if I'm about to jump off a cliff. "Life's so very short, Jade. Before we know it, it's over. It may seem ridiculously fast and irrational to be making this decision given the amount of time we've known each other. But since meeting you my life has changed for the better and I want to spend as much of what I have left of it with you … if you'll let me."

She leans forward and kisses me on the lips. She tastes like mayonnaise and beer. "Nothing would make me happier, Jax," she says with a sigh.

I pull her into my arms and hold her for a moment, feeling the love flow between us, like a wild river that is pushing us towards the ocean so fast we have no control over it. Even if we wanted it.

"What will Ash think of this?" she says, pulling back from me but keeping her hands on my thighs.

"He wants me to be happy."

She nods slowly and then reaches down to stroke Bob as if she needs a moment to think without looking at me. "Will he be happy if you leave him alone in the city?"

I laugh. "Ash is never alone, Jade."

She bites her lip. "You need him. And he needs you, Jax. I don't want to come between you two."

I take her hand and squeeze it reassuringly. "You won't."

She continues to bite her bottom lip, deep in thought. "Where will you live? What will you do for work?"

I release her hand and reach for my Marlboro Lights. "I have my eye on a place not far from you, I'm not sure what I'll do for work yet." I keep both statements as vague as possible so that she will have absolutely no idea that I am already very close to receiving the keys for the little cottage on the canal and that I will most likely never have to work again if I handle my new wealth properly.

"Okay."

And, just like that, I feel like a huge weight has been lifted from my shoulders. She is accepting me – and all my secrets – into her life without a second thought.

She really does live each day as if it were her last. Something I also intend to do from now on.

Chapter Thirty-Eight

Returning to *The Water Nymph*, I make love to her feeling a new sense of hope and depth to our relationship. She lies with her head on my chest after, trailing her fingers across my chest. "I'd like you to meet my family, Jax." I'm surprised but honoured she would want to introduce me to them.

"Of course," I say, taking her hand and intertwining my fingers with hers.

She looks up at me with an expression of wariness. "They'll probably grill you like you're some shady gangster who's unworthy of their daughter's attention. I warn you now."

I chuckle at this statement. "I *am* unworthy of your attention but I'm not a gangster, Jade." She grins and snuggles back down onto my chest.

That evening on *The Water Nymph*, over a bottle of wine, I sneakily ask her if she has done anything about the cottage yet. I want to know if she has approached the estate agent and discovered it has been sold. She is sitting crossed-legged on the floor, wearing one of my T-shirts again. She seems to like stealing my clothes as well as my cigarettes.

"I haven't called the estate agents yet but I've spoken to my accountant and asked him if he can put my books together so that I can speak to some banks about getting a mortgage first. I don't want to go in and make an offer if I can't actually borrow any money."

I take a sip of my wine and light up. I really do need to

quit soon; I've been smoking like a chimney lately and am starting to feel it when I run in the mornings now. "I'm sure you'll be pleasantly surprised very soon, Jade," I say with a smile. She looks at me strangely for a moment then her face changes again.

"I don't suppose you'll have any problem getting another mortgage to buy a house here, seeing as you're in finance." It sounds like *she* is fishing for information but I smile smugly. She still has no idea I won't need a mortgage. I am still reluctant to tell her about my win. I don't want it to change the way she looks at me. She is clearly unimpressed with money – her comments on the car were enough to tell me so – and it may just scare her to think I can lavish her with wealth and gifts she is neither accustomed to nor wants.

"The sale of my flat will cover the cost of a new house here, Jade."

She nods slowly. "I guessed you would have a fair amount of money, City Boy," she says, laughing a little. If only she knew exactly how much a 'fair amount' was.

Instinctively, I feel that I will know when it is the right time to reveal the extent of my wealth to her and reassure her that it will change nothing between us. The love I have for this unique woman is worth more money than I could ever want anyway. It's priceless. But right now, while we are having such an open discussion, it seems the perfect opportunity to probe a little deeper. I place my wine on the table beside me and lean forward. "Money doesn't always make people happy Jade. It makes life easier for sure. But it's the connections we have in life that give us real abundance."

She raises a brow, her lips quirking upwards. "I agree. Extreme wealth can make people fearful. They fear losing it or that other people will only want to be with them because of it."

"Would you be fearful if you were in a position of

wealth?"

She laughs. "No. I'd continue living the way I do but use it wisely. Help others perhaps, but no, it wouldn't make me fearful."

We stare at each other for a moment. I take a drag on my cigarette and swallow hard before I speak. "I have a fear. One that has nothing to do with money but now seems a good enough time to be honest about it."

Her eyes grow wide as she waits for me to speak. My eyes fall to the ground for a second as I pluck up the courage to voice my true feelings.

"My life is changing quickly, Jade. These past few weeks have taken me on a new path; one I did not expect or foresee. Meeting you has changed it the most. You've given me a unique opportunity, as a bisexual man, to have the best of both worlds," I pause, shaking my head with a smile. "Well, it seems that way for now. But I'm not stupid enough to think it will always be this way. You're still young and may grow and change into someone entirely different over the next few years. The pressure of being with a man that wants a piece of every cake may take its toll on us both over time."

She continues to stare at me her expression giving nothing away as I confess my worst fears.

"But, I'm trusting, for now, that we can make this work somehow. Ash will always accept me, no matter what choices I make. He has, so far, even when it hasn't been easy. He's never complained about sharing my dick before."

She laughs but it's not filled with contempt. "Jax, I live one day at a time. I look no further into the future than that. I appreciate what life sends my way and I relish it. Whether it be money, a beautiful sunny day or a very handsome man that appears on my doorstep. I'm not being flippant. Just honest. And I appreciate your honesty." She takes my hand and kisses my knuckles tenderly.

"You have nothing to fear right now. I hope that you can begin to live like I do. One day at a time without fear for the future. Whatever that future may be. I'm very happy you are choosing to spend it with me. I accept that Ash is a big part of your life."

I stub out my cigarette and take her hands within my own leaning my head against hers. "Thank you. I know it's a lot to ask of you."

She squeezes my fingers and raises her head kissing me on the forehead. "One day at a time, Jax," she whispers, as she pulls me into her arms and gives me a hug that is filled with so much love it makes my heart thump faster.

I am more than grateful that Jade has accepted Ash in my life. And Ash seems to love her just as much as I do. But he is just indulging me for now and I know I will have to handle him carefully in the future. I will never be able to give Jade all my heart; part of it will always belong to him.

Fate decided that when I was born that it would be split in two and never be whole. Until now, I kept it dark and hidden so that it would never be broken but now I feel it splintering apart and changing colour. I can feel a sense of lightness pushing through, a type of love that I have never experienced before. I have been so accustomed to my dark, loveless world; it has taken me by surprise that I could have it any other way. Jade has given me the opportunity to really feel loved and accepted just the way I am: complicated and imperfect.

Just as the chart she plotted for me said, I now have two people in my life – two people to fulfil my every desire. The love of a man *and* the love of a woman. A love that includes both physical and emotional connections to make my broken heart feel whole and complete.

We speak no more about money, sharing partners or of any fears we may have for the future. There is only so much truth that can be spilt in one go. And after Bob's evening walk, we go back to bed, alternating between smoking joints and exploring each other. I find myself falling even deeper into her beautiful soul as we continue to discover what makes our bodies tick.

For the first time, we indulge in a little bondage together and I discover she is not averse to my slightly kinkier nature. Using her black and white stockings, I tie her to the bed and blindfold her using one of her silk scarves. Tonight, I show her the bittersweetness of using only the sense of touch and sound as I make love to her tenderly and then fuck her hard.

I love watching the way her body responds to mine: the noises she makes, the way her face changes from a look of sublime bliss to exquisite torture as I play with her like she is my personal toy. Her body is so very beautiful and she is extremely flexible. I bend and twist her into all kinds of unusual positions. I'm glad I brought a whole box of condoms with me. I'm now always prepared. Something that has definitely changed since meeting Jade. I wasn't always so careful in the past.

We fall asleep in the early hours of the morning, exhausted but blissfully happy. That night, I dream of the little white cottage and, strangely, of Ash living on *The Water Nymph* beside us. That would never ever happen and I wonder why I would dream such a thing until I realise my subconscious is just being overly greedy.

Besides, I know we would all drive each other crazy if we did live together in such a scenario. Jade would most likely run after living with Ash for longer than a week.

The demanding bastard that he is, he even invades my dreams.

Chapter Thirty-Nine

I wake up the next morning, alone in the bed. Jade is singing along to the radio in the kitchen. The smell of coffee and bacon makes my stomach growl. I pull on my shorts and wander down to the kitchen. Outside it's another warm day and the sun is shining again, the windows are open and I hear moorhens outside on the water, their distinct chatter breaking in as they float past us. Bob jumps up and greets me.

"Morning sleepyhead," she says smiling at me and cracking eggs into a saucepan, mixing them up into a frothy blend ready to scramble them just the way I like them.

"Hey, Fairy Girl," I say, scratching at my stubble and sitting down on the floor to make a joint for after breakfast. Bob flops beside me and puts his head on my leg.

"What do you want to do today?"

"I'm easy," I say, laying a large rolling paper out on her battered table to make the joint.

"Oh, I know that, City Boy. But what would you like to actually do today?"

I laugh and stroke Bob before focussing on grinding my purple haze. "I could take you out to lunch somewhere if you like."

She nods and continues to mix the eggs. "Are you trying to fatten me up, Jax?" she says walking over to me with my coffee and kissing me on the head before walking back to the hob in the kitchen.

I grin. "Maybe. It's fun working off the calories with

you."

We eat breakfast sitting on the back of her boat and I am amused to see my old friend, the swan. He glides up and sticks his head over the side, begging for his piece of bread. Bob barks at him and he hisses back.

"There's a good pub in Great Bedwyn. We could go there. They do the best roast in the area," Jade says, slipping a rasher of bacon into her mouth.

"Sounds good, how far is it from here?"

"In that beast you brought with you, not far at all," she says laughing.

I narrow my eyes at her. "You really don't like the car, do you Jade?"

She leans back against the side of the boat and sips her coffee. "It's a little … pretentious."

I smile at her and light up the spliff, I literally inhaled my plate of eggs and bacon and am ready to slip into the hazy world of stoned-ness for a while before we leave *The Nymph* for the day. "What sort of car would you buy if you could?"

"I don't need a car Jax, I have my bike to get around on."

I laugh. "But if you could, Jade, what would be your ideal runabout?"

She seems to think about this for a moment before answering me with a grin. "Probably some beaten-up, old Land Rover." I nod and take a hit on my spliff, making a note to start looking for one. "It would have to be something practical and not too precious if Bob is going to be jumping in and out the back covered in mud," she says.

"I assume you can actually drive?" I say, lying back on the cushions she has scattered over the floor and put my hand behind my head. The sky is dotted with fluffy white clouds today and they float slowly above us in strange animal-like shapes and distorted patterns.

"I can drive but I choose not to." I knew she would

probably say that the eco-hippy that she is.

We lie down together for a while, looking at the sky and enjoying the warmth of the sun on our faces. The spliff gets passed back and forth. Now suitably hazy, we shower together which results in much laughter as we both squeeze into her tiny cubicle. No wonder she visits her friend in Devizes for a proper bath.

We head out in my 'pretentious beast' with Bob in the back, sleeping on his blanket. I note that his doggy smell is already permeating the air inside the car and think that Jade is probably right: an old Land Rover would be best. Less precious and much more practical than this bad boy.

We arrive shortly after at The Cross Keys in Great Bedwyn, a little village that is cut in half by the canal. Life seems to revolve around the water here, just as it does at Honey Street, and as we walk into the pub to order our Sunday roast, I take note of the locals and the comfortable feeling of familiarity between them.

They stare at me and Jade but smile with amiable curiosity. We sit in the garden and drink a pint of shandy each. I will be driving back to London later and don't want to push it. Jade sits next to me on the wooden bench seat, her thigh pressed against mine. She is looking at me with a soft smile on her face.

"I'll speak to my parents about us visiting next weekend if you'd like?" she says, brushing my unruly hair away from my eyes. "We could go up for lunch next Sunday, take a day out to see them. You can drive us there in your dick extension."

I turn to face her and place my hand on her thigh stroking her silky soft skin with my thumb. "Sounds good. I need to impress them with the size of my assets."

She laughs then bites her bottom lip again indicating she is thinking and is, perhaps, a little nervous again. "I'll see if my brother can make it over as well, you can meet them all together, get it over with in one trip."

"Is your brother likely to grill me as well?" I quip.

She looks down at my hand on her thigh and smiles. "Oh, he's likely to threaten you at some point if he thinks you're only interested in me for sex."

I grin. "I *am* only interested in you for sex." She punches me on the arm. I turn her face to me gently making her look at me properly. "I'll be on my best behaviour and let them see that I'm head over heels for their girl."

She blinks her big blue eyes sparkling brightly. "Head over heels, eh?"

I nod licking my lips slowly. I want to say that I am head over heels in love with her but it still feels too soon. The moment of tenderness is broken when the server arrives with two big plates of roast beef with all the trimmings. Bob jumps up and starts sniffing with avid interest.

It's after we finish our lunch – which is exactly as Jade said it would be, delicious – and we're sitting in the garden when she surprises me again.

"You don't really work in finance, do you, Jax?" It's completely out of the blue. I almost jolt in shock as she stares at me daring me to deny the truth. I take a long slow drag on my cigarette before answering.

"What makes you say that?"

She grins slyly. "I did a little stalking on the internet this week."

I raise a brow, my heart starting to thump in my chest as I wonder what she found out about me. How did she find my last name? I haven't mentioned it to her. Maybe she opened my wallet? It's been sitting on the counter a few times. I am listed on the web as a psychologist at my practice. It is all there for the world to see and find me if they wish to seek help.

“I see.” I’m waiting for her to tell me I am a big fat liar and she finds it either amusing or frustrating that I have kept my job a secret up until now.

“I knew you were lying to me the first time you told me you worked in finance. It didn’t quite fit who you were. Unravelling people’s problems and analysing them seems more appropriate for you.”

I am flabbergasted, she had me sussed from day one. Not that I’m surprised, this girl is far too clever to be fooled by my bullshit. “And how do you feel about the fact that I psychoanalyse people for a living?”

She sighs heavily and flicks her ash into the ashtray flippantly. “I feel the same as I did before I found out, Jax. I don’t judge people on what they do for a living, I judge them on how they conduct themselves in their lives.”

I laugh. “I’m fucked then.”

She laughs with me and nudges my shoulder with hers. “You could be a dustman and I wouldn’t give a shit, City Boy.”

I snort a laugh at that one. “I was never destined to pick up rubbish, Jade.”

She stares at me again, her eyes wandering across my features longingly and runs her finger across my lip, making me shiver. “No, you most certainly were not.”

We leave The Cross Keys and take Bob for a walk along the towpath. It is a pretty place, dotted with cosy cottages and barges along the canal bank that all fit into the country water life I am beginning to love more and more. We sit on the bench next to the lock for a while gongoozling as a boat rises in the water as its owner opens the gates and lets the water flood in to take him to the next level on the canal.

I feel full and content. We leave the village shortly after four and I know I don’t have much time left with my girl before I head back to London. As usual, I don’t want to go but it won't be long before I can shut the door on my life in the city permanently and start this new adventure. We spend the remaining time in bed. It's probably just as well I am only seeing her on the weekends. Her body will be bruised and battered from all the demands I am making on it right now.

We part ways in the early evening, saying nothing to each other as we embrace in the car park. We speak with our mouths joined in a slow sensual kiss. I slide into the Range Rover and spin it around without looking in the rear-view mirror. I never want to see her walk away from me. I arrive back at my flat by nine feeling happy but twitchy.

I take a shower and smoke another joint before flopping back into my cold and empty bed. My mind is spinning with all the thoughts of what is happening in my life right now. It takes me a staggeringly long time to fall asleep without Jade beside me.

Something I hope won't be a regular occurrence for much longer.

Chapter Forty

The next day I do something very out of character. It's Monday and I walk to the corner shop where I bought my winning lottery ticket from and buy the last pack of Marlboro Lights I intend to smoke. I have decided it is finally time to quit.

I know I will most likely cave by the end of day one but I am determined to keep myself alive now instead of living with a death wish. I savour each cigarette, telling myself as I do that it will be good for me to stop. I wonder how Jade will cope without her complimentary cigarettes when I go back down to visit her next weekend.

By Tuesday evening I have been to the pharmacy and brought some nicotine patches. I stick two on my upper arm just to be sure I get my fix and roll a joint. Neat. No tobacco. I'm not willing to give up the weed, that would just be pushing things too far. I sit on my sofa and take quick hits on the blunt and within five minutes I'm grinning like the Cheshire cat in *Alice In Wonderland*. That's the way to do it.

Ash comes over on Wednesday evening with a takeaway. "I'm taking you to Heaven on Saturday night, Jax. Make sure you're ready by eleven," he says to me as I dish up the Indian takeaway he has brought over for us. He lounges on my sofa like Cleopatra, a glass of wine in his hand.

"I can't, Ash. I'm heading back to Honey Street to see Jade again. She's taking me to Somerset to meet her family on Sunday."

Ash spits wine all down the front of his shirt. "You're fucking what?"

I laugh grabbing some cutlery from the drawer. "You heard me, Ash."

He stands up and marches over to me, his energy bristling. I know he's as angry as a wasp's nest poked with a stick. "For fuck's sake, Jax. You've spent every weekend down there since you met her, don't you think she could do with a break from your dick for just one weekend before you disappear from my life altogether."

Oh, here we go.

I stop what I am doing and look at him standing there like a sulky Adonis and give him a sympathetic smile. "Ash, I'm not disappearing from your life, you know I would never do that to you. It's just one more weekend, then I'll be all yours the weekend after. We can go to Heaven then."

He pouts at me and pulls his plate off the counter, heading back to the sofa with a stomp. "I'll go without you then," he sulks as he spoons chicken tikka into his mouth. I just continue to smile at him and switch the TV on. He usually gets his way with me no matter what. It might just do him some good to find I am less compliant than normal.

I arrange for a brand-new mobile phone to be couriered to Jade on Thursday, with my number already programmed in. I send it to *The Water Nymph* care of The Barge Inn and hope they get someone to deliver it to her. I want to be able to speak to her when we are not together. I am turning into a grumpy bastard without her close by. It may also be because I haven't smoked a cigarette since Tuesday and the patches just don't seem to be hitting the spot. I'm determined, however, to keep on this path as I can already feel the difference when I'm running in the mornings before work.

I sent a note with the phone. *Now we can have phone sex, Fairy Girl*. She will, no doubt, grin at that suggestion.

Friday morning, I find a text on my phone from Jade, *'I am sitting on the front of my boat naked and thinking about you, City Boy. See you tomorrow xx'*. My dick twitches eagerly, even though I am just walking into the office for the day and can't do a thing about it until later.

After her naughty text, I want to get in the car and drive down to see her tonight but haven't arranged to pick up a car until tomorrow morning. I call Ash after I finish work and he tells me he is going out with Jo tonight to some new restaurant in Covent Garden. I decline his offer of joining them and opt instead for my neat weed joint and some porn. I don't want to get too loaded tonight if I'm driving early tomorrow. By midnight my brain is a little fried and I am bored with looking at people having sex when I am not. I call Jade. She picks up after two rings.

"Hey, City Boy. Are you bored with watching porn and wanted some real action down the phone with me?"

I laugh, she seems to know me very well now. "I always want real action with you, Fairy Girl," I reply with a growl. I hear her breath catch and I sit back further in my chair stroking my chin with a salacious smile.

"Thank you for the phone, by the way, I've already stuck some sequins on it so it doesn't look quite so boring."

I take a hit on my joint and cough as it hits the back of my throat. "Can you put sequins on your nipples for me tomorrow when I arrive?"

She laughs and the conversation turns decidedly dirty. I am a hopeless pervert. Some things never change.

Standing in the bathroom and brushing my teeth, I think about my conversation with Jade. There's a massive smile on my face. She really is a very naughty fairy. I am just about to slip into bed when I hear someone knocking, or rather banging, on the front door. My entire body begins to tingle as the hairs on my forearms rise. No one should be knocking on my door this late at night, it's gone one and Ash would have just let himself in with his key if it were him.

I grab a pair of boxer shorts and stumble about as I try to pull them up quickly while heading to the front door. I reach for the baseball bat tucked behind the table by the doorway as I look through the peephole. Call me paranoid but it's always there. Just in case.

I am greeted by the sight of a petite blonde who is staring up at me with a saucy grin on her face. Fuck. This is the last thing I want the night before I head back to see Jade. As if she can see me standing there on the other side of the door contemplating whether to open it, she stands up on her tiptoes and peers through the hole banging her knuckles against it again just for good measure.

"Jax! I know you're there, open the fucking door!"

She is smiling but I can see the frustration in her eyes and know that if I don't open the 'fucking' door she will continue to keep bashing it until she wakes all my neighbours up. Not good on any level in this fancy block of flats that only houses respectable citizens. Unlike myself.

Placing the bat back behind the table I open the door, the keychain in place. She steps forward grinning and places her hand on the door frame clearly expecting me to open the door fully.

"Samantha," I say, displeasure dripping from my tone.

She frowns a little, looking confused as to why I have not let her in immediately and tilts her head to one side, her brown eyes growing wide as she sees the keychain. "Why's the chain on, Jax?"

I let out a sigh wishing she would just fuck off. "It's one in the morning, Sam, this isn't a good time. And how the fuck did you get in the front door without buzzing?"

She lets out a low whining sound that immediately annoys the shit out of me before she begins to speak. "I must have pressed the wrong buzzer, someone let me in anyway. Why haven't you returned any of my calls, Jax? You told me you'd call me, that we'd meet up again. But I've not heard a thing from you. That's just rude and mean."

Two thoughts instantaneously pop into my head. First, it was a big mistake to fuck this woman more than once. Second, it was an even bigger mistake to bring her back to my flat the second time we did fuck.

I vaguely remember manipulating her into some of the perhaps riskier sexual bondage acts I like by promising her I would call her again. We were both as high as kites on a particularly good ecstasy pill and, regrettably, I was too engrossed in her *assets* at the time to catch any indication she was a potential stalker. I'm amazed I still remember her name.

She licks her top lip slowly then pouts before sucking in her mouth and then releasing her lush lips in a loud pop as if she is thinking about what to do next. Probably with my dick.

"It's Friday night, Jax. The night's still young. Please, let me in," she whimpers in a very irritating tone. Oh God, now she is pleading with me. No doubt she had her finger pressed on one of my poor neighbours' buzzer for so long they let her in just to shut her up.

This situation could quickly get out of control if I continue to hold her at arm's length with the chain still in place on my door. Her grin returns when I do finally open the door. Instantly I regret it as she stumbles through, showing me that she is clearly drunk. She is wearing a long black coat and stiletto heels that are so high they are adding at least six inches to her tiny frame. Fuck-me heels!

Pushing my hands into the back of my hair and interlinking my fingers at the back of my neck, I watch her as she flops down onto my couch her hair falling across her face for a second before she regains her composure and flicks it back over her shoulder and crosses her legs. I get a flash of creamy white skin and little else. It looks like she is possibly naked except for the coat and heels.

This is not how I envisioned my Friday night ending. And especially not with her.

Chapter Forty-One

Samantha was, the time I first met her, a very appealing plaything. Pretty and petite, with amazing tits and a mouth that could suck like a vacuum cleaner. Easily charmed and very compliant in the bedroom, she was an easy conquest. Plus, she reminded me of my first ever love, the kind of puppy love you have at sixteen.

That girl was Tina. She found her way into my heart in a way I had never experienced before. I knew, very quickly however, that I would never be good enough, or normal enough, to pursue the tender love we shared at that naïve age. Tina was heartbroken when I called off our relationship. It was the first time in my life I had allowed someone into my heart and it broke us both when I finally accepted that I could never give her what she wanted: complete monogamy and a 'normal' life.

Samantha had managed to hold my attention longer than normal – being a doppelganger of Tina who I still held some regret for. Ash and I enjoyed a night with Samantha together that first time we met; I made the stupid mistake of enjoying her two more times without Ash. Something I never usually do, for exactly the predicament I am now in. They always want more.

Now inside my flat again, she leans back into the sofa and places her arms over the cushions scattered across the leather couch, giving me an open invitation to join her. Despite the fact it is so late – and I have just finished a very saucy phone call with the young woman I am very much involved with – I feel a jolt of excitement in my lower regions. The woman before me sees it in my eyes and leans her head back slightly opening her mouth a little before sliding one of her hands inside her coat where she begins to slowly release the buttons.

I know I'm in trouble as she slips the coat open and reveals her bare chest to me, one of her perfectly manicured fingernails trailing across her hardened nipple. "We had some good times together before, Jax. I thought we'd have some more fun tonight."

I stand and watch her as she plays with her nipple wishing that my past actions had not decided to catch up with me, tonight of all nights.

Part of me almost wants to just dive in and just take advantage of the free booty call. But the other part of me, the new Jax that has found something special, is punching me in the nuts in frustration. Why would I even want to go there when I have the most amazing woman waiting for me in the countryside?

Because I am greedy, selfish and a brilliant liar.

I could lie to Jade and pretend this never happened. She would never know. As I walk towards Samantha, who is now taking my steps towards her as a green light and sliding her hand down towards her black silk underwear, I feel something bubble up inside of me. Contempt. Both for her and for myself.

This is how she sees me: as a piece of meat that will fuck her so hard, she won't be able to sit down for a day after. I stop inches from her and crouch down slowly so that my face is directly in line with her crutch. She lifts the hand that was about to slip inside her underwear and places it on my cheek. Her fingers are warm but the action is strangely cold. Predictable.

We could so easily just fall into what we have done in the past: hours of mindless fucking.

I place my hand on hers and remove it slowly without saying a word. I stand again and pull her up with me where she staggers a little on her heels, her coat slipping down her arms and falling at her back. She stares up at me, her chest rising and falling rapidly as she waits for my next move. Her pupils begin to dilate confirming her growing excitement. I have no doubt she is anticipating my mouth against her own in a ferocious battle of lips and tongue any second.

I have every intention of throwing her out my front door with a scowl and a few choice words thrown in for good measure.

That is what I intend to do. That is the right thing to do. But something else happens instead.

As I open my mouth, to tell her she was nothing but a distraction in the past and I want nothing more to do with her, a cold, uninvited voice inside my head interrupts and stops me in my tracks.

Take her, you idiot! You know you're weak … you know you're afraid of committing to anyone but yourself. Do you really want to change your life after meeting a girl in the countryside that you hardly know? My inner dialogue chastises me. *Go on. I dare you. It's just a quick taste. Just one more time before you turn into a complete pussy.* I recognise this voice, it's 'old Jackson'. He would never hesitate to grab an opportunity like this and has decided to rear his ugly head and give me a ball slap.

My eyes wander across Samantha's face as I consider my inner demon's goading. While I hesitate, battling with myself and my conflicting thoughts, she steps closer to me and presses her body against mine. The warmth of her ample chest without the barrier of clothing sends an instant signal to my dick and he springs into action. The arousal from the call I took with Jade floods through my system again. It can't differentiate between her and the woman currently in my grip.

"What are you waiting for Jax?" Sam hums low in her throat. Her eyes narrow as she pulls her arm from my grip and reaches down into her coat pocket. She pulls out a condom and slips it into my hand. Tilting her head to one side she flashes me a sexy grin and thrusts her hips into my erection.

An image of Jade flashes into my mind again and I try to fight against what is unfolding. I try for exactly five seconds and then fail. My basic, primal needs, mixed with my fear of falling too far and too fast for the girl who has captivated me, turn me into the old creature of habit. The one that will just take what is being offered to him.

My inner demon growls in victory. He knows he's won. He knows me. Full Stop.

I spin her around so that she's facing away from me and dive in, losing myself fully in the blurred lines of what I am now doing on autopilot. It's ridiculously fast, brutal – without emotion. A simple transaction between two people that results in one thing and one thing only. A quick orgasm followed by an instant sense of guilt and impending doom.

With the act completed, I step away and turn my back to her. Instantly dismissing her. I can hear her panting as she watches me stalk to my kitchen where I can grab a bottle of water before going back to bed.

She is expecting another round, that this is just the interval. I'm usually a sure thing with that. But not tonight. I turn one last time to face her before I switch off the kitchen light and head down my hallway to my bedroom. "Show's over, Sam. Make sure you shut the door properly on your way out," I say as she continues to stare at me in shock, her arms still braced against my sofa.

She gives me an incredulous look; totally sober now, I've made it perfectly clear I'm done. She stands, grabs her coat from the floor and shoves her arms into the sleeves, pulling the belt around her waist with a vicious snap.

"Fuck you, Jackson! You're nothing but a player and a tease." I hear her shout as she stomps towards the front door. It slams behind her as she leaves. I hope she hasn't woken up my neighbours. Again.

The terrible thing about the whole situation is I feel a surge of power flow through me as I go back into my bedroom and shut the door.

Being a complete bastard is still such a thrill.

Chapter Forty-Two

It's Saturday morning and I throw my duffel and suit bag into the back of the Range Rover and work out that I have almost completed my notice period at work. In another week I will be free to do exactly as I please. The thought makes me both happy and sad.

I turn up the music as I drive down the motorway towards Jade and a weekend of bliss, smiling as the bass vibrates up my legs. Last night's strange turn of events gave me the answer I was looking for. Physical release without emotion is no longer on my agenda. It is soulless and toxic.

Despite the niggling guilt that I have effectively cheated on Jade before I've even started a real relationship with her, I am pleased that I can at least recognise how much damage I was causing my own emotional state in behaving that way for so long. I may have failed the test of remaining faithful to Jade but without tapping into my old self, the Jackson Doyle that was cold and calculated and did not feel emotion, I would be none the wiser as to what I really wanted.

Even if it was at Samantha's expense. Hopefully, she has also learnt something positive from that experience.

Jade would not approve, I'm sure, but she doesn't need to know that I played the bastard card last night. Something I never intend to do with her. That part of my character needs to stay firmly locked away and only let free in extreme circumstances from now on. For preservation purposes only.

What happened last night will remain a secret. No one else needs to know. Not even Ash. It's in the past. Done. Over.

I'm a little nervous about meeting Jade's family on Sunday but know it is important to her. I just hope they don't see through my carefully constructed walls and see that I am a dark and deadly predator that has just swept up their precious daughter and stolen her away from any kind of 'normal' life they may have wished for her. Not that she has been living a particularly 'normal' life so far by the looks of things. But none the less, this is going to be a key event if we are to continue down this path together.

I put my foot down to arrive in good time. When I do step down into *The Water Nymph* that morning Jade is naked and wearing diamond sequins on her nipples. The perfect welcome home present.

We spend the whole day laughing and doing what we do best: ignoring the outside world and staying hidden within our bubble. We walk Bob and hold hands. We eat when we are hungry and drink when we are thirsty. Jade makes me laugh when I tell her I have quit smoking cigarettes and that I am only smoking weed neat from now on.

"Good. I only smoke when I'm around you anyway, City Boy. The bad influence that you are." She tells me she has always been a social smoker anyway, until I came along. I wish I had her discipline but the patches seem to be working a little better now and it is getting easier.

It rains on Saturday night and we sit in bed and listen to it pounding on the roof while we smoke my haze from her wooden pipe and drink hot chocolate with marshmallows. There is something quite sublime about listening to the rain hitting the metal on the roof of a boat. It's as if you are so close to nature you can really feel her in the rawest way. The sounds, the smells, everything is heightened; it's almost dream-like.

I feel as if I am in a permanent dream right now. The money. The girl. The contentment.

It all seems just a little too perfect and, as Jade slips down and wraps her mouth around me again, I have the strangest thought that it seems all too good to be true and that at any moment it will change. Perhaps more ghastly playthings from my past will reappear to fuck it up.

The thought disappears as she takes me in her mouth and shows me just how lucky I am right now.

We are up early on Sunday and I dress in dark jeans and a smart but casual shirt. Jade laughs at me as I get ready. "Seriously, Jax. You don't need to dress up to meet my family, they'll love you however you dress."

I tie the top part of my hair back and splash on some Calvin Klein. "I understand how this works Jade, if I turn up in my Metallica T-shirt and Doc Martin boots, they won't give me the time of day."

She just laughs at me and dresses suitably Jade in a funky tie-dyed mini dress in baby pink with her biker boots. She braids her hair and spikes the top section just the way I like it.

I no longer need big busty blondes when I have the most beautiful girl in the world on my arm. With her wrists covered in bangles and bracelets, as usual, she grabs a red scarf – which looks like it has seen better days – throwing it around her neck to finish her look. I will buy her expensive silk scarves from now on, if she will allow me.

We put Bob in the back of the car, on his blanket. Jade gave him a tiny piece of hashish with his breakfast again so that knocks him out for the journey. She says she doesn't want him to be sick all over the back of the hire car; secretly, I think she wants him to do just that. We leave Honey Street heading to Somerset with the sound of drum and bass playing on the stereo.

An hour and a half later, we are driving down a country lane and my heart is thumping in my chest. I feel like it might be me who vomits, not Bob. Jade grins at me, loving my discomfort. Her amusement at my obvious nervous anticipation rolling off her in waves of delight. She directs me to a turn off that leads to a set of large gates with the sign to *Folly Farm* nailed on the outside. I take a deep breath before putting my foot down slowly on the accelerator and gliding inside.

The farm is sprawled out before us, with horses in the fields and a beautiful country farmhouse sitting in a dip in the landscape. A Harley Davidson is parked outside and two other cars. One is a beaten-up Land Rover and the other a top of the range BMW.

She is tapping her foot now – from excitement or nerves, I am not entirely sure. Her eyes are sparkling and she is biting her bottom lip. I pull up beside the Harley and put my hand on her thigh to stop it tapping. "Ready, Fairy Girl?" I ask her, fixing my face with a false grin.

She places her hand over mine and smiles. "Are you?"

"Hell no." She just laughs.

As we are stepping out of the car, the door to the farmhouse opens and her parents emerge. They are a handsome couple in their early to mid-fifties by the looks of things. Jade's mother is stunning and has the same ebony black hair as Jade. Her father is tall and slim and equally as impressive in his looks, he grins at Jade as she runs up to him and flings her arms around his waist. She is clearly a Daddy's girl.

I stand back for a moment feeling completely out of my depth. I have never, in my entire life, been in this situation before and I am suddenly reduced to feeling like a teenage boy intimidated by the parents of his girl. Jade's mother walks towards me smiling. "You must be Jax." I smile back and am a little shocked when she steps closer and kisses me on both cheeks while gripping my hands.

She looks me up and down, giving me the once over, her lips twitching as if she is suppressing the need to laugh. I try not to break out in a sweat at her scrutiny. "Well, you really are *very* handsome. Our little girl failed to tell me that piece of information," she says with a wry smile. I laugh looking away for a second as I run my hand across my jaw feeling slightly awkward at her comment.

Jade has finally extracted herself from her father and is holding his hand leading him over to me. "Jax, this is my father, Michael, and my mother, Maria." I hold out my hand to her father and he takes it in a firm grip giving it a good hard shake. We are already jostling for the supreme male position; I think with a repressed smirk.

"I'll get Bob out of the car," Jade says, leaving me standing with her parents.

I try not to fidget and show how uncomfortable I am with this situation. "It's a pleasure to meet you both," I say, putting on my best smile. The one without my shark's teeth showing. Maria smiles and slips her arm into mine pulling me towards the house.

"I hope you had a good journey here; the traffic can be a pig sometimes on a Sunday," she says to me amiably. Michael gives me an 'I'm not sure about you yet' smile and follows Jade to help her with Bob who is probably still comatose in the boot.

Maria leads me into the house, which is just as beautiful on the inside as it is on the outside. It has a warm and cosy air about it and is filled with comfortable furnishings and, by the looks of things, a lot of antiques. I am suitably impressed.

Inside, we are greeted by two small scruffy dogs and a

Labrador, who all proceed to try and lick me clean. I am getting used to fur babies now, after spending time with Bob, and pet and fuss them while Maria tries to pull them off me.

I hear Jade step inside the house with her father, they are talking quietly and I am guessing he is already giving her a hard time about me. Bob joins the melee of dogs and they all bound off barking and yapping like a wild pack of wolves, out into the kitchen, then disappearing through the back door leading out to a large garden. He clearly knows them all very well and is off to play.

I'd go with him if I could get away with it.

Maria guides me into the large kitchen, a huge wooden table to one side looking out over the garden and an island in the middle with pots and pans hanging over the top on a wooden frame hanging from the ceiling. It is decorated with hops and wild dried flowers and looks like something out of the *Country Life Magazine*. "Sit, Jax, please. You must be a little tired after the drive. What would you like to drink?"

Jade is suddenly beside me and takes my hand, squeezing it gently. "I'd love a coffee thank you," I say. Jade pulls out one of the chairs sitting flush to the island and indicates I should sit. I do so like a good little boyfriend, smiling at her appreciatively, as she plonks herself next to me and puts her hand possessively on my thigh.

I can literally feel her father's eyes boring into the back of my head as she does. Oh, this is going to be a lot of fun. *Not.*

Maria starts to make us all a drink. Her father goes to the fridge and pulls himself out a beer. "Wouldn't you rather a beer, Jax?" he asks me as if it's a trick question and he is trying to see whether I will trip up and show my true colours.

"I'm good for now, thanks," I say.

Jade is trying not to laugh and I visualise spanking her

hard later for that. "Dad, he's driving. Stop trying to ply him with booze already." Her father sniffs but smiles and opens the beer before grabbing a glass to pour it into.

"Where's Ben?" Jade asks. This must be her brother.

"He'll be back in a minute, sweetheart. He's just in the paddock with Justin, looking at the new mare we brought last week."

I wonder who Justin is and whether her brother will be giving me the same once over her father is currently doing. I try my best to relax and remember I am the one usually in control. I can smell something divine coming from the range cooker and wonder what we are having for lunch. If Jade's mother taught her how to cook so well, I'm guessing it will be delicious.

We all head outside at Jade's suggestion, as the weather is dry and warm again and we settle at a large table. The pack of dogs, including Bob, come back from their romp and lie down beside us, heads resting on their paws ready for a snooze. Maria has set the coffee and some water on the table and is pouring for us all. Michael is sitting opposite Jade and me. He is definitely checking me out, as any father would, trying to work out if I'm a villain or my intentions towards his daughter are actually good. I'm probably his worst fucking nightmare.

Jade has chosen to sit on my lap, much to my surprise and discomfort, and is doing her best to wind her father up it seems, toying with my hair and whispering naughty things into my ear. We have only been here twenty minutes and she is already playing with fire. Her mother seems to have no problem with her daughter's behaviour and I wonder if that is where Jade gets her mischievous and sassy streak from. Michael, on the other hand, is gripping his beer as if he will shatter the glass at any second.

It both amuses me and worries me a little. I'm not sure

what she is hoping to achieve. But she seems to be enjoying herself, the little vixen that she is.

"Hey there, little sis. Come and give your bro a hug." A guy in his mid-twenties appears from around the corner of the farmhouse. He is about the same height as his father but his hair is much lighter than Maria's and Jade's. He has a cute and friendly face and, without even thinking about what I am doing, I check him out and note that he is very fit indeed. Good genes seem to run in this family.

Jade jumps off my lap and into her brother's arms, where he swings her around and around until she shrieks at him to stop. I am smiling as I watch them. I can tell they are very close. And I have already deduced that she talks to her brother a lot more than she does her parents, who are most likely clueless as to what Jade really gets up to in Wiltshire. Thank God.

He puts her down and walks over to me and grins. "So, you're the fiend that has stolen my sister's heart and turned it into mush then?"

I like him instantly and smile at him. "I assume I am, yes."

Jade glares at him and I laugh, standing so that I can shake his hand. He ignores my outstretched hand and grabs me into a bear hug instead, slapping me on the back heartily. I like him even more now. "Good to meet you at last, Jax. Don't let the old man freak you out today, he's just miffed Jade's found another man to give all her attention to," he says with a chuckle.

Everyone – except Michael – laughs at that comment.

We drink our coffee and then go back inside for the lunch Maria has prepared for us. A hearty roast lamb dinner with all the trimmings. I am starting to feel less anxious as a warm and comfortable conversation starts up around the table. This family are clearly unique in the way they interact with each other. They are extremely close in many ways but seem to give each other the space they all need. Especially Jade. Her father asks me what I do for a living and I tell him the truth. He seems very surprised by my response and I chalk up a point to me for this reaction.

I do like to surprise people. It gives me a sadistic little kick.

I don't tell him, however, that I will no longer be employed in a week and that, if I don't want to, I will no longer have to work. I am happy that Jade says nothing about my impending unemployment or the fact that I am intending to move closer to her very soon. She still has no idea how close that will be.

After dinner, Jade takes my hand under the table and places it on her thigh making me jump a little as she slides it up her skirt. "I'm going to take Jax over to see the horses, Dad. Ben, do you want to come with us?"

"Sure thing, sis."

Michael is wiping his mouth with his napkin, still looking a little uneasy about the fact Jade is clearly stating a big claim on me and is not afraid to show her affection, even if it is under the table. I am sure he knows I currently have my hand very close to his daughter's underwear.

I release my hold on her upper thigh and stand up. "Would you like any help clearing up, Maria?" I ask like the perfect guest.

She smiles at me and shakes her head. "No, of course not, Jax. You are our guest today. Go out to the paddock with Jade and Ben. Michael will help me with the dishes." I know I am digging myself a big hole here but – fuck it. I am perversely starting to enjoy this little game with the alpha male of the house.

I head out with Jade holding my hand and her brother beside us. Bob is following us with his new pack trailing behind. I feel like the pied piper. "You're being very touchy-feely in front of your father today, Jade," I whisper into her ear as we walk.

She chuckles. "It annoys the fuck out of my Dad when I touch you and I like to see him squirm," she whispers back to me. I laugh at her brazenness and find myself grinning as we walk across the garden and then out to the paddocks at the back of the farmhouse.

"Do you ride, Jax?" Ben asks as we reach an area with several stables and farm machinery scattered around.

I shake my head surveying the area. "No. I've always been a city boy, never had the opportunity."

Ben grins at me. "Fancy a go?"

I look across the paddock at the horses chewing grass and flicking their tails in a vain attempt to remove the flies from around them. "I think it would be best if I didn't," I say.

Jade laughs. "Scaredy cat," she teases me. Ben smiles as he opens one of the stable doors and the head of a large grey horse pops out.

"Jade's an excellent rider, she could teach you if you come down more regularly."

I turn and look at her raising a brow. "Is she now?" She blushes slightly and I am amused at her reaction. Another little secret she has kept from me that has now been revealed, although it doesn't surprise me that much. She certainly knows how to ride me very well indeed.

Ben leads the horse out into the courtyard and lets me stroke him, telling me he is an Andalusian and very docile. He starts to saddle him up and then opens another stable, leading out a similar, but slightly shorter, horse.

"Fancy a quick gallop, sis?"

She nods eagerly and I am delighted to see her so animated. In fact, I find myself feeling aroused at the thought of her astride a horse and cantering off down the field. They laugh and joke as they start to put on the horses' tack and get ready for their ride. I stand with Bob and watch them, taking in the way they talk to each other, teasing and joking with a familiarity I have never known.

I lost my parents the day I walked out of my home at the tender age of seventeen and never had any siblings. It makes me feel a little strange for a second until I brush it off and regain my emotional balance once more.

Ben finds them both a riding hat and jumps up on his Andalusian like a graceful athlete. Jade faces me as she tightens the strap of her riding hat under her chin. "We won't be long, City Boy. Take a wander around with the pack." She grins at me surrounded by Bob and his friends, their tails all wagging as if they know I am now their walking master.

"No problem," I say and she leans in to kiss me quickly on the mouth before jumping up on her horse like a nimble cat. I get a flash of her red underwear as she mounts the horse and my mouth starts to salivate. Neither she, nor Ben, are wearing the clothes you normally see riders in, but they look so at home on their horses it makes me a little envious for a moment.

Jade winks at me and then kicks her horse with her biker boots and is off.

I watch her and her brother take off across the field like two crazy Native Americans shouting and whooping at each other. I laugh and amble across the courtyard with my new friends in tow. I walk for a while across the paddocks and see Jade and Ben in the distance, running wild and free with their horses. I feel a real sense of happiness and contentment as I watch them until I feel a presence behind me and it makes me jump instinctively as if I am about to be attacked.

"My daughter, as you can see, is a very free spirit, Jax,"

Michael has crept up on me like a ninja and is standing next to me now with a tumbler in his hand. I turn to face him and give him a slight smile.

"Yes, she is." He takes a sip of his drink – it smells like whisky – and narrows his eyes slightly.

The *talk* is coming.

"Jade has been through a lot in her life already, Jax, and is actually very vulnerable, despite her bravado and seemingly unbreakable outer shell. In fact, we are very lucky to still have her with us at all," he says. I know he is referring to her difficult journey with cancer and turn to face him and nod slowly.

"I have no intentions of hurting your daughter, Michael."

He sighs heavily and looks out across the field at his daughter and son who are now cantering back towards us in a plume of dust. "I have never seen her behave like this with any other man, Jax. She clearly has strong feelings for you." I wait for the threat to come. He looks back at me and I see the shift in his eyes, the love and fierce protectiveness surface like a lion about to roar. "I will seek you out and make you wish your life was not worth living if you break her heart and I will have no remorse in doing so. Do I make myself clear?"

I try not to laugh. "Absolutely," I say in the most serious voice I can muster.

He nods slowly and I know he feels like he has just regained his position as alpha again. "Good. Now, let's get you a proper drink before you have to go back to that bloody boat she insists on living in." I laugh as he thumps me on the back and we walk slowly back to the house. The dogs following happily behind us.

We return to the house where Michael pours me a finger of whisky as if we have just sealed a deal and are celebrating the fact. I allow him this luxury and wait for Jade and her brother to return from their ride. Maria asks me how I like the boat life and if it is something I would think about doing permanently in the future. She is also fishing to see how serious I am about Jade.

"I love the outdoor life the boat gives but I think it would be a little more difficult in the winter," I say to her sipping my whisky and trying to hide a grimace – it's not my favourite drink at all.

She smiles and nods. "It is a lovely way to live and suits Jade very well. She prefers the privacy and freedom it gives her." She pauses her face becoming a little pinched. "But I do worry about her sometimes, there all alone. Especially in the winter."

I place the whisky down; I intend not to drink it all as I am driving us back. "She seems very resilient, Maria. From the short time I've known your daughter, I know she can take care of herself very well." Michael makes a snorting sound as if he disagrees but says nothing. Maria nods and takes my hand making me feel a little uncomfortable as she stares into my eyes with an imploring look on her face.

"And she has you to take care of her now, Jax." Before I can answer that, Jade and her brother burst through the back door laughing loudly. Close shave, thank God.

Jade and I leave shortly after and I am still laughing to myself at how Ben discretely pulled me to one side as Jade loaded Bob into the car and told me that 'I'd better not break her heart, or he will break my legs'. I have been threatened by both men of the house and it is making me feel a lot happier knowing they both care about her enough to do such a thing. It means they love her enough to pick up the pieces if I do 'fuck this up' and break her heart.

I have every intention of doing the exact opposite – proving them both wrong. But I am no fool and know that, with the life I am about to pull Jade into, it may be a possibility at some point.

I hope and pray that day never comes.

Chapter Forty-Three

We are just pulling into the car park of The Barge Inn when my phone rings. Grabbing it from the holder on the dash I press answer before I check the caller ID. The sound that erupts from the speaker as I place it to my ear makes my whole body go rigid and the hairs on the back of my neck rise in fear.

It's Jo and she is crying hysterically.

Jade looks at me, her eyes growing wide at the horrendous sound my friend is making down the phone. Slamming my foot on the brake we skid on the gravel for a second before coming to a halt.

"Jo? What's happened? Calm down honey, I can't understand you." She is sobbing uncontrollably and takes a while to make any sense whatsoever. What she does say next makes my blood run cold.

"Jax. You have to get back here right now. It's Ash. Someone beat him up so badly he's in intensive care. They've put him into a coma to try and stop the swelling in his brain." She hiccups between sobs.

And just like that my whole world comes tumbling down, as if a tower made from stone has been shattered above me and is suddenly falling straight on top of me, crushing me beneath the debris.

Everything else becomes irrelevant once I end the call with Jo and literally run to collect my things from *The Nymph*. My focus is now on one thing and one thing only.

Getting to Ash as fast as I can.

"I'm coming with you," Jade says as I toss my duffel bag into the boot of the Range Rover. I am shaking from head to toe.

"No, Jade. Stay here. I'll call you when I know what's happening."

She grabs my arm trying to force me to stop what I am doing and look at her. "Jax, you need me. You both need me."

I turn and look at her, trying not to lose it completely. "I need to see him, alone. Please understand this. I'll call you when I can."

Jade lets go of my arm and her eyes go suddenly dark and cold. She nods once and steps back from me. I see something flash across her face but I am too focussed on Ash to even worry about what it could mean right now.

After a quick kiss on her forehead, I slip back into the driver's seat and watch her in the rear-view mirror. She stands and watches me leave, her face in shadow and Bob by her side. I feel like I may have just broken something between us but I don't know how to deal with it right now.

I drive like a mad man back to London and to the hospital, beating myself up. I was not there for him; I was with Jade. He must have gone to Heaven last night and got himself into trouble. I hit the steering wheel repeatedly with the palm of my hand and swear loudly.

Eventually, I reach the A & E, where I find a receptionist who confirms that Ash was brought in three hours ago and is in intensive care still. Before she can even give me directions, I tear off to the lifts and make my way up to the ward. My body is shaking; my head is a mess. I want to kill whichever motherfucker did this. I have always taken care of Ash, protected him in the world that we play within, where we often push the boundaries – take risks with the strangers that we indulge with. I stepped out of that world for a moment and now his life is possibly hanging by a thread because of my selfishness.

Jo is sitting in a side room. She looks terrible and flings herself at me, sobbing and clinging to me as if her life depends on it. I hold her tightly and stroke her hair until she calms down. She looks up at me with her big green eyes. "I went around to check on him, Jax. I let myself in when he didn't answer the door." She screws her face up as fresh tears begin to fall down her cheeks. "I found him tied to his bed. He was so badly beaten I thought he was dead. If I hadn't found him when I did, he probably would be. Thank God I still have a key to his flat."

I wipe a tear away from her cheek with my thumb and feel like my heart is already broken and beyond repair. "You did good, Jo. Real good."

She shakes her head slowly. "We went to Heaven together last night. He insisted we go out without you, he left before me with that guy you picked up a while ago. I remember Ash said you bumped into him on your birthday."

I feel like I have been punched in the gut. The same bastard who kissed me in front of Jade. He was aggressive – sexually – and liked to be excessively dominant. I was the one that took charge the night the three of us were together, I kept everything under control as I always do. Ash alone with him would have been a big mistake. One that he has obviously paid for ten-fold. "Where is he?" I ask, my heart thumping like it is about to jump out of my chest.

Jo takes me to the intensive care reception where the ward sister on duty quizzes me as to who I am and what my relationship is to Ash. I tell her to mind her own fucking business and let me see him immediately. Jo takes over by lying and persuading the nurse that I am his brother, as only family can see him in the ICU. The nurse reluctantly takes us down the corridor to where my only true friend – and lover – is lying in a bed, hooked up to so many machines. I cannot quite believe it is him.

My beautiful man is so broken I do not recognise him at first. I take his hand and collapse on my knees beside him and sob like a baby. I am vaguely aware of Jo behind me, her hand on my back.

I failed him. I failed him in the worst possible way and now I must pay the price.

I leave the ICU sometime after and walk to a quiet corridor in the stairwell. The clock on my phone says it's two in the morning but I call Jade anyway. She picks up immediately. "Tell me he's okay, Jax. Please tell me he's okay." I can tell by the tone of her voice that she has been crying. My heart feels so incredibly heavy right now, I want to curl up in a ball on the floor and pretend this is all a bad dream.

"He's alive, Jade. They've induced a coma so that his brain doesn't continue to swell. It's bad. Very bad."

She sobs down the phone and I sink to the floor, my back against the wall with my head in my hand. "I'll come up in the morning, Jax. Please, let me come up. I can't stay here and not be with you. Both of you."

It becomes clear to me, in that moment, that she really does love me and will do anything for me, including accepting Ash. "I'll arrange a taxi for you," I whisper. She sniffs and I hear her flick a lighter. She is probably smoking her pipe. I could do with a hit myself.

"He'll be okay, Jax. I know he will," she says reassuringly. I take a deep breath before exhaling again, all my anguish rushing out in that one strained breath.

I hang up, unable to say anything more.

Chapter Forty-Four

I stay by his bed all night talking to him quietly.

I tell him how sorry I am and how I will never leave him again. I threaten him that if he doesn't pull through, I will beat him myself. I fall back on my old Catholic upbringing praying to the God I was told would always support me in my hour of need. I cry and swear and then cry some more.

By the morning, I have fallen asleep in the chair next to him, almost as broken as he is. I am woken sometime later by a nurse who tells me I must leave the room for a moment while the doctor carries out his checks. I leave and stumble along the corridor to find something to drink – and someone I can bum a cigarette from if I'm lucky. My willpower to stay off the nicotine vanishing like a puff of smoke on the breeze. Jo is asleep in the side room, her arms tucked under her head which is falling off the seat at an awkward angle. I take off my jacket and place it over her, moving her into a more comfortable position before leaving her again and heading out.

There's a vending machine down the corridor and so I buy a coffee. Outside, in the smoking shelter, I am glad to find a few people out there chuffing away. I bum a cigarette and sit down with it in my hand staring at the floor. It tastes disgusting but I smoke it anyway. I am already plotting my revenge on the bastard and go over various scenarios repeatedly as I smoke and drink the bitter coffee. By the time I walk back into the intensive care unit I know what I will do and how I will do it.

Jo is awake when I return. She hugs me and says she needs to go home for a while but will return as soon as she can, letting me do the same. I don't care if I never shower again; I will not leave this place until I see Ash open his beautiful eyes again. I want to be there when he does.

He must wake up. I cannot live without him.

I go back to his room and find the doctor still there talking to the nurse. He smiles at me with a look that I am sure he gives all relatives in this situation. A feeble 'I'm so sorry' smile. "Thankfully, Mr Spencer is starting to recover but it will take some time before we can take him off the ventilator. The swelling is starting to reduce now, so we can feel a little more positive about his recovery."

"Thank you," I say and slump back into the chair beside Ash, taking his hand in my own. It feels cold and lifeless as if he is not even in his body. What is laying in the bed beside me is just a broken shell – the man I love has disappeared.

The police arrive sometime after and take a statement from Jo. She does not tell them about the man we know nearly beat Ash to death. She knows our code – she knows I will deal with this. But she tells them she found him tied to the bed and they take notes as if this is a regular occurrence in their world. It probably is. They say they will return when Ash wakes up to take a statement from him. I hope he regains consciousness sooner rather than later but I will speak to him first before they can interrogate him. I know the justice system will not be able to carry out the same type of sentence I intend to give the man who did this to my lover. They would put him in a comfy cell at best, after months of wasted, unnecessary court time.

I will make it a lot easier for the world by carrying out my own form of punishment. I will do this carefully and I will do it soon.

Jade arrives shortly after the police leave. She pulls me into her arms and I allow her to hold me as I cry again like a child with no shame. She sits with me by Ash and strokes my hair, kissing me and talking to me in a whisper, telling me over and over that Ash will recover and that it wasn't my fault.

She is wrong. It *was* my fault. I have tried to live the impossible dream with two people and it has backfired on me. All the money in the world cannot put this right but I still spend the rest of the day arranging for private medical care and rehabilitation for him when he is well enough to be moved.

That evening I tell Jade I need to go for a walk. She stays with Ash and I leave the hospital for a while to clear my head. I walk – and walk – and walk some more.

I think about my life and how much it has changed in such a short space of time. How I love two people with equal ferocity now and how difficult it will be for me to share my time between them to keep them both safe and happy. I reflect on how much I have cheated fate and that I am now paying for all the dark and horrible things I have done to other people over the last few years. How I have taken what I wanted, when I wanted without even thinking of the consequences.

An hour or so later I find Jade sitting in the same spot I left her. She is holding Ash's hand and is talking to him. For a moment, I stand by the door quietly, looking at the two of them and feeling like my heart is going to shatter completely if I ever lose them.

"Jax needs you, Ash. So, you see, you have to wake up. He can't survive without you, even with me in his life. He won't be able to survive with just one of us. I need you to know that, Ash. We both need you more than you know. Don't let go, Ash. Don't let go," she pleads and I step back out of the room for a moment so that I can compose myself again. Watching her talk to Ash in such an empathic way has twisted my heart and pulled it kicking and screaming out through my rib cage.

She is the most beautiful soul I have ever known. Her compassion and understanding for both Ash and me are all too much and it's killing me. I step back into the room again shortly after, smiling at her as if I hadn't just heard her speaking to him.

"Hey, City Boy," she says looking up at me with a gentle smile on her beautiful face. "I think he'll wake up any minute you know." I sit down beside her and take her hand from Ash and raise it to my lips where I place a kiss on her knuckles. She stares at me for a moment her eyes dark and wide. I cannot believe how beautiful she is, inside and out, or how much I have come to love her. I touch her lush bottom lip with my finger and trail it across the soft plump flesh.

"I love you, Jade."

She chokes back a sob and pulls me to her, pushing her fingers into my hair at the back of my neck as if she wants to climb inside me. My declaration of love hangs in the air between us as she holds me. It's like a living thing, palpable with intensity.

"I've loved you from the moment I saw you sitting on top of *The Water Witch*, Jax," she replies with a sweetness to her voice that tugs further on my heart. I pull her onto my lap and she curls herself around me.

I hope she still feels that way when she discovers what I plan to do to the man who nearly broke us all.

Chapter Forty-Five

Ash comes out of the coma three hours later. He is not fully conscious but he is able to breathe without the ventilator and his vitals are back up. The doctor says he should make a full recovery within the next twenty-four hours. Still, he will need hospital care over the next few weeks giving his broken ribs time to heal. He'll need a second MRI scan too, to make sure there is no permanent damage to his brain.

Jade and I stay the night in a room at the hospital squeezed into a single bed I insisted they find us. I am not leaving this place until I know Ash is fully conscious. I hold her tightly and listen to her breathing as she sleeps in my arms.

I have a lot to thank Ash for and a lot to make up for. Eventually, I fall asleep, dreaming of how I am going to take my revenge on the man that created this bittersweet mess. It's not the best sleep, filled with visions of blood and twisted bodies and I wake early the next day. Jade is still sleeping, and I extract myself from her gently, trying not to wake her.

I head back to Ash and find a nurse at his bed, checking his progress. She smiles at me with empathy and, not so subtly, checks me out with hungry eyes, as if I am not grieving and, in a state worse than a tramp on the street would be. But it makes me smile.

"Everything's looking really good, Mr Spencer. I think your brother will open his eyes today," she says. I give her a curt nod and sit down beside him again, not bothering to tell her we do not share the same surname and he is not my brother but my lover. She leaves shutting the door behind her.

I take his hand again and lean my head back in the high-backed chair, trying in vain to get comfortable and close my eyes for a moment. I feel like utter shit and my head is thick and woozy from the lack of any proper sleep. I am just drifting off again when I feel his hand twitch beneath my own and I jump on reflex as if someone has just poked me with a stick.

"Jax?" he manages to croak. His voice is so quiet I almost think it's a figment of my imagination.

I am sitting on the edge of the chair staring at him while I hold my breath in excited anticipation. "Ash … I'm right here. Open your eyes, you bastard."

He finally manages to prise them open. And, in that moment, I feel as though my head is going to explode, I'm so pumped up with relief and adrenaline. His eyes are still swollen but, through tiny slits, I can tell he is looking at me, his lips twisted into what looks like a grimace. "You're the fucking bastard," he whispers and I feel the tears begin to fall again.

He starts to laugh and then chokes and coughs. I grab the buzzer for the nurse, pressing it over and over as if it is my own personal lifeline, not Ash's.

"I'm sorry, Ash. I'm so, so sorry," I groan as I bend over and kiss him with all the emotion I'm feeling spilling out of me like water from a broken pipe. He lifts his hand slowly, too slowly and places it on my arm.

"Stop being so dramatic you prick." My Ash is back – he is going to be okay.

By that evening, Ash is sitting up in bed and teasing the nurses in only the way he can.

Jade is sitting on my lap as we watch him, laughing as he tells the nurse taking his temperature that he would love to take her out for dinner sometime. I never imagined Jade would cry in the way she did when she knew Ash would be okay. The nurse smiles at him, makes a note of the reading on his records, before telling him she is happily married but is very flattered by the invite. The doctor cannot quite believe how quickly he has snapped back into his old self. But Ash has been through a lot and he is a stubborn and tough character, regardless of his seemingly soft and effeminate ways.

He has learnt how to take a beating, just as much as I have. It seems he is not destined to leave the planet just yet after all.

I have already given my soul to both God – and the devil – in exchange for this man's life while he was unconscious. I prayed silently throughout the hours he lay there resembling a corpse. I wonder if they will step forward now and take it. I would still give it gladly.

"You both look like shit, why don't you go home and get a shower and some sleep?" Ash says to us when the nurse has gone. He is still almost unrecognisable and his voice is low and gravelly with a slight slur.

"I'm not leaving you, Ash." Jade is stroking my arm gently as she sits on my lap her head tucked into the crook of my neck.

"Oh, just fuck off, will you! Jo will be back in soon and, quite frankly, I need to sleep for a while."

Typical Ash. I know he is being flippant for Jade's sake but I really do want to stay with him. Make up for the mistake I made of leaving him alone at the weekend. He was clearly feeling rejected and a little jealous that I had taken off to Wiltshire again. His visit to Heaven, and the sex that followed, resulting in him ending up here was his way of dealing with it.

When he is feeling a little better we will need to talk – alone – to reassure him that I am still committed to him and that he never has to feel pushed out or unwanted again. I underestimated the way he was handling my new relationship with Jade. He seemed fully on board with me pursuing my dream but it's obvious now that he wasn't handling it very well at all. He is as good a liar as I am and was allowing me to step away from him because he loves me. But it made him reckless and he was also giving me the 'fuck you' finger at the same time.

I don't blame him. We have always been a team, always worked our darker deeds together. I have never given my heart to anyone else but him before.

It has been hard on him and he hid the fact very well.

Chapter Forty-Six

Reluctantly, I leave with Jade and we head back to my flat. The nurse on duty promises me she will call immediately if anything changes. She reassured me that he is over the worst now and will be fine. Jo text to let me know she will visit him for a while this evening, which made me feel a little better.

We walk into my flat in silence. It occurs to me that something is missing. "What did you do with Bob?" I ask as I throw my keys into the bowl on the table by my door. She sighs wearily and strokes my arm as she walks past me to the kitchen.

"Chloe has him, he's fine." She opens the fridge and pulls out a bottle of water, leaning back against the counter and unscrewing the lid. She looks just as exhausted as I feel. She dropped everything just to support me and Ash. It's been an intense emotional ride for both of us since Jo's frantic phone call.

I love this girl so much right now it hurts.

She is watching me as I pull the packet of cigarettes I bought on the way home out of my pocket and take one out. My determination to stay off the nicotine has gone right out the window and I don't give a shit. She says nothing as I light it up and throw the packet on the coffee table flopping down on my sofa in defeat. "Do you want anything to eat or drink?"

I flick on the TV for distraction. "I'm fine," I say, numb.

She begins to rummage through the cupboards, clearly ignoring me and looking for something she can rustle up. She walks over with a cold beer and places it in front of me, taking a cigarette from the packet and lighting one up for herself. She goes back into the kitchen and I hear her banging pots and pans.

She has managed to cobble together stir fry, and we sit and eat on the sofa with some American sitcom playing in the background. The drama is so fake and beyond reality that it makes me smile a little. After our supper, Jade pulls out her wooden pipe and loads it up curled up beside me. "Do you think the police will find the person that attacked Ash?" she asks as she passes me the pipe.

I close my eyes for a moment thinking about what I am going to say next. "I know exactly who did it, Jade."

She looks startled for a second. "Then why haven't you told them already, they could be arrested for assault or even attempted murder for what they did to him, Jax."

I turn to face her, and she stares at me with those beautiful dark blue eyes questioning why I have not already given them this vital piece of information. "I'll deal with this myself."

She sits up and places her hand on my thigh. "Fighting violence with violence will solve nothing. Karma doesn't allow it." She's adamant.

I push her hand away and stand up abruptly, suddenly very angry. "Fuck 'karma', Jade. The man that did this to Ash didn't give a flying fuck that he almost killed him. The police will do nothing to make this situation better."

She leans back in the sofa and crosses her legs slowly. Just watching me as I rant. "Use your wisdom on this, Jax, not your anger," she says quietly, her energy calm and cool. I stare at her as if she is crazy. What does she know of my anger or my wisdom? She does not understand my world at all.

I say nothing in return. If I did, I would regret it. Instead, I walk to the kitchen and stand at the sink, my hands gripping the edge of the counter so hard it makes my knuckles turn white. She comes up behind me and places her hands on my waist leaning into me.

"I know you feel guilty, I see it in your eyes. But if you take this into your own hands, you'll only make it worse. You may even end up in prison yourself. That will help no one, especially not Ash." She is right, I know, but I cannot seem to control this urge inside of me to find the sick motherfucker and torture him slowly. The need is burning inside me, turning me inside out with its intensity.

I turn around and take her into my arms shaking with frustration. "Let's take a shower and go to bed," I whisper into her hair. She squeezes me and nods once in reply.

We shower together and I end up taking her quickly and viciously as the water crashes over us, as if I need to take out my anger on her instead. She takes my pounding without question and makes me come so hard I almost fall to her feet after.

She dries me like a child and soothes me as I cry silently, again wrapped in her arms. She leads me to bed and helps me inside where she kisses me and strokes my hair.

I feel like an utter bastard for fucking her so hard in the shower and then allowing her to be so tender towards me after. I do not deserve her love. I do not deserve her. Full stop.

I fall asleep with her wrapped around me like a warm soft blanket. I am so out of control right now I do not recognise myself or what I have become.

Chapter Forty-Seven

The next morning, I wake with a jolt in my solar plexus as if someone has just hit me there, making me feel uneasy and disorientated. I sit up and sigh in relief when I see Jade is sleeping beside me and hasn't left in the night.

She has now seen me at my very best – and my very worst. I brush a lock of her hair away from her face and kiss her gently on the cheek. She murmurs in her sleep and stretches a little. I slip into the kitchen and put the kettle on.

We have both slept heavily after our gruelling vigil at the hospital with Ash. I check my mobile for any missed calls or messages. There are none and I assume that all is well, so I can take a little time before going back to the hospital. I left Hilary a message on Monday morning to say that I would not be able to come in this week. My time in Harley Street is done. Finished. Over.

I make coffee and smoke while I spoon two sugars into Jade's cup. I am going to send her back to *The Water Nymph* later today, she needs to get back to Bob and her own life after running around after me and Ash for the last two days. She will push back against this, I know, but I have some things I want to do before I go back to Wiltshire. I need a clear head before I can focus on her again. What she said last night – my plans for revenge, the violence – is there under my skin, scratching and itching like a disease that is spreading across my body like an unwanted parasite.

Jade is still sleeping as I sit down beside her and run my

finger across her shoulder down to her breast in a slow tease to see if I can wake her up gently. She stirs and opens her eyes blinking up at me for a moment before smiling. "Did you manage to sleep?" she asks me before yawning. I can't help but smile back at her, she looks so young and beautiful like this, all sleepy and soft. She pushes herself up and grins when she sees the coffee. "Do you want to head back to the hospital?"

I am blatantly staring at her perfect breasts as she sits up fully and drinks her coffee without bothering to cover herself. "I'll take you for some breakfast first, then we can head back to see Ash. I'll arrange for a taxi to take you back to Honey Street tonight."

She frowns at me. "I don't need to go back so soon. Chloe said she'd keep Bob for as long as I needed her to." Her voice is firm but I detect the undercurrent of fear running through it. She doesn't want to leave me or Ash right now.

I can't say I blame her but I'm adamant on this one. I run my finger across her cheek slowly, deliberately trying to distract her. "I need you to go back for a while, Jade. I've a lot to sort out for Ash in the next few days and you'll only be bored if you stay here. I'll come back and see you at the weekend again."

She sips her coffee looking at me over the rim of the cup and I know she is thinking about how angry I was last night. "Don't do anything crazy, Jax," she says, her eyes wandering across my face.

I laugh grimly. "My whole life is one big crazy, Jade."

"You know what I mean."I know exactly what she means but say nothing in response.

I take her back to the same café not far from my flat and buy us both a cooked breakfast. My appetite is returning and I can eat today knowing that Ash is recovering now. We take a cab to the hospital and find Ash sitting up and being spoon-fed by the nurse he was flirting with yesterday.

His eyes are looking a little brighter today and his face is less swollen. It's turned a nasty blue-black but, despite this, he is still smiling. He is keen to get out of the hospital but he isn't going anywhere for another few days. They are insisting that he remain with them until they have done the MRI scan and checked the results.

Jade and I sit with him for the rest of the day. He asks how my visit to Jade's family went and I tell him about her riding with her brother and how both her father and her brother threatened me. She laughs when I tell him, rolling her eyes as I say how much it amused me.

"Well, you have a new family now by the sounds of it." It's sarcastic. A typical Ash response when he's feeling disgruntled.

Jade stands up and reaches for him kissing him on the cheek. "*We* are your family now," she says, then quietly leaves the room looking at me with sadness in her eyes as she does. She knows I need to talk to him alone.

Ash watches her leave but says nothing more.

I drag the chair closer to his bed and lean forward slightly. "Stop with the guilt trip, Ash. It doesn't suit you. Jade cares about you as much as I do, she knows this situation is difficult for you. She begged me to let her come and see you."

He turns his head away from me and I can see him struggling with the reality of what is happening between the three of us. "I don't want you to tell the police about the guy that did this to you, Ash. I'm going to deal with him."

He looks back at me and his eyes glisten as if he is about to cry. "You'll do no such thing, Jax. He isn't worth the trouble. I did this to myself and I'm just being a bitch because I know I was stupid and can't admit it in front of her."

I take his hand and squeeze it gently. "I was stupid. I

had no idea you were struggling with all the time I've been spending with Jade. I was too wrapped up in the novelty of it all."

He shakes his head slowly. "You love her, it's blatantly obvious and I don't want to take that away from you, I want you to be happy with her. I've already told you that. I was just blowing off steam and … well, it went tits up, that's all."

I stand up and begin to pace across the room raking my hand through my hair.

"Blowing off steam almost got you killed! You picked the wrong guy to play with. He *will* pay for what he did to you. You were a fucking idiot to go out alone that night with him. You should have known better. But he won't get away with it. I won't let him get away with it. I forgive you for being so reckless, but I won't forgive him. Ever." I turn my back to him for a moment trying to reign in my temper that is fizzing up in my veins again.

"Talking of blowing off steam and being reckless. Who did you fuck the night before you left to see Jade and her parents?" Ash says catching me completely off guard.

"What?"

"You heard me, Jax. I found a discarded pair of tacky looking knickers on the floor in the lounge and a used condom in your bin the day you left to see her."

My head begins to throb as the memory of Samantha slams into me like a wrecking ball. I was in such a rush to leave the following morning I didn't think to do a sweep of my flat. He's a bugger for helping himself to my weed stash when he runs low. "You went through my rubbish?"

He lets out a heavy sigh and begins to tap a finger against the bed. "That's irrelevant. What is relevant right now, Jax, is why you would be stupid enough to dip your wick into someone else and screw up what you've been desperately trying to create with Jade." He pauses letting out a rattled cough. "She may be happy to share you with me. But another random you decide to screw while juggling between the two of us? Not so much, Jax. Are you delusional or just becoming exceptionally greedy now you've been given everything you could ever have wanted?"

My cheeks begin to burn with both guilt and anger. I know he's right. I thought I'd got away with my indiscretion. But, as usual, Ash was straight on the scent of another predator threatening to take his superior position. No wonder he went straight out for a fix at the club, despite my insistence he should wait for my return from the countryside.

This is such a fuck-up.

If he tells Jade what he knows, this will all be over. Regardless of my own decision to stop acting like a man-slut she would be well within her rights to doubt my commitment to her in the future. I've literally just declared my love for her, given her the green light to open her heart to me and she will think it's total bullshit. She'd be devastated. And rightly so.

"It was a mistake and one I won't ever repeat again."

He stares at me for a moment, his eyes emotionless, cold even, before he blinks and they return to their usual soulful brown. "How are we going to do this, Jax?" he says, his voice still a little gravelly.

I turn to face him again and take a deep breath. I'm not sure if he is referring to the three of us, my bad decision to screw Samantha or my intentions of revenge.

"We will find a way."

Chapter Forty-Eight

I leave Ash later that evening, telling him I will be back tomorrow, despite his insistence I don't need to keep babying him and that he is fine without me sitting beside him twenty-four hours a day. Jade kisses him goodbye and this time he holds her as she does, gripping her tightly to him as if he is trying to convey how sorry he is through touch alone.

My heart is pounding in my chest as I wait for him to expose my fuck up after our conversation.

But he says nothing. One more thing I'm grateful for. But this secret between Ash and I now hangs like a dark cloud in the distance; I will have to trust him to be discreet. The threat of my slip up with Samantha being revealed is enough to make my stomach churn and shatter any dream I may have for an easy future between the three of us.

Refusing to think about the consequences if Jade does hear about this monumental fuck-up, I do what every other man does in this situation: I ignore it and dump the memory into a secure box inside the back of my brain. Locking it away with all the other things I no longer wish to revisit.

We grab a takeaway on the way back to my flat. It's too late for Jade to head home now so I order a taxi for the morning. I don't really want to let her go again. It's a constant push-pull on my heart. The only light is from a candle burning and the end of a joint we smoke together as we lie on the sofa, listening to music. I can't wait to get rid of this flat now. It feels alien to me. I miss the gentle sway of the boat and the sounds of the water against the hull of *The Water Nymph*.

It's midnight by the time we get into bed and I make love to Jade slowly and leisurely, my eyes locked on to hers the whole time. Our connection is so solid now it makes me feel both strong and ridiculously weak. She breaks beneath me and trembles within my arms like a beautiful angel.

I am so confused it makes me want to weep. I have done enough crying in the last few days. I cannot remember the last time I cried so much – I was probably a child. It's as if the floodgates holding back my shitty existence have broken and a tidal wave of emotion has come crashing down around me in one great wash. I'm afraid of losing her. I'm afraid of losing Ash. I'm weak and vulnerable right now. Something I've not felt in a very long time.

Jade leaves in the morning. She kisses me in such an intense way it feels almost desperate and then tilts her head looking up at me with a smile that looks a little sad as she slides into the taxi. "See you soon, City Boy."

Her acceptance leaves me in total awe of her once again and I head back inside feeling instantly empty. To fill the void, I make several calls to the solicitors regarding the house and the estate agents who are advertising the flat. The house is almost mine and there are two offers on the flat. It seems there is a silver lining to the dark cloud that descended over me. I have one other thing to deal with.

I roll a joint and stare out the window of my flat. The skyline before me now evokes a sense of claustrophobia. I miss the open space of the countryside, the ducks, my swan on the canal and I know that I am no longer a city boy. I have disconnected from this place.

Jo calls and says she is with Ash and he is looking a lot better today. I tell her that I will visit him tomorrow, he needs a day off from my 'babying him'. Around six, I take a long, hot shower and then dress robotically, my mind focussing on what I have planned for the evening.

I leave the flat and know exactly where I am going – and what I hope to find.

A cab takes me to Soho and I hit a few of the bars. It is Thursday evening and the beautiful people of the city are already out and about, starting their weekends early. I was one of them for many years. I have a beer in the first bar and sit quietly by myself for a while, waiting, but leave after an hour and walk to the next bar.

Nothing.

I head to the last bar on my hit list and order another beer. I am starting to think I have wasted my time when I see what I am looking for. He is sitting in the corner with a group of young guys laughing and joking. My heart starts to pound and I feel the rush of adrenaline I have been waiting for a surge through my veins.

I am ready.

But I bide my time, wait at the bar and sip at my beer. A guy comes up to me and starts to try and talk to me but I ignore him and he quickly moves on. The music is loud and it's getting packed as I see my man get up and walk away from his table, heading to the restrooms.

I slide off the barstool and follow him. There's one other, standing at the urinals. My prey is taking a shit by the looks of things as one of the cubicles is shut. Perfect.

I stand next to the random guy and give him a smile. He grins back looking at my dick as I pull it out and join him. I can't produce a single drop under his scrutiny. He shakes his head at me with a chuckle and then turns around to the sinks where he washes his hands and leaves. I button my jeans back up and grab the chair that is sitting by the door, where the attendant would normally sit. I place it under the door handle and jam it tight with a kick of my boot.

I wait, leaning back against the sink, my arms crossed in front of me as I hear the toilet flush and the door to the stall opens. He looks up as he is buttoning up his jeans. His eyes flash when he sees me, then he blinks and grins at me. "Hey, Jax. How are you, man?"

My whole body is primed and pumped with adrenaline. I push myself away from the sink and walk towards him slowly. My whole body is primed and pumped with adrenaline. I can see a red tinge in my peripheral vision and feel a tingle at the base of my spine as if a spark of electricity is beginning to power up. I want to kill this man and my body is responding at a frighteningly quick pace.

He steps back a little as he sees the anger in my eyes and the tension in my body. The way his expression changes shows me he knows his night is about to very much take a turn for the worse.

"How am I?" I say, my voice is deep and low. "I'm fine and dandy, you piece of shit."

He holds his hands up in a gesture of surrender as I back him up slowly against the stall door.

"I can't say the same about Ash though."

He is backing further away from me now, his eyes wide and flicking over to the door where he sees the chair tipped up against it, locking us both in.

"Hey, Jax, calm down man. What's going on here?"

I grab him by the throat before he can say another word and his head slams against the door of the cubicle which bangs open and makes him groan. His hands shoot up to his throat and they scramble wildly as he tries desperately to peel my fingers away from his windpipe. "What's going on here?" I growl at him, repeating his stupid question. "Your worst fucking nightmare, that's what's going on *man*." I spit the last word out at him.

He tries to take a punch at my kidneys but I'm already on top of him before he can even take the jab. I punch him so hard in the jaw, the most perfect uppercut from my right hand, his head bounces back again and he slips down to the floor moaning.

I am just about to kick him in the ribs and lose myself to the red-tinted anger flowing through my veins when I feel like I am having an out of body experience and am floating above myself looking down at the scene before me. I see myself standing over the man; I look like a feral creature, my face twisted and evil. Blood is trickling down his jaw and he is holding his hands up to protect his face. I hear a voice in my head. A sweet familiar voice. "What are you doing, City Boy?" and I gag violently, feeling like I am about to vomit all over the man lying at my feet.

He lies crumpled on the floor like a broken doll; I stumble away from him.

In my mind, I see Jade, her eyes beautifully outlined by smoky grey eyeliner, they stare at me like two soulful pools of blue liquid. She is frowning slightly and I know, in that moment, I cannot do this. I cannot carry out the revenge I so desperately want to inflict on this man at my feet. I stare at him and feel sick to the stomach. He looks up at me his eyes filled with fear. I find myself grinning.

"I should kick the shit out of you until *you* find yourself in a coma in hospital. But you're just not worth the time or effort. You'd better keep some eyes in the back of your head from now on. If you go to the police and tell them about our 'little talk' tonight, I'll tell them what you did to Ash and I *will* make sure you go to jail for a very long time."

I pause, my breathing heaving, my body vibrating with repressed violence. "Do you understand?" I spit out.

He nods just the once.

I glare at him conveying exactly how serious I am

with just my facial expression, before turning around and removing the chair from under the door handle. I take one last look at him, still heaped on the floor and know I have done what I needed to do.

He will never beat another man in his life. I have made sure of that. And Jade made sure I didn't kill him.

Chapter Forty-Nine

My phone rings: It's Jade. "Jax? Where are you? Are you okay?" I'm still breathing heavily but find myself smiling as I walk.

"I'm taking a walk Jade, I'm fine." She pauses, I can hear her moving around on her boat and Bob barking.

"I had this awful feeling that something was wrong, is Ash okay?" Her voice is unsteady and edged with panic. Is she fucking psychic?

"Everything's fine, Jade. I'm just heading home. Ash is okay, I'm seeing him again tomorrow. Go back to bed, Fairy Girl."

She sighs heavily. "Okay, call me tomorrow."

I hail a cab and slip the phone under my ear as I get inside. "I love you, Jade," I say and hang up.

The taxi driver eyes me warily in the mirror as he pulls away from the kerb but says nothing. I'm still pumped up ready for a fight and no doubt look like a potentially bad fare. He has no idea just how much.

When I get back to my flat, I strip, putting my clothes straight in the washing machine, and step into the shower, turning it up to scalding hot. I wash away my anger and scrub off the scent of revenge from my body. My right hand is slightly swollen, my knuckles bruised from where I hit the guy.

In bed, I lie on my back, staring at the ceiling for a long time, replaying what happened tonight, the surrealistic enormity of it all. I finally slip into a deep but peaceful sleep. The following day, I visit Ash and tell him what happened at the bar.

He listens without saying anything – his face says it all. He is grateful for what I have done but equally grateful that I didn't inflict more harm on the man. He didn't want me being arrested. I tell him we have Jade to thank for that. He takes my hand and wraps his beautifully manicured fingers around my still swollen hand. "We never talk of this again, Jax. Never." I nod in agreement. What is done, is done.

And we will no longer look back, only forward to a future that will be bright. I have enough money to provide for us all and the love from two people that is so strong, it can, seemingly, survive anything.

He insists that I go back to Wiltshire on Saturday to spend the weekend with Jade. He is going to be stuck in the hospital until Monday when I have arranged for him to move to a private hospital with five-star care. The MRI scan came back with positive results, he has a thicker skull than any of us imagined!

We talk about the house on the canal and the sale of my flat and I promise to take him away to a place in the sun when he is fully recovered. He accepts this with a grin on his face. The swelling around his eyes is starting to reduce and his body is less fragile. He is recovering well. He is one hell of a lucky bastard.

Friday night, I begin to pack some of my belongings, knowing that I will be moving soon and don't want to leave it all to the last minute. As I wrap some of my personal items, I discover I have very little material belongings that mean anything to me. Most of my furniture, I decide, will go to a local charity. Packed up and in a rapidly emptying flat, I feel like a nomad.

I call Jade and we talk for over an hour about everything

and nothing, although I leave out the part about punching and threatening the scumbag that put Ash in hospital. She seems a little distant, distracted even, but it's no surprise considering what we have both experienced in the last few days. I am itching to get back in the Range Rover again and drive down to see her. I browse the internet looking for a car to buy for myself, smiling as I trawl through the listings of old Land Rovers.

I visit Ash early Saturday morning just to see him one last time before I disappear. The last time I left him alone for the weekend he ended up tied to his bed and beaten to within an inch of his life. I don't ever want him to be in that situation again and need to show him how much I care and that he will always be on my mind.

He tells me to give Jade a big sloppy kiss from him and I leave him, promising that I will check in over the weekend to make sure he is okay. I drive down the motorway listening to Bob Marley singing 'Everything's Gonna Be Alright'. I'm finally beginning to think it will.

I arrive in Honey Street and find Jade sitting on the wooden bench table in The Barge Inn's garden. Bob sits next to her, looking suitably shaggy and happy. They are both waiting for me and I am bursting with happiness at the sight of the pair of them. I park up and jump out striding across the car park as she sits and waits for me to walk over with a smile on her face. Bob runs over to me and jumps around like Zebedee for a moment.

"You look much better," she says to me as I reach her and place my hands on her cheeks holding her as I scan her face taking her all in.

"I feel better." She smiles as I lean in to kiss her and we melt into each other as if nothing else exists around us and we are in our own bubble of bliss.

We walk down the towpath to *The Water Nymph*, and

I breathe a sigh of relief as I step down inside the boat that has now become my real home. She makes us both coffee and we sit on the back of the boat smoking her pipe and watching the world go by.

"What really happened Thursday night, Jax?" she asks suddenly as she lies on my chest playing with the bracelet on my wrist.

"I know you weren't just out for a walk, City Boy." I chuckle and slip my hand down her waist, touching the exposed skin peeking out from under her cropped top.

"Do you really want to know?"

She continues to play with the bracelet her breathing a little hitched. "Yes."

I give her the basic details, toning down the violence but including the moment I heard her voice in my head and stepped back from the situation that was beginning to spiral out of control. She listens to me relay the story without interrupting. When I finish, she looks up at me and smiles.

"I'm proud of you. Karma will do the rest now."

My lips curl into a droll smile before I pull her to me and lavish her with another toe-curling kiss.

Karma seems to be smiling on me now, that's for sure.

Jade is making us supper and I am sitting at the front of the boat with Bob when I receive a call. The solicitors tell me that the cottage in Honey Street is now officially mine and I can pick the keys up whenever I am ready.

I wander back through the boat with a smile on my face. I decide that I won't wait for the keys but will break into my new home with her tonight. Now will be a good time to tell her everything she needs to know about my wealth and the life I intend to live with her and Ash by my side. She looks at me with a quirk to her brow as we eat. "What's going on? You've done nothing but grin at me since you got that call."

I laugh slipping a forkful of the delicious pesto pasta she

has made us into my mouth. "I have a surprise for you," I say playfully. Her eyes widen a little and she licks her bottom lip which is currently slick with oil from the pasta.

"Oh, really?" I lean back and stretch my arms up and over my head enjoying this moment immensely as she squirms a little before me.

"Yes, really."

She tries to make me fold and tell her my secret throughout the rest of dinner. But I resist and tell her she needs to be patient, something she is not very good at. After our supper, I roll us a joint and take her hand, pulling her up from the floor where she has been sitting with Bob reading through her astrology charts. She stares up at me with nervous excitement in her eyes as I lead her towards the back of the boat with Bob following us.

"Put your sexy boots on, Fairy Girl, we're going for a walk." She gives me a little pout but complies, clearly not understanding why I am still grinning like an idiot. I grab some candles from the pot in her kitchen and shove them into my jacket pocket as it is just beginning to turn dark now and I want to sit with her in our new home for a while.

I am shaking with excitement as I take her hand and lead her out of the boat.

Chapter Fifty

Jade walks beside me, looking up at me with a mixture of curiosity and frustration. Bob runs back and forth along the towpath finding new sticks. "Where are you taking me?"

I smile widely. "You'll see." She almost stamps her foot in frustration, which makes me laugh. She knows I am building this up somewhat and she still has no clue as to what 'the secret' is. I stop her at the hidden entrance to the cottage and pull her into my arms for a moment wrapping my arms around her. "Don't be cross with me, Jade," I whisper into her hair. "I've done this for both of us and I've done it because you deserve it."

She pulls back from me looking up with a slight frown on her face. "What have you done, Jax?"

I smile again and then tug on her hand pulling her along so that she has no choice but to follow me through the overgrown pathway to the cottage. I feel her energy change as we walk into the secret garden, her body becomes stiff for a second as she registers that the sign outside now has a *Sold* sticker stamped across the front. I turn and grin at her again and I see her eyes widen as she processes what this may mean. Bob runs ahead of us and is lost in the grass for a moment.

The cottage sits like an apparition in the slight mist that is beginning to rise as the sun falls beneath the horizon. It looks so beautiful in the grey light, filtered with the soft pink hues of the sunset. Almost otherworldly. But one thing is certain at this moment as I appreciate it fully now that it is mine. It has always been waiting for us to claim it.

I lead her to the front door and turn her around. She is shaking slightly as she looks up at me her eyes filled with anticipation of what I am about to reveal.

"I bought this cottage for you. It belongs to us now."

She stares up at me, her eyes swimming with tears as she shakes her head slowly. "When? How?" she stutters.

I laugh at the irony that she is, for the first time since I met her, unable to respond with a sharp comment.

"After you brought me here the first time, I approached the estate agents and made an offer. I pushed through for a fast exchange and tonight I received the call that it is mine. I don't have the keys yet but, seeing as it belongs to us now, I think we can just break a window and go inside, don't you?"

She lets out a strange, strangled noise and flings her arms around me. Her tears are falling now, and I am the happiest I have ever been as I feel her tremble in my arms for the best reason of all. The deepest kind of joy.

We laugh as we discover the back door is so worn and old, it only takes the weight of my shoulder to break it open and we step inside. Bob follows us, sniffing around with his tail wagging. Jade walks through the cottage touching everything, taking it all in and digesting the fact that this place is now hers.

An old sofa in the lounge has been covered by a dust sheet. I light the candles on the floor in the shape of a heart which makes her laugh and I pull her onto the sofa and sit her on my lap. She tucks her head into my neck and kisses me.

"Thank you, City Boy," she says, her warm breath caressing my skin.

"You are most welcome."

We sit in silence. Both of us digesting the enormity of this new situation. As I hold her in my arms, my subconscious gives me a not-so-subtle nudge. There is one last thing we need to discuss, the reason I came here in the first place and this is the right time to tell her.

"There's something else I need to tell you, Jade. It's been troubling me that I haven't told you."

She swivels her head to look at me, her expression switches from serene to wary.

"I'm not sure I could take another revelation tonight, to be honest, Jax. Let's not spoil this lovely moment. Save it for another time," she mumbles.

Closing my eyes and resting my cheek against her head, I take a deep breath. It's ridiculous I'm finding it so difficult to disclose the one thing that led to the ownership of this place. My lottery windfall. "I need to tell you this. It's important. I don't want any more secrets between us."

She sighs heavily. "Some secrets are best kept hidden, Jax. That way they can't hurt anyone."

I'm confused as to why she would say this but want to get this off my chest. The money I now have is something she should know about. It's about to change our lives in a big way and she needs to understand this. "You need to hear this, Jade," I state.

"Spit it out then," she sighs in defeat.

My throat bobs as I swallow hard. Her breathing has accelerated and I'm not sure which one of us is more nervous at my next revelation. Oddly, I'm not sure why.

"The reason I rented *The Witch* this summer was that my life changed very suddenly and I needed some space and time to think about my future." She says nothing but I feel her grow tense against me. "I bought a lottery ticket and it turned out to be the jackpot winner. The amount took me by surprise. I needed to find somewhere away from my usual distractions to really think about what I was going to do with it."

Her head swivels and as she looks up at me her perfect brows crinkle in what looks like confusion. She looks a little agitated. Now I'm the confused one. "Wow. You won the lottery and ran to the countryside. That's what you wanted to share with me?" Her voice is laced with sarcasm.

Ignoring the spikiness in her voice, I run my fingers down her arm and take her hand lifting it to my lips where I kiss her knuckles. "I won twenty-five million, Jade."

Curling her fingers around my own she shifts in my lap so that we are face-to-face. Her grip tightens on my hand. "That's a lot of money." Her eyes are wandering across my face as she gnaws at her bottom lip. I wait for her to continue but it seems to take her some time before she decides what she is going to say next. "I'm sure you deserve all the happiness it can help bring into your life."

Her cool response makes me feel a little uncomfortable but confirms that the amount means little to her in her simple world filled with simple things. Tilting my head, I assess her for a moment, trying to work out what's really going on in her pretty head right now.

"All the happiness it can bring *us*, Jade. What's mine is now yours. I've been blessed with something most people only ever dream of. I intend to use this wealth wisely. I may be faced with other obstacles in the future but a lack of money will never be one of them. And that includes you and Ash, neither of you will ever need to worry about money again."

She snorts a laugh. "Did you worry I'd feel threatened by your millionaire status, City Boy? Is that what you've been worrying about."

"I had no idea how you would feel, to be honest," I reply twisting her in my arms so that she is snug against my chest again.

There is a moment of silence between us before she speaks again. "Money's just another exchange of energy, Jax. It comes; it goes. But I'm happy you were the one to win it. I have no doubt you'll make good use of it."

I squeeze her against me breathing in her unique scent. "I wasn't sure how to handle it at first. Of course, I knew it would make things easier for my future but it was you, not the money, that changed everything for the better. This cottage is just my way of showing you how much I appreciate that." My heart clenches as I think about how much she has helped me break free from my old patterns. "I was lost until I met you. Now I've found the perfect home *and* the perfect person I want to share it with. That's priceless. Even twenty-five million can't compete with that."

Another snort vibrates against my chest. "Well, I'll remind you of that fact when you get bored and cranky with me in the future. I hope you feel happier now you've got that off your chest."

My own response is to squeeze her harder. I ignore the weird vibe that she seems to be giving off. I'm glad I've finally told her about the money. It was weighing heavily on my mind. I'm relieved there are no more secrets between us.

We sit in the cottage and smoke a joint, listening to the sounds of nature – both inside and outside the cottage. It's like a living breathing thing, just as *The Water Nymph* is and I know, as I hold Jade close to me in this dark and dirty tumbledown cottage, that it will be the most perfect place to live. I visualise Jade in the garden, planting herbs and standing in the kitchen barefoot, making delicious meals from everything she has grown in the garden. I see Ash sitting in our cosy lounge by the wood burner, warming his feet on a winters evening with a smile on his beautiful face. Life feels perfect right now. Perfect in every way.

Jade finishes the joint and stubs it out a little ferociously on the floor under her boot.

"Actually, there's something I'd like to get off *my* chest. I'd like to ask you a question, Jax. And I want you to answer me honestly. Is there anything else you want to share with me? Anything else you've been keeping from me because you were too afraid to tell me? Some small piece of information that could, perhaps, affect our future together."

The blissful contentment I was wallowing in is instantly broken. Her unexpected question jolts me abruptly from my daydream. Her voice has switched from her usual sultry tone into something else I'm not entirely comfortable with. The blissful contentment I was wallowing in is instantly broken. Poked with a sharp stick, my happy balloon pops as the only other thing I have kept from her jumps like a sadistic madwoman into my mind. She's wearing a long trench coat, stiletto heels and nothing else.

Bollocks.

Now it all makes sense. Her weird behaviour. The strange vibe that has been permeating the air, tainting this wonderful moment between us. It hits me like a truck. The reason she has been acting just that little bit cagey lately. Still attached but slightly disconnected.

Jade knows. She knows about Samantha.

Somehow, she's found out. She thought I was about to confess what a wanker I'd been when I said I needed to tell her something. No wonder she responded strangely when I told her about my lottery win. She was waiting for me to tell her about Samantha, not the fact I'm a multi-millionaire.

What an utter prick I was to think she wouldn't find out. Ash must have told her. It would have taken just one text to detonate the bomb. One message from him on a mission to force me to be honest with her and clear the messy carnage of my past actions. He knows if we are to move forward together, I need to stop lying to her. I need to become the man they both need me to be: trustworthy, faithful, honest.

Jade has obviously been privy to this secret and kept it to herself, allowing me to believe I'd gotten away with it. Fuck. She must have been digesting what to do with that piece of nasty information while I was still in London.

I panic. Backpedalling in my mind like someone heading straight for a brick wall with no crash helmet. But I decide to play dumb.

"Like what?" I ask playing with her hair, my breathing slow and even. I'm praying silently in my head that it's something else. Something that won't crush our relationship like an old car thrown to the scrap yard.

"I heard the conversation you had with Ash in the hospital, Jax. The door to his room wasn't shut properly and I could hear you as I waited outside. I know you slept with someone the night before we went to visit my parents."

And just like that, I feel the world fall out from beneath my feet. It wasn't Ash that dropped the bomb after all. But it has finally detonated.

The secret I've kept hidden within a cage in my mind springs free like a demon hell-bent on devouring us. Here we are, in the perfect setting with the perfect future laid out before us, and she has been waiting for me to step up. To be the man I've claimed to have become. Waiting for me to reveal my fuck-up and be honest for once in my life.

I'm up against the wall, the firing squad ready to pull the trigger. This is my last chance. The last words of a condemned man. Whatever I chose to say now will either finish us permanently or give us a slither of a chance to repair the damage.

I don't have any time to play with a response. No time to carefully construct my answer. I need to be honest. No calculating. No manipulation. No more deception.

"It was a mistake, Jade. And as I said to Ash, a mistake

I never intend to make again. You are the most important person in my life now. You and Ash. No one else." My heart thuds loudly in my chest.

The silence before she answers me is deafening. I think I may be experiencing the start of a heart attack as it begins to bang against my rib cage erratically.

"I'm not so sure, Jax. I'd like to believe you but it seems you're incapable of saying no when you're offered that extra slice of cake. It's obviously something I'll have to accept if I want a piece of your heart. You explained how you lived your life that night after the festival. You were totally honest with me. I accepted at the time that you were incapable of monogamy, I thought I could handle it." Laughter spills from her lips. A crazed type of laughter.

"I was falling for you so hard, Jax. I ignored the complexity of that part of your character. I really thought you were changing, falling in love with me in the same way I was with you. I thought the love growing between us would be enough. You already had Ash. With me in the mix, I thought it would be enough. And then when I heard Ash confront you about the person you saw the night before you came back to me … well it seemed I was wrong. I made the same mistake so many women do when they fall in love. I thought I could be the one to change you. Change your basic instincts."

Squeezing my eyes shut I clench my fist before letting go of the strand of her hair in my fingers.

"No. You weren't wrong Jade."

"I wasn't?"

I pull her onto my lap so that she's straddling me and take her face in my hands. My eyes lock onto hers and I find myself frowning with frustration. I can't lose her. Not now. Not when we're so close to obtaining Utopia. My heart is breaking right now. Desperation to repair this shitty situation flooding my system.

"I've no intention of being *that* person ever again, Jade. That old part of me is dead. Gone. Over. Having sex with someone else that night was stupid. It meant nothing. I felt nothing. But it did help me understand that a revolving line of random partners is not what I want or need from now on. I need a physical and emotional connection with someone I love. No more sleeping around. No more soulless sex that hurts the people I really care for. My heart belongs to you and Ash. He's the only person you will need to share me with Jade … if that's something you can do. I know it's still a selfish thing to ask for. But he is the one thing I can't give up."

Pausing for breath, I close my eyes for a second. She is still staring at me when I open them, staring into my soul waiting for me to continue with my brutal confession.

"There will be no more casual booty calls. No more revolving sexual partners. I promise you this, Jade. I made that decision seconds after I stupidly took what that person offered me. The only reason I kept it from you and Ash was to avoid either of you feeling hurt by my own stupidity. I did it to protect you. And I did it because I was ashamed of my weakness in that moment." My fingers are gripping her tightly and my entire body is now vibrating with emotion.

She shakes her head, her eyes locked onto mine. We stare at each other frustration radiating from both of us for different reasons. Neither of us backing down. "I'll need some time to think this through, Jax. I want this future with you. This cottage. Everything you could offer me … but I'll need some time."

I nod. It's all I can do. She is in control now. I'm numb. Cold. Screaming inside with the need to atone and force her to understand why I did such a stupid thing right in the middle of our love story. My body has frozen; my head feels woozy. Despite all the wonderful things that have happened I could still lose everything I have gained since meeting her.

This is the one thing I feared the most but refused to think about. The possibility she would doubt my sincerity. My love for her. The commitment I'm willing to make. But I created this doubt within her mind. I am the one responsible for her hesitation. I chose to dive in with Samantha. I stepped over the line when I had everything within my grasp.

Stupid. Reckless. Predictable Jax.

Jade takes my hands away from her face and places them on her waist. She slides her fingers up and down my arms for a moment as if contemplating her next move and then surprises me by leaning forward and placing her lips against my own. She kisses me and then pulls away with another sad smile. "Let's go, City Boy. It's getting cold."

Lifting herself from my lap she stands before me and takes my hand, urging me to get up off the sofa. Bob lets out a low grumbling noise, stretches and then stands wagging his tail. I wish I could be him right now. Blissfully ignorant to the disaster that is now unfolding around him.

We leave the cottage and walk back to *The Nymph* in silence. She holds my hand but there is now a tension radiating between us. I try not to dissolve into a pathetic mess at her feet.

Only Jade can decide if the dream I had for us can now become a reality.

When we return to *The Nymph*, Jade leads me to her bedroom and begins to instigate sex. It doesn't make any sense to me that she allows me to touch her at all, worship her in the only way I can after our conversation. But she does. Selflessly, with all the depth and sincerity I have felt from her since the moment we met.

I take whatever I can in that moment. Just like I always have. But this time it's because I want to prove that I'm hers and she has nothing to fear. I will always belong to her.

As I make love to Jade that night, I realise that I am both the luckiest and stupidest man on the planet. And everything hangs in the balance. This beautiful woman has given me her heart and trusted me with her future. But now it is clouded with uncertainty.

Perhaps by allowing me to make love to her it is her way of punishing me for what I did. Forcing me to experience one last time what I may now lose after everything we've been through. The unique connection I have with this woman both physically, emotionally and, it seems, spiritually.

After we both explode in a spectacular release, which is coated with a bittersweetness I can feel throughout every nerve ending in my body, she falls asleep in my arms. I lie awake staring at the ceiling until the early hours of the morning, going over and over what I should have done, what I haven't done and how I will feel if Jade tells me she can no longer be a part of my life.

By the time dawn makes an appearance I've exhausted both my body and mind from fighting my demons and twisting in the sheets all night while Jade slept soundly beside me. Slipping out of bed as quietly as I can, I head for the shower and blast myself with cold water so I can at least function again before driving back to London.

Jade finds me sitting on the floor in her lounge sometime later nursing a cup of black coffee with Bob sitting beside me. He's been staring up at me with pitiful eyes as I stroke him. He knows somethings changed. He's not stupid. Unlike me.

"Did you sleep?" she asks as she rubs her eyes.

I give her a wry smile. "What do you think?"

Placing her hand on her hip she sighs heavily. "I just need a little time, Jax. Just give me some time. I have a lot to think about. The cottage. You. Ash. What the future may hold. It's a lot for me to process."

I nod. "I'm sorry, Jade. I'm sorry I've put you in this position. And I'm sorry I lied to you."

"Don't," she waves her hand at me dismissively. "Please don't do that."

I shake my head, feeling a mixture of sadness and anger at what I've created between us. I push myself up from the floor place the coffee cup on the table and step towards her. She steps back from me and I instantly see the confirmation in her expression that last night was perhaps her way of saying goodbye. She needed to feel me inside her one last time before she decides.

Bob looks up and his head swivels between us with confusion. His tail thumps just once in a pathetic attempt to make a happy sound. Raking my fingers through my hair, I close my eyes and nod. "Okay. You're right. I won't do that. I'm going to give you all the time you need. I'm going to get in the car and drive back to London. I'll check on Ash and I'll wait to hear from you."

Her eyes glisten with tears as she clenches her fists, her chest rising and falling rapidly. "Thank you."

I grab my car keys from her battered table and glance one more time at her as I walk towards the back of the boat and the outside world. The world that I no longer want to be a part of. She stares at me with such intense emotion reflected in her eyes I almost falter and fall to my knees at her feet. Beg her to let me stay. Beg for her forgiveness.

But I don't. I keep walking.

It is up to her now and I will have to wait. Wait patiently for her to decide.

Chapter Fifty-One

"You have no one but yourself to blame," Ash says as I sit and watch him finish his lunch.

It's been days since I left Jade and I've done nothing but feel sorry for myself. I've not heard from her. Not a text, call or letter. Nothing. Not that I expected anything. She is one for disappearing for long periods even before this catastrophe. Ash is now in the private hospital and it won't be long before they release him.

"Yes, thank you for that reminder, Ash," I reply crossing my legs at the ankles and leaning back in the chair with my hands linked behind my head. I close my eyes and clench my jaw. I'm angry with everyone and everything right now. Especially myself.

"I'm glad she heard the conversation we had about that incident." The word 'incident' is pushed out from his perfect lips as a hiss as if he finds it revolting and literally needs to spit it out. "I'm glad she's making you wait. I hope she keeps you waiting for at least another month," he adds.

I open my eyes and release my hands from the death grip they have on the back of my head. Flopping forward I rest my elbows against my thighs and uncross my legs spreading them wide. "Stop being such a cunt."

He raises a brow and throws me a sultry smile. "You love it. You crave the punishment."

I laugh; he's right. I could do with a good beating right now. Someone should tie me to a whipping post, serve me the rightful punishment for my wrongdoing and then I could wipe the slate clean once my back is a tattered mess of fleshy ribbons with blood dripping down my spine. Okay, that's a little dramatic – and inappropriate considering what Ash has just been through – but hey that's how I feel. It would be a lot easier than the mental torture I'm currently experiencing.

Ash sips the last of his orange juice and then pushes the tray table away from his bed. His room is like a five-star hotel, light and airy, beautifully decorated and comfortable. He has been holding court here as he does everywhere else and the nursing staff are already in love with him.

"She'll come around, Jax. I know she will. Just give her the time she needs." His eyes soften and he smiles at me again, a sympathetic and knowing smile. "Jade loves you just as much as I do, you lucky bastard. It'll be okay. Trust me on this. She'll forgive you eventually for being such a twat."

Shaking my head, I return his smile. I hope he's right. Waiting for her to contact me is like waiting for that final walk down death row. Terrifying but I know I deserve this. I'd taken both her and Ash for granted in so many ways before it all fell apart. I was lost in my own little fantasy and was cocky enough to think they would both just fit in around me; fit in around whatever I chose to do with whomever I chose to do it with.

"I'll be back tomorrow. Get some sleep," I grumble as I push myself up ready to leave.

He grins. "Of course, you will. And stop telling me what to do, prick."

I plant a kiss on his forehead before I leave and then head back to my flat. It's the last place I want to be in but the only place I can find sanctuary until Jade gives me her answer.

Most of my belongings have been packed up and a lot

of the furniture has been removed. It feels like a prison cell now. But I'm willing to take the punishment. I'm in a prison of my own making and I need to do the time. Complete the sentence that the judge and jury have decided is adequate for my crime.

Falling into my chair when I get back, I flick on the TV and start to build a joint. I will do what I always do when faced with misery. Block out reality with a haze of smoke, bad TV choices and a shitload of chocolate.

After the first week of hearing nothing from Jade, I manage to pull myself together a little. Ash is now out of the hospital and I spend my time taking care of him and getting back into a fitness routine. I run every day, twice a day sometimes, and cut out all the crap in my diet. I slow down on the smoke, only consuming one joint at the end of the evening before I go to bed to help me sleep.

When I can sleep.

Jade continues to leave me hanging. No messages. Nothing. Just silence.

One day slips into the next. The sale of my flat is almost complete and I'll need to think about where I'm going to live. I can't go to the cottage. That is not an option unless Jade takes me back. Thinking about the cottage just makes me sick to the stomach right now. If Jade decides she wants no part of this life with me, I'll have to accept I'll never enjoy it with her. But I will transfer the deeds into her name and give it to her. It was always meant to be hers.

I start to look at rentals. Ash has said I can stay with him for a while but that isn't something I want to do. I need some space and time to think away from him.

On the nights I do finally achieve sleep, my dreams revolve around Jade, Ash and my many, many faceless conquests. They become a mixture of nightmares and soothing memories of happy times on the boat wrapped in Jade's arms. I'm not sure which is worse. The happy memories or harsh night terrors.

Time passes in a foggy blur. One minute in brutal clarity, the other in a haze of despair.

The night before I am due to leave my flat for the very last time, I find myself sitting on the floor with my back to the wall with the same duffel bag I took to *The Witch* beside me. Reluctantly, I've agreed to stay with Ash until I find a decent rental. He is waiting for me to arrive but I'm delaying my departure. Not because I hold any sentimental feelings for this place but because when I walk out this door it will be the final nail in the coffin. My former life will officially be over but the one I had hoped to start may not begin.

It's depressing the fuck out of me and I can't seem to get off this floor. I take a drag on my joint and lean my head back against the wall. My eyes close and I hold the smoke in my lungs for as long as I can before letting it back out. The THC floods my system and sends a swirl of colours filtering through my mind. I float for a while enjoying the effects of the weed. Time is ticking by and I know it's getting late, but I have zero enthusiasm to get up off this damn floor. Ash will be getting impatient, but I'd rather stay here in a state of drug induced numbness.

As I lift the joint to my lips for another hit I hear a knock on my front door.

I decide to ignore whoever is standing on the other side but, after several more thumps, I find myself robotically pushing myself up and walking towards it before I can even register that I'm moving. Being stoned tends to do that to you. Autopilot kicks in.

Releasing the chain on the door as the person trying to get my attention knocks again, I find myself shivering as a scattering of goosebumps travel up my arm and reach the back of my neck. I pause for a moment dropping the butt of the joint on the floor and stubbing it out with my boot. Finally, I open the door and the scent of vanilla and incense saturates my system.

Jade stands in the doorway. There are dark shadows under her eyes, and she looks like she's lost a little weight. Her hair is loose around her shoulders and she's wearing an oversized woollen jumper that falls to her knees. She still looks ravishingly beautiful and perfect to me in every way despite her slightly dishevelled appearance.

My eyes scan her entire body landing on her biker boots before travelling back up again. She stands perfectly still her dark blue eyes glistening under the hallway lights as she waits for me to speak.

I haven't seen or heard from her for a month. Ash must have manifested that timeline. But now she's here, standing before me like a ghost from the past. But this time I'm glad to see this ghost at my door. She has haunted me every single day since I last saw her in the flesh.

Finally, my brain kicks into action and, without further hesitation, I pull her into my arms crushing her against me. I need to make sure she is real, not just a figment of my imagination.

"What took you so long to answer the door, City Boy?" she whispers as I hold her tightly against my chest.

"The last time I answered this door late at night I made the biggest mistake of my life." I reply.

She lets out a deep sigh. It is loaded with so many unspoken words, so much emotion. I continue to hold her waiting for her to push me away. But she doesn't. Instead, her arms tighten around my waist. She slips her fingers under my shirt and presses them against my skin sending sparks of electricity up my spine.

It's still there. The connection we had. The unique bond we formed. I feel a glimmer of hope begin to form. Jade leans further into my embrace. I wait for her to speak, to tell me what she has decided.

Several minutes pass before she puts me out of my misery. "Are we going to stand here on your doorstep all night or are you going to invite me in?"

Releasing her from my arms I step back and gesture for her to walk inside. I follow her silently as she makes her way into my lounge. The sound of her boots echoes loudly against the walls as she walks to the centre of the room and turns around to face me.

We stare at each other for a moment. Just soaking up the fact we are both in the same room together again after what feels like an eternity. I shake myself out of the silent stupor I've slipped into. I need to start the conversation. Say something to get the ball rolling.

"I'd offer you a seat, but as you can see there aren't any. The sale goes through tomorrow. I've been clearing out for the last month."

"I know."

"You do?"

"Yes, Ash told me."

I nod a small smile slipping onto my lips. "You've been in contact with *him* then."

She returns my smile. "I've spoken to him a few times in the last few weeks, yes. He also sent me a set of your keys." Uncurling her right hand, she reveals the two keys that give access to my lobby and front door.

My lips twitch with amusement. "I'm glad he did."

Her eyes flick around the room. With nothing in this flat now except me and my duffel bag it seems to ironically reflect how I've felt without her in my life for the past month. Bare. Cold. Soulless.

She walks towards the window places the set of keys on the ledge and then presses her hands against the glass staring out at the twinkling lights in the distance. "So many people out there living their lives Jax. Living in different ways with different people. Some breaking all the usual rules … just like we were."

Her voice is soft, melancholy.

I follow her to the window and stand directly behind her. She lets out a sigh again as I place my hands on her waist and lean into her. I am unable to resist touching her right now. We both stare at London's skyline for a moment before she takes her hands away from the glass and presses them against my own. I wait for her to continue. This is her moment and I'm going to give it to her. Whatever the outcome.

"Talking to Ash helped me make peace with what happened. He explained why you did what you did. Why you needed that last soulless fuck to make you see clearly what you really wanted and what you had waiting for you. It's taken me a while to accept that it was fear that made you fall back into your old patterns. But I've surrendered to it now. Let go and accepted that I'm just as lost without you as you are without us. I'm sorry I doubted you for a while. But I'm grateful you gave me the time I needed to come to my decision, Jax."

She swivels in my arms and looks up at me. There's nothing but love reflected in her beautiful blue eyes now and at that moment, I know everything is going to be okay.

"I'm ready to start that new life you promised me, Jax. Are you ready to start a new life with me?"

I kiss the top of her head and smile with relief. "Yes. Yes, I am."

Epilogue

It's been six months since I won the lottery and went to *The Water Witch* to think about what I was going to do with the money. Six months since I found, and almost lost, Jade. And five months since Ash found himself in a coma in hospital and I nearly beat a man to death for doing it.

I am now sitting on the back of a yacht in the Caribbean Sea, sipping a beer and, of course, smoking a spliff – some things never change. I put my feet up and smile as Jade pops up from under the water, her braided ebony hair glistening wet in the glorious sunshine. Her cherry-red bikini cuts clearly through the turquoise blue of the sea. Ash is swimming up to her and I laugh as he dunks her under the water just as she resurfaces. They are like two children. Playful and mischievous. It is perfect.

Our little cottage is coming along nicely and Ash has just come out of rehab. I insisted he gets clean of cocaine. I quit nicotine four months ago and only smoke the herb straight from now on – for medicinal purposes only, of course.

I no longer need to trawl the clubs and bars to feed my other addictions. I have Jade. I have Ash. We are one big happy family. Oh, and Bob, who is currently residing in the best kennel I could find, probably sulking.

My life changed the day I took that lottery ticket out of my pocket and handed it to the guy in the corner shop. It changed even more the day I stepped foot onto *The Water Witch*. Living on the canal is a way of life for me now. Jade and I plan to live on *The Water Nymph* in the summer months, cruising up and down the Kennet & Avon like water gypsies, then hibernate in the cottage in the winter. Ash visits us regularly and I visit him in London when I need to be alone with him.

Jade accepts he is part of my life and Ash accepts she has now also become an extension of me.

I have my eye on a property in the south of France so that we can drive over with Bob and Ash when we need a change of scenery. I no longer work. Fixing other people's problems to avoid resolving my own is now a distant memory. Instead, I help Jade with her jewellery making (who would have thought it?) and spend time renovating the cottage and digging in the garden. I'm now quite a handyman and gardener. I love the simplicity.

I'm not sure what I will do when the cottage is finished but I know I will find something. Jade still works for the magazines and plots her astrology charts for people wanting to know what their future holds. She enjoys her work too much to give it up. I just persuade her to take more days out to spend in bed with me now. Ash has started his own recruitment company with the money I gifted him. He plans to work part-time overseeing it and reaping the benefits, rather than having to do all the hard slog.

I take a hit from the spliff and wander to the back of the boat, leaning over the edge as they swim up to the steps and grin at me. Two beautiful souls that I love equally. They smile up at me and try to coax me into the water. They have given me everything I could have ever wanted in this life. The money has just helped me to make this life easier.

And it was a journey I could not have foreseen.

I've ridden this rollercoaster the best I can. Sometimes with my arms up in absolute joy. Other times gripping the bar filled with terror. But right now, I'm taking it all in with a new appreciation and love for what I have.

It's just a ride after all.

And it's been one hell of a ride for me so far, thank you very much.

My name is Jackson Doyle and this is my story.

How does it continue? Who the hell knows?

The End

Afterword from Author

Perfect Twist has been a real journey for me.

I wrote the first draft in October of 2016. It took me two weeks to literally throw the initial bones of the story onto my laptop in such a frenzy my husband wondered if he would ever see me again. I wrote from the moment I woke up, between clients, and after I'd finished work until the early hours of the morning. It was a necessity to 'get it out' and was channelled to me so quickly I just couldn't type fast enough (and I can type very quickly). I then spent the next three years trying to find an agent or publisher for this piece of work that I felt instinctively 'was the one'.

Despite all my efforts, money and time painfully spent consulting professionals and submitting, nothing happened except a mixture of nice feedback with regards to my writing and the concept, but plenty of 'it's not right for our readership'. The classic thanks but no thanks. Everyone seemed terrified at the content of this story and said it was too risky to publish. Not a good bet for sales.

I tweaked and rewrote so much of the original manuscript it felt like I had lost my way. Then several things happened and as it always does in my world, I suddenly found myself having a bit of an epiphany. I went back to the original manuscript, polished but kept the content as I had originally written it and decided to go back to the self-publishing world.

I realised after a lot of soul searching that Perfect

Twist is perhaps a risk and it is different with the aspects of bisexuality and polyamory key to the story. But this is a modern world now and these aspects of life are more current than ever. I knew that I needed to be true to what was channelled to me in the first place and just give it to the world as it came to me.

It is Jax's individual story, but I know many can relate to it in their own way.

The idea was to originally write a book based on a time when I lived on a wide beam canal barge on the Kennet and Avon canal with my now husband. It was a magical time in my life. I had not expected it to come to me in the form of a bisexual man struggling with his internal demons who begins a 'coming of age' journey.

I also realised that I needed to be patient (something like Jade, I'm not good at!) I have a lot of people to thank for helping me keep my sanity during this transition. They know who they are, and I am eternally grateful. Darren, my husband who has supported me from the beginning. I can't thank you enough for the constant encouragement and helping me stay on track. You have been my inspiration and helped me every step of the way, drawing the initial cover design, building me a wonderful 'hippy hut' to write in our field, helping me overcome my fear of diving into the world of social media and giving me the push in the right direction when I veered off the path. You have always championed me to become the writer I have longed to become.

Nick Taylor at Just Write Right became my fabulous editor who not only champions stories in the LGBTQ genre but is incredibly good at his job! Without him the story would not have been set in the year 2000 where gay rights were still being established and bisexuality was still somewhat of an odd mix to the rainbow flag.

Gabriel, James and Stefan at SpiffingCovers for their

hard work and countless tweaks on the cover and putting the book together for me. Thank you, guys, you seriously worked hard for your money! Hours of listening to Liquid Drum and Bass by Sound Territory (thank you) also helped get me in the right energy space. And a soundtrack of its own to the movie I have played in my head for the characters involved on Spotify.

This story is raw and sometimes dark but filled with so much light. I am grateful we now live in a world where we can love whomever we like and however many people we like through connections of love and joy. But I know it has not always been that way and there has been so much judgement and struggle for those who love in different ways from what 'normal' society saw as acceptable.

So, this story I believe is to show that no matter our gender, sexual preferences or choices of the amount of partners we have at any one time, we must always be honest, truthful and follow our own path to love and connect with the people that make us truly happy. No matter the consequence.

I hope it touches your heart as it did mine. And I hope Perfect Twist has caught your interest enough to read Ash and Jade's stories in the next two books that will follow. Perfect Fool is Ash's story and Perfect Paradox is Jade's story and will complete the twists and turns of their journey with Jax.

With love, light, and blessings,

Tara xx

Find me on Instagram @tjgristwood

Find me on Twitter @GristwoodT

Find me on Facebook Tara Gristwood

Printed in Great Britain
by Amazon

65290467R00206